# HERO

# WORSHIP

# AMELIA
# WILDE

For more books by Amelia Wilde, visit her online at www.awilderomance.com

# HERO

# WORSHIP

# CHAPTER
# ONE

*Daisy*

I USED TO DREAM ABOUT ART GALLERIES.

Clean spaces. Hardwood floors. Champagne and hushed voices. People admiring the pieces on the walls for their artistic merit and nothing else. Not the artist's mark in the corner. Not the rumored wealth or danger of her father. Just paint on canvas.

I still love the *idea* of art galleries.

The reality of art galleries is that they're a headache.

Cream or white makes inescapably logical sense for a gallery. It puts the focus on the pieces, where it belongs. But Jesus, it's *bright*.

Every ritzy gallery in LA has gone with this motif,

and it's hell. Although an artistic rendering of hell would be dark. I'd rather look at brimstone than all this off-white. My head hurt before I got here. Now, an hour into Marie's show, it spears through my temples and into a dull ache at the top of my spine.

Lovely.

If *I* owned a gallery, I'd make the walls black. Navy at the brightest. Curators and gallery owners who think it's only possible to draw attention to art with white walls suffer from a shocking lack of imagination.

Unfortunately, having a powerful imagination doesn't transform the white walls into anything but what they are. It also doesn't transform the show from *ongoing* to *over*. Marie's garnered a decent crowd, but not large enough for me to slip away unnoticed.

I don't *want* to sneak away. That's why it's such bull-shit to have this reaction to something as common and innocent as white gallery walls. That's why it's so incredibly frustrating to be so sensitive to things like…light-bulbs. Sunlight. Illumination in general. I'm trying to be a decent friend, for God's sake, and it would be easier if I wasn't always teetering on the edge of a migraine.

The sensible thing would be to text my driver now and make apologies later.

I type out the text and delete it.

"Daisy!" Marie's arms go around my neck with nervous force. Champagne sloshes in my glass, but I don't let it spill. "Thank God you're here. I didn't think anyone would come."

I hug her back, never mind that her body bumping into mine has made the headache worse. "What are you talking about? You have a crowd. These are men with money."

She pulls away and sneaks a look over her shoulder. "Are they?"

"...yes." I turn her to face the gallery with a hand on her elbow and gesture with my champagne glass. "The one in the blue suit is a supplier for a luxury interior decorating company. And the man he's next to—"

"The one with dark hair?"

"Yes, him. He buys his wife fine art as foreplay."

Marie gasps, her cheeks flushing pink. "I can't believe you said that."

"It's true. And he's obviously on the hunt tonight. Look at him."

The dark-haired man studies the pieces on the walls with a gleam in his eyes, ignoring everyone else in the room, including the artist. Marie's auburn-haired and unassuming, and she's been mistaken for a caterer's assistant once already this evening.

"Do you think..." She drops her voice. "Do you think he'll buy one?"

"Yes. Watch."

The man steps closer to one of her pieces. It's smaller, tucked into the corner of the gallery, but I know exactly why he's attracted to it. Marie's other work is like her. Bright. Kind. Unassuming. She does landscapes, which I'll freely admit doesn't sound like the kind of thing a man would buy as an erotic gift, except that *these* landscapes are different. Not because she's chosen unique subjects, but because of the light.

Marie's pieces are sunny and warm. They're bathed in a summer glow. It makes me jealous. Not of her, but of the light. I've never been able to spend as long as I wanted outside in the summer. As a child, I forced the issue more often. All children think they can be invincible if only they believe it hard enough.

I'm not invincible. If I spend too long in the sun, or in the light at all, my own brain will remind me of how fragile it is.

So Marie's landscapes make my chest hurt. They're paintings of a warmth that will always be out of reach.

Other people, like the man who wants a piece for his wife, see that gold haze and feel nostalgia. They have wonderful memories in light like that, and I'd bet most of those memories aren't bookended by being in pain, and being sick, and finally blacking out.

The dark-haired man shakes his head like he's waking up and reaches for his wallet.

"Oh my God." Marie clutches at my arm. "I don't know what to say. If he comes over here—I don't know what to *say*."

"He's not going to come over here."

Her grip relaxes. "What?"

"He'll buy from the owner, not from you. But don't be surprised if he comes over afterward to talk to you about the piece and shake your hand."

"But it's—but that one—"

"He picked out the moody one."

"I didn't think anyone would choose that one," she whispers.

"It's okay," I whisper back. "It's great work. It will make great foreplay."

"Daisy, it's a painting of an approaching storm!"

"Haven't you ever had an orgasm?"

Marie dissolves into laughter. "Oh, no. I'm never going to make it here."

"You already made it here."

"I mean…*here*." She waves a hand at the men and women attending her show. All of them have money. I can tell by the clothes. By the way they stand. By their faces as they take in the work. People born to wealth have a certain kind of aura. I would know. "I'm not like these people. I'm not even like you."

"Ouch."

She puts a hand on my arm, apologetic. "I just meant this is *easy* for you. You know what to say. You know all the jokes to make."

"I would save the orgasm jokes for friends."

Marie's eyes light up. "Are we friends?"

I laugh like it's a hilarious joke, but a little part of my heart dies. "Of course we are. That's why I'm at your show."

"Of course we are," she echoes.

Of course.

The gallery owner calls to Marie, and she squeezes

me, a tight, close hug, and lets go. "I'm so glad you came. If I don't see you, I'll text you, okay?"

"You'd better."

She flits off into the gallery.

I smile after her, hyperaware of my expression. Marie doesn't think anyone noticed her, but everyone in the room saw her come over to hug me, and now they're taking the opportunity to stare.

I'm used to the staring. On average, it takes people thirty seconds to figure out what's *wrong* with me, and another thirty seconds to figure out if their eyes are playing tricks. To wonder what kind of a freak I am. Then, if I'm very unlucky, they'll connect me with my dad.

Don't misunderstand me. He's one of my favorite people in the world. *Nobody* has a better dad than I do. But when I'm recognized as his daughter rather than a woman with monstrous eyes, some people feel entitled to ask questions. Sometimes personal questions. Sometimes, if they're particularly pushy, they'll make requests.

Usually, those requests involve delivering a message, or arranging a phone call or a meeting. They're too scared to ask him themselves. They're not afraid to bother *me*.

I'm not into that.

So I make zero eye contact with the people in the gallery. I put my champagne glass on an empty standing table and slowly, casually make my way to one of the gallery assistants. One of Marie's bigger, more expensive pieces reminds me of the beach where I learned to swim, so I buy it and give the assistant the address to deliver it to my house.

It doesn't matter that we're not *really* friends. It stings a little bit, but it doesn't surprise me. My childhood was beyond excellent, as far as childhoods go, but from what I gather, I spent more time alone or with my parents than other people. I had a close circle of friends, and my family, and by the time I left New York to come to California it was easier to stick with what I had.

Explaining myself to someone new is exhausting.

I text my driver, Shane, who doubles as my bodyguard, that I'm ready to leave. He's just sent me a thumbs-up emoji when my phone rings.

My cousin Artemis is already talking when I accept the call, drifting into an out-of-the-way corner so I can close my eyes.

"—can't do that. I've said it so many times, and I *know* you heard me, so, like—"

"Artemis. *Artemis*. Did you mean to call me?"

"Oh my *God*, Daisy, of course I meant to call you!"

"Sorry." I can't help laughing at how all-out she goes. "It sounded like you were arguing with Apollo again."

"I *am* arguing with Apollo again. That doesn't mean I can't talk to you at the same time."

"You can text me. Seriously. Don't interrupt your argument on my behalf."

7

"You *shh*. I'm not interrupting anything except Apollo insisting that I haven't told him—"

Apollo's voice, muffled in the background, interrupts her.

"I am right," Artemis insists to him. "You will not win this battle."

I catch a barely audible *put your money where your mouth is.*

"Hi, Apollo," I shout into the phone, wincing at the sound even as I do.

"Hey, Daisy," he shouts from the background of the call.

"You're not going to win," I whisper-shout back. Ironic, since winning battles of diplomacy is his literal day job.

"I know," he answers, and then he laughs, which makes Artemis laugh, which makes me laugh, too. Which makes me wish, not for the first time, that I lived in New York with my cousins and my parents and my aunts and my uncles. It makes me wish I didn't have to hide. It was never my plan to live at home forever, but it gives me a pang of homesickness and regret that I *have* to live in California now. Verbal battles would make a nice change from the one raging in my retinas. Except I can't go back, no matter how much I miss them.

"Are you ever going to get somebody else to fight with?" I tease Artemis. I've known her since we were babies, and she's always stuck close to our family, too.

Especially once her dad adopted Ares and Apollo when we were six.

"No," she answers, prim. "I prefer a well-matched opponent."

"You don't act like I'm well-matched," Apollo says, close to the phone.

"Is it worse than that?" I drop my voice like I'm about to question her about a terrible secret. "Will you die without him? Is there a ticking clock the moment he leaves the room?"

Artemis laughs, and then laughs harder, and it's... actually kind of forceful and weird.

"Um...are you okay?"

"She's going to snort-laugh herself to death," says Apollo, directly into the speaker. I'm sure I'm imagining any weirdness in *his* voice. It's probably the sight of Artemis ugly-laughing. A rare thing to see, since she's normally the definition of beauty. She has her dad's golden eyes and her mom's supermodel looks. I'm only a little jealous.

Of her, *and* how good she looks with Apollo, who has dark hair and blue eyes. They would make the perfect celebrity couple if they weren't best friends.

Some people might argue that they're siblings, but they're not blood related, so if they choose to be obsessed with each other, all I can do is tease Artemis relentlessly about it.

"She's still going," comments Apollo.

"Get *away*," chokes Artemis. It takes her a few beats

to regain control. "I'm trying to ask Daisy about her art. What did the gallery guy say?"

The *gallery guy* is a curator I met with earlier this week after months of persistence on his part. He saw one of my pieces in the catalog for a charity auction and has been asking for a meeting ever since. I finally agreed, mainly because daytime meetings are going to be beyond me soon, and I don't want to explain why.

It was a mistake. He liked the wrong work. I offered him a car-sized study in all the shades of black that exist, so many more than most people ever notice during the day. It's studded with orbs of light that allow a further range of tones to celebrate the dark. He didn't even give me a chance to begin explaining how personal the piece is before pulling out first one, then another of the wrong paintings to crow over instead.

"He said my work is great."

I make my voice so sparkly and positive that Artemis snorts. "Daisy. Come on."

"He said it was transcendent. He said it was like nothing he'd ever seen. He wants to arrange a show." These are all objectively good things, but they make my stomach feel like an empty pit. I don't want to be celebrated for the art I have no control over. Even if it is the only kind I've made for the last few years.

"I knew it! I *knew* it! When's it going to be? In LA, right? I'm flying out."

"Don't." It comes out too fast. I massage my temples with my free hand, willing the pain and panic out of my voice. "I mean—it's not a sure thing yet. I haven't given him a date."

"Why not?"

"Because—" Because if I have an in-person show at a gallery, my entire family is going to come to LA. There won't be any stopping them. They'll come to the show, and they'll see my pieces, and they'll know.

They'll *know.*

"I feel weird about it."

"Everybody's going to love your work." Artemis uses the same confident, reassuring tone she always does. "We *already* love your work. A *lot* of people already love your work."

Artemis hasn't seen my work. Not my *real* work. She and the rest of my family have only seen my display pieces. The few I've sold. The few I've put up for auction, or donated.

Letting them see my real paintings in a bright-white hell gallery would be...uncomfortable.

But not as uncomfortable as letting them see me.

I'm in California for a reason. My family doesn't need to worry.

"I know you do, I just—"

My phone buzzes.

**Shane:** Out front. Coming in to get you.

I move toward the gallery exit and exchange fake-brisk nods with him. Shane is ultra-professional, but that doesn't mean we can't have a few inside jokes about how weird the idea of a bodyguard is.

"I know," I tell Artemis as we go out into the night. The heat feels heavy. My head gives a deep, painful throb. Shadows in the corners of my vision say I should've left Marie's show already. "I'll think about it. It's not that—"

Shane wraps one arm around me and *shoves*. My periphery warps again.

"Jesus, Shane, what—"

"Keep your head down," he barks. A *bang* rattles my skull, sending a shooting pain through my temples. It's so strong that my vision goes, my knees wobble, and Shane manhandles me across the sidewalk toward my black SUV. Another *bang* makes my brain short-circuit. That *hurts*. A woman on the sidewalk screams. People run, shadows blurring. Shane shouts over his shoulder. I'm dimly aware of him wrenching open the back door and putting me inside. He climbs in after me, launches himself into the front seat, and drives.

The acceleration knocks me against the seat. My phone skids onto the floor. A muffled *thud* on my side of the SUV sends me scrambling for the other side. "Shane. What was that? What *was* that?"

"A bullet." The light from the navigation screen hurts, so I cover my eyes. A phone rings over the SUV's sound system. My heart races in the dark, pain rising and rising. I'm not letting this happen now. Not now.

*Deep breaths*, I tell myself, as though it's ever worked before. As though I could get one in through my shaking anyway.

His call connects to the man who heads up my full team. "Report."

"This is Shane." His voice is loud and clear and the hurt reverberates like a bell. "I have Daisy in the car. There was a shooter at the art gallery."

"Injuries?"

"No. She wasn't hit. But I need backup at the house."

My vision goes fuzzy, like static, the pattern imprinting on the dark. It's a harsh, wailing pain in my head, like an alarm that won't turn off. I want to scream, but the sound gets choked off. No, damn it, *no*—

*Shane*, I try to say.

I'm sick on the floor of the SUV instead.

The last thing I hear is Shane. His terse reports are broken up by my failing brain.

"—seizure." A sound like static. "—at the house before—" More static, and then: "Daisy was the target. Yes. I'm sure."

Then the darkness closes in.

It's not a dream.

It's not a nightmare.

It's worse than that. It's nothing, pitch-black nothing, forever and ever and ever.

# CHAPTER
# TWO

*Hercules*

**M**IDNIGHT, WE MEET AGAIN.

There was a time in my life when I slept whenever I could. Thirty minutes in a quiet public park. A nap in class, if I had to be in school. When our apartment was free of the sounds of my mother's clients.

When I didn't have to be awake to drag the assholes out by the shirt collar.

My time in the Army only played into the pattern. Boot camp did its best to turn me into a morning person. Ran on that schedule until I joined the Green Berets and parachuted into shitshows all around the globe, and what the fuck do you know? I was right back where I started, sleeping when the opportunity presented itself.

I pull down on the heaviest resistance band that's commercially available, gritting my teeth against my stubborn shoulder, and keep an eye on myself in the mirror.

My body no longer gives a fuck about conventional sleep schedules. There's no fighting it, so I have come to the gym in my building to run on the treadmill and zone out to loud music while I complete all the exercise reps recommended for my shoulder.

It'll never be the same. That's not what the exercises are for. Their purpose is to head off muscle atrophy and work on my range of motion.

I hate these fucking exercises. *Hate* them. But I'll do them, because I couldn't *die* when Ollie and I hit the ground. That would've been acceptable. I'd have traded my life for his.

Instead, I got to keep living with a shoulder so fucked up that I got an honorable discharge and a ticket back to the place I was trying to avoid.

My phone rings, cutting off the music in my headphones.

I keep tension on the band and tap my headphones to answer. It doesn't matter who it is. Nobody calls about anything good past midnight. Best-case scenario, it's nobody who considers themselves family.

"Hercules."

"Hey, prick. Do you have to answer my calls like I'm some peon in the mailroom?" No such luck, because the voice on the line belongs to my brother—adoptive brother—Ares.

"What do you want?"

"Listen. Dad's going to call you. Don't do your usual thing."

"Fuck off. I don't have a *usual thing*. And—*Dad*? That's cute."

Ares clears his throat. "Right. Zeus, the man who housed us and raised us until we left for—"

"Shut the fuck up. Why are you calling to warn me about a phone call?"

"Because I'm a decent human being, unlike you." This teasing, dry-humor motherfucker. "I thought you'd want a heads-up, since you're not going to like—"

A two-toned beep alerts me that Zeus—*Dad,* for fuck's sake—is indeed calling. "Time's up." I switch calls, disconnecting from Ares. "This is Hercules. What's your emergency?"

"I hope I didn't wake you," Zeus, my not-Dad says, as if he can't hear that I'm using full sentences and was obviously not in the middle of a REM cycle.

"You didn't. I'm at the gym."

There's an exceptionally brief pause, during which Zeus is probably debating whether to mention that it's almost one a.m. "I'm glad you're up. I need you to clear your schedule and take a job for me."

I release the band on a count of five and pull it back

again. "What job? If somebody hacked into your shit at the shelter, that's not—"

I'm interrupted by an enormous *crash* in the background of the call, followed by shouting.

"You pirate-ass *motherfucker.* I'm so fucking done. I will *end* you." My not-Uncle Hades.

"You'll have to try harder than that, sweet pea." My other not-Uncle Poseidon.

An even louder *crash.* Wood splinters.

Zeus sighs. "Hades, you're paying to replace the table."

"If you think for one second that I won't tear this house down with my bare fucking hands—don't *touch* me, Poseidon, I swear on the graves of every—"

"It's a hug!" bellows Poseidon. "I'm trying to hug you! It's an expression of comfort, you obstinate asshole."

"I don't want a hug, *I want to find that motherfucker* and *snap his*—"

Hades's voice fades, like he's chasing Poseidon elsewhere. I can almost see Zeus in his house—in the house where I lived for a year and a half, which doesn't make it mine—on the other side of the city. He'll have his thumb and index finger to the bridge of his nose. He'll still manage to make his exasperation charming. He'll be trying his best to temper the mood in the room. I don't know how he does it. Could be sheer force of will. But if Hades and Poseidon are at each other's throats in Zeus's house, then...

Things are not good.

"This is a mindset issue," Zeus says, mostly to himself. "*Mindset.*"

"Want to fill me in on why your brothers are in a fight to the death?"

"It may surprise you to hear this, but that wasn't a mortal battle."

"Oh? What was it?"

"That was Poseidon doing me a favor. Hercules, I need you to get on a plane. There's been a situation with Daisy."

My heart falls out of my chest. I haven't moved from the bench, but the adrenaline rush is as powerful as it was in the field. My face goes hot, then cold, then numb. If she's dead—

"Daisy who?"

My adoptive father's niece, that's who. I met her when I was seventeen and some prick had pushed her into an alcove. He had his hands on her, she didn't want it, I stepped in.

I didn't want her to save me from my life.

She insisted on it. I was living in her uncle Zeus's house within forty-eight hours, right next door to her.

It's been torture ever since.

"Hercules."

Heavy footsteps speed into wherever Zeus is standing, and there's the sound of a collision, one body against another. Zeus grunts, and something slams on the floor, and I can't tell what any of them are saying. A dog barks, loud and frantic, and doesn't stop barking. That's Hades's dog.

Zeus's voice rises above the fray. "Sit the *fuck* down, Hades. Poseidon—"

"Give me the phone," Hades demands.

"Do you need me to come over there and break up—whatever the hell this is?" I ask.

"Hades. *Hades.*" Someone—Zeus?—snaps his fingers. "*Look at me.* Conor's losing his fucking mind. You know what that means. Hades. Come on. You have to get ahead of this. That's the only option. Otherwise, I have to—"

"*No,*" Hades snaps. "Don't touch me."

"I'm handling this. Here. I'll sit on the floor, too."

"Look." The strain shows in Poseidon's voice. "We're all here, sitting on the goddamn floor. To be honest, I thought we were past this."

"Hades. I have it," Zeus says. "Now let me finish this conversation and get Hercules—"

Hades makes a sound that would've scared the fuck out of me if I heard it during a mission.

"It has to be him. You know we can't go. It's not what Daisy wants, either, and if we show up there..."

Zeus doesn't say what will happen if they go to where Daisy lives in California.

"I can't go to California." It comes out flat and empty. My brain doesn't know what the hell to do in this information vacuum. Daisy isn't important to me. She's my not-cousin with whom I have never gotten along and never will. The fact that she gathered the combined power of her family to get me out of jail after I beat up a guy for her doesn't mean I owe her anything.

"Herc. Please."

When Zeus bailed me out of jail and brought me to live at his house, he framed it like he owed me the bedroom and the fancy school and the place in his family. It was nothing less than he'd do for any of the children born to women who worked for him at his whorehouse. It had been his mistake that my mother and I slipped through the cracks, and his alone, and he insisted I owed him nothing in return.

I'd love to believe that, but it's not true. He offered me more than I can repay, even if I've never been his son. Even if I never will be.

"It's against policy."

"You make your own policy."

He's right. I *do* make my own policy. I'm a highly sought-after security consultant. Most of my work revolves around digital security for firms with government contracts, which require a higher clearance level than most people in my field have have. Occasionally, though, I protect people on the ground. It's a personal rule that I don't protect family, and I made that rule for a reason.

"You're going to get me killed over this."

Silence.

In that quiet, my face burns with shame. My shoulder aches. I've been holding this rep too long, and I've been holding myself away from Daisy and *her family,* not mine, never really mine, for even longer. It's a flimsy fucking excuse, too, because nothing has managed to kill me yet. I've survived beatings and shootings and hitting the ground from a height presumed to be unsurvivable.

What I want to do is the simple, easy thing—offer my life for hers. Daisy's parents and her aunts and uncles and her cousins want her to come home. They can live without me. If I could give my life over the phone, I'd do it.

I'd have done it several times over by now. I'd have done it for my mother. I'd have done it for Ollie. I'd do it right now, but I can't.

Deep down, I think Zeus knows this inconvenient unproven fact about me. At the very least, he has his suspicions.

Across the city, he's sitting on the floor with his brothers because this is clearly so stressful for Hades that he's having a brain problem. I've never seen the full result of one of those in person. If I refuse to take this job, will it kill him?

Will Zeus kill me?

If I hurt his brother, he'll try, and then we'll know for sure if I can die.

If I *can't*, I'm in for a lifetime of torture.

But the idea of being in the same room with Daisy again has my stomach in knots. My heart runs an obstacle course in my chest. I feel feverish, and chilled, and what the fuck am I supposed to do? Look at her like she's not the most beautiful person I've ever seen? Talk to her like I don't resent, with every cell in my body, that I can never have her? She is named after a *Daisy,* for the love of Christ. She's delicate and pure, and I'm a tattooed asshole whose primary talents are brute strength and violence. It was bad enough when we lived next door to each other. Bad enough sitting across from her at dinner. Bad enough breathing the scent of her shampoo during all the bullshit family events Zeus and his brothers forced us all to attend.

I'm scraping the bottom of the barrel for excuses, and I know it, like I knew my parachute wasn't going to be enough to save Ollie.

Fuck. They can all hear me.

It's a phone call, but the ask feels like a physical pressure. I don't know which one of them is doing that over cellular data or if it's my own jackass of a body trying to get me to agree. Out of nowhere, I think of a cool, shiny quarter in my palm. Handing it over to someone who needed it more. Being *proud.*

"She won't want me. We don't get along."

"Someone shot at Daisy tonight." Zeus delivers this like he's mentioning an inoffensive weather forecast.

The resistance band rips in two in my hand. The metal loop it was attached to flies out of the wall. I duck before it tears out one of my eyes, and then I'm on my feet, half the shredded band clutched in my fist.

"She wasn't hit." My mouth gets there before my

22

brain does. If a bullet so much as grazed Daisy's skin, her father and uncles would already be on a plane. "They didn't get her."

"No. Shane got her in the car and got her home."

*Move. Go.* I'm in New York. She's all the way across the country. There's nothing I can do to protect her now. All I can do is get my ass to the airport.

"When?" The door to the gym *thud*s behind me. I take the stairs up to my floor two at a time, then three.

"About an hour ago. We need someone from the family at her house, and we—I know," Zeus says, though nobody else has spoken. He's probably talking to Hades. "I know. We're doing our best to respect Daisy's wishes. You're all we've got, Hercules. There's nobody else we trust."

I only pause to punch in the code at my door, and then I'm inside. There's a bag in the coat closet with a set of clothes, a black plastic case, an all-in-one charger, a set of ID documents, a box of bullets, and a pistol. I swing it over my shoulder and it drops into place like my old Army gear. I'm not a soldier anymore, and I'm all but certain that I can't give my life for Daisy. I can't give her father what he wants, which is a guarantee. Those aren't real.

"Is the plane ready?"

"Fueled and on the tarmac." Knowing Zeus and his brothers, that plane had a full crew and was cleared for takeoff before the call connected. I yank the apartment door shut, punch in the code to lock it, and keep moving.

"I'm doing this," I tell Zeus. My vision is clearer than ever. All the adrenaline has my body prepared for a fight. I have one objective only: get to her. Get to her as quickly as possible, so I can keep her safe. "But I hate you for it."

*I hate you for pulling the family card. I hate you for trusting me. I hate you for making me see her when I can't touch her, when I can't kiss her, when I can hardly fucking look at her. I hate you. I hate you. I hate you.*

What he should say is *I hate you too. You've always been difficult. You've never been grateful. You make everything harder, and you're a constant reminder of the ways I fucked up in the past.*

"Hercules."

"Yeah?" I cross the sidewalk in front of my building and step out into the road, waving my good arm over my head. A cab leaves the flow of traffic and slows to a stop.

"Thank you."

"Don't thank me yet." I slam the door shut behind me and tell the driver to take me to Republic. Anything could happen between here and California. "I'll let you know when I land."

I take three separate naps on the flight, all of them less than half an hour. The only thing worse than falling out of an aircraft is being trapped in one. It's a new sensation. In the Army, long flights were a chance to sleep for at least a full, uninterrupted hour.

Now it's time that I'm separated from Daisy by the distance of cruising altitude and hundreds of miles.

I'd like to *stay* separated from her. That would be ideal. She doesn't want me to be in her house any more than I want to be in her house, but she won't die under my protection. I've accepted the mission. The next step is to carry it out.

*Not* because I have feelings for her. The only thing I feel about Daisy is frustration.

My plane touches down at a private airstrip west of LA as the sky is turning gray, gearing up for dawn. There's a car waiting by the hangar, a driver standing at the door.

The driver gives me the code phrase for the mission. *Midnight blooms*. He's brisk about shutting the SUV's door behind me and driving off. No doubt he's been given explicit instructions from Zeus. The man isn't wasting a second, even from all the way across the country.

> **Hercules:** Landed. In the car en route to her house
>
> **Zeus:** No trouble on the flight?
>
> **Hercules**: Tell me you didn't stay up all night tracking the damn thing
>
> **Zeus:** I would, but I'd be lying
>
> **Hercules:** Go the fuck to sleep

Zeus doesn't answer, and I know that's not because

he trotted off to bed. All three of those overprotective pricks are probably still sitting on his kitchen floor in a huddle, waiting for confirmation that Daisy's fine. As if she doesn't have security already.

Somehow, the thought isn't comforting. Her security wasn't enough to keep someone from shooting at her at an art gallery. That's why I'm here.

It's a short drive from the airstrip to Daisy's house, which is immediately recognizable as a property her father bought for her.

It's beachside property, for one thing. Her yard is grass on one side and a sandy beach on the other. Waves roll on the shore under the lightening sky. The houses on either side are a good distance away, giving her privacy, and every window in view has a subtle tint to it that says it's the ultra-expensive filtering glass that her father and both her uncles have in their giant-ass houses.

Daisy's is neat and elegant. One story. White siding. Black frames around the windows. The driver enters a code at the gated driveway, and we go through.

A lantern hangs above the front door, its glow fainter by the second as the sun begins to rise. I sling my bag over my shoulder, put my phone in my pocket, and go.

Daisy's front door opens before I can touch it. A man in a suit sans jacket stands inside. "Code."

"Midnight blooms."

He gives a terse wave to the driver, takes my shirt in

his fist, and hauls me over the threshold. Doesn't seem to care at all how loud the door slams. He locks it and turns his back on me, heading into the house.

What the fuck?

"You're Shane, right?"

He pauses, halfway around a corner. "Yes."

"The hell is going on?"

Shane doesn't answer, and it doesn't matter that I hardly slept on the plane. I'm wide awake, because this is off. Hades would've had a hand in hiring this guy. There's no way he's this shaken by a near miss.

I follow him into the house. Through a neat living area with a picture window overlooking the ocean. Through the kitchen. A short hallway leads past a walk-in closet and into the main bedroom.

Dawn is beginning to filter through the windows. The glass makes it more shadow than light. The brightest spot in the room is Shane's phone. It washes all the color from his face and makes it hard to see anything else. He sits on a chair next to the bed, watching the screen.

Daisy comes into view as my eyes adjust.

She's on top of the covers in a black cocktail dress, and she's dead.

Fuck, no, she's not dead. I've taken a few involuntary steps closer, and I can see her chest rising and falling. Her eyes are open and staring, no reaction at all to the light of Shane's phone.

It would be impossible to tell if she was reacting,

anyway, because her pupils are about the size of her irises. According to family lore, they were like that when she was born. If she hadn't inherited her father's sensitivity to light, she'd have blue eyes.

But this stillness, this staring—this is not fucking normal.

It's not rage that floods my body. It's bloodlust. I want to find the person to blame for this and fucking *kill him.*

First, I have to deal with the liar in the room.

"Shane."

He doesn't look up from his phone. "It's my understanding that you're—"

I don't know I've gone for him until his shirt is in my fist. Until his feet are about to lift off the ground. We're the same height, but I could do it. "Tell me what the *fuck* is going on. Tell me why she's like that if the bullet didn't touch her."

Shane shoves his phone into my chest. "That."

I put his feet firmly on the ground, let my bag slide off my shoulder, and look at the screen. It's a graph. Some kind of medical printout. A blue wave is spiky and high and thrashing, like a storm, and it's way above a thick red line in the middle. "What am I looking at?"

"A seizure."

"Are you fucking with me? Why didn't you take her to the hospital?"

"Hercules—"

"I *know* you have orders for this, motherfucker. If

you're more concerned with your job than with *her safety,* then get the fuck off this property before I tear you limb from—"

"They're *her* orders," he snaps. "I'm following her orders. She hired me, she pays me, they're *her orders.*"

He's shaking. This close, there's no denying that the man looks like shit. Dark circles under his eyes. A wild look about him.

I let go of his shirt but keep my hand on his chest in case he loses his mind. "Has she been like this since the shooting?"

"Yes. She had the first one in the car."

"The *first* one? How many have there been?"

"This is the fifth."

"Okay." I can't fucking breathe. This is not the job I agreed to. This is not the job Zeus thought he was sending me on. "Shane, did she give you specific orders not to tell her dad about this?"

"Yes. She did."

"Anybody else?"

"Her mother. Her uncles. Her aunts."

"She left her cousins out of your deal, then?"

"She didn't mention any of her other relatives."

Shane's not only scared shitless. He's at the worst possible crossroads of loyalty and duty. He has an equal obligation to protect her secrets and her life, and in this situation, he's equally fucked. It's a lonely place to be.

He takes a deep breath. "It was my understanding

that you're taking over inside the house. If you've changed your mind, or if you're not equipped—"

"Shane."

"Yes?"

"You're relieved. You and your guys have the perimeter. I'll take it from here."

He blinks down at his phone in my hand like he's never seen it before, then shakes himself out of it. "You'll need this. Get your phone out."

A couple swipes on his screen, and a window pops up on my phone. **Do you want to accept this download?** I'd like this to be not fucking happening, but I accept the download along with his contact information. We go through the obnoxious process of letting Shane thumbprint into my phone, then adding my print to the app. Jesus, it takes forever.

"Sometimes the patch throws a false alarm, but you'll be able to tell," he says.

"How?"

"Because if it's a false alarm, she doesn't look like *that*."

"Got it."

Shane shoves a hand through his hair, then steps to the side of Daisy's bed. He pats her shoulder, a brief, professional touch, and straightens up.

"Gatehouse at the end of the driveway. Call if *any-thing*—" His voice breaks. "Call if you need anything."

Then he brushes past me. A few seconds later, the

app pops up another notification. Her front door is open. Now it's closed.

I pull up my recent calls and dial Zeus's number. It's only hundreds of hours in hostile territory that's keeping my mind in check.

"Hercules? Is everything—"

"Are you alone?"

"Brigit's with me."

"You need to be alone."

Fuck, fuck, *fuck*. This is not the call I thought I'd be making. I thought I would be overkill. That I'd stroll in, identify any flaws in her security and fix them. I thought I'd be telling my not-Dad that he and his brothers could relax, that I'd neutralized any threat. Not announcing that she's a threat to herself.

The background noise changes. "I'm alone. What is it?"

"She gave her guy orders not to tell anyone if she had a seizure."

Zeus curses under his breath.

"Anything she tells me after she wakes up has to stay between us. I can't tell you a goddamn thing after this phone call unless she talks to you first. Do you understand?"

"Is it happening now?"

"Yes. And according to Shane, it's the fifth one since the shooting."

A long, deep breath, audible over the phone. "Do you have a kit with you?"

"It's always in my bag. It's there now."

"Get it."

I'm already on one knee, digging through my bag. The kit's in a black, shatterproof box the size of a brick and has traveled with me all over the world. Everyone in my not-family travels with one on their person at all times. I pop it open on the chair by the bed. There are two pill bottles, a vial with liquid, and five syringes waiting, safe in customized cutouts in thick foam lining. A side pocket contains individually wrapped alcohol wipes.

"I'm assuming pills aren't going to be an option."

"I doubt you can get her to swallow at this point. Have you given field injections before?"

"Yes."

"You know what to do?"

Now *my* hands are shaking, and I'm not fucking scared. I've done this before in far worse situations.

"Walk me through it anyway."

"Take out the vial and a syringe. Undo the cap. You'll need—"

I follow along. Take off the cap. Sterilize the top of the vial. Flip. Push air in. Check for bubbles. Zeus gives me the amount to draw into the syringe.

"Two? Are you sure?"

"It's five milligrams per milliliter. If it doesn't stop in ten minutes, you follow with another two."

"And if it doesn't stop *then*?"

"It'll stop."

"How the fuck can you know that?"

"I'd go for the arm, if I were you, and I'd do it now."

I approach the bed, drop the phone next to Daisy, and find her arm. One more alcohol swipe. My heart has never gone harder, or faster. I've done this a million times. Battlefield medicine is nothing. But the way she doesn't react, doesn't so much as *blink*, has my mouth dry and my jaw aching.

She doesn't flinch at the injection. I swipe a hand over her eyes.

They stay closed.

Phone in hand, I drop into the chair next to the bed. "It's done."

It's not *done*. None of this is *done*. Daisy's been keeping a massive secret, and I've walked straight into it. My body drops the bottom out of the adrenaline rush, replacing it with all kinds of inconvenient emotions.

"Okay. Wait there. Do you have the app?"

"Of fucking course I have the app." I flip to it on the screen. That wave, which apparently represents Daisy's brain, is still at a fever pitch. "Did you do this on purpose?"

"Hercules, I didn't know."

"Yes, you fucking did. You *knew* she didn't want you to come here." It's a rush of anger now. Bloodlust on top of bloodlust. "You set me up."

"I swear I—" Zeus's voice falters, then cracks, and it's like a sucker punch. He's telling the truth. "I swear to you. I didn't know it was like this."

"What—" A million dickhead questions come to mind. "What's going on with you? Are you afraid your brother's going to kill you?"

"No. I *know* he's going to kill me."

"Because you're…" What the actual fuck have I can-nonballed into? "You're not going to tell him what's happening with Daisy?"

"Shane isn't the only one who's made promises."

"Explain." I actually don't care what promises Zeus has made to anyone, but it hasn't been ten minutes.

Zeus laughs. Sounds painful. "I was her favorite."

"Her dad's her favorite."

"I took care of her when she was a baby. She came to me when she didn't want to tell her parents things. I didn't think she would keep—"

The sentence ends so abruptly that I think the call's failed.

It hasn't. This asshole is emotional.

"*Stop it.* Cry on your own time."

"I'm not crying." All at once, Zeus sounds like he's at a cocktail party.

"You're not going to fuck me over, either."

"No. I'm not."

"I don't believe you."

"It's not a requirement."

Jesus, I hate him. He sent me across the country for this woman, and now her life is in my hands, and it's not just bullets I have to protect her from.

"Did you even tell her I was coming?"

His huff of a sigh says *no*. "I called. She didn't answer. I guess she didn't want to chat between seizures."

"*Fantastic*. You're telling her in the morning, then. Or whenever she wakes up. I'm not going to be standing over her goddamn bed without any warning."

"I'll do that."

"She wouldn't want me to see her like this. She doesn't need to know. It's what I'd do for anybody on the battlefield."

"Understood."

"I don't *like* this." Because no matter what he says, how is it not a fucking trick? How does he not want me to fail this task so he can stop pretending he wants me in his *family*?

"I don't like it, either."

I shouldn't feel anything about that statement. Of course the man wishes I didn't exist. Of course he wishes my mother had been honest with him so he could pay her off and never think of me again. Of course he didn't want to choose me.

I'm the ex-soldier with time on his hands. Ares and Apollo are busy running the world from behind the curtain.

"Check the app," Zeus prompts.

The blue wave is calm. Well below the red line.

"It stopped, I think. The graph went down. It looks like it's breathing."

"That's sleep." The cocktail party persona slips,

just a little, into sheer relief. "That means she's asleep. Everything should be fine if you let her sleep."

"Great."

"Don't make her any promises."

"...what?"

"Don't promise her anything, Hercules. Don't promise to keep her there."

"*Keep* her here?"

"If this keeps happening, you have to get her home."

I stand up and pace away from the bed. "You don't want me to make any promises, but you want me to promise *you* to bring her home."

"Yes." There's a long pause, and everything from the day crashes into me at high speed. Exhaustion from the flight. Stress. Adrenaline. The persistent ache of not belonging in what everyone says is supposed to be my *family*. "Please."

"I hate you so much."

"That's okay."

"I'll bring her home if it comes to that."

I hang up before he can say anything else.

# CHAPTER THREE

*Daisy*

**U**GH.

I am garbage incarnate. Every muscle hurts. My skull aches. My teeth. I reach for the bottle on my bedside table without opening my eyes. Uncap it. Swallow the pill dry.

Then I lie still and think about silence and darkness until it kicks in.

Thankfully, the painkillers don't take long to work. Pain melts out of my head first, relieving the scratchy pressure at my eyes, and works its way down to my toes.

Which is exactly the moment my phone buzzes on the bedside table.

I reach for that without looking, too, and find it in place on the wireless charger. I have a vague memory of the phone sliding to the floor of my SUV last night, which means the seizure situation was handled by Shane, which means I owe him.

"Hello?"

"Daisy!" My uncle Zeus's voice is warm and bright. He's so full of shit. "It's me, but you knew that. How are you?"

Because Zeus sounds like he does, I know they found out about the shooting. I'm sure my dad was beside himself.

A wave of guilt, followed by more hatred, followed by a strong urge to give up on all this and go back to New York, pins me to the mattress.

I let out the loudest possible sigh. "Who called my dad about the thing last night? I know it wasn't Shane."

"There was no call."

"Who sent the *courtesy text*, then? I'm going to fire that person."

"Come to think of it, I don't remember. You could ask your dad."

My heart rate is up. I hate this. I don't hate talking on the phone to Zeus. I hate this game we're playing. And yes, I'm the one who started it. I'm the one who insisted on moving to California. I'm the one who won't give them a full explanation. I'm the one who's hiding.

"Please tell me you're not outside my house right now."

"We're not outside your house."

My mind is almost finished processing the scene that probably happened in New York last night. "Uncle Zeus."

"Yes?"

"Is someone *else* outside my house?"

"I wanted to let you know before he arrived."

"Before *who* arrived?" His hesitation tells me exactly who. I slap my hand over my eyes and instantly regret it. "You did not. You did *not* send Hercules here because one random person—"

"Daze, the courtesy text said it's an ongoing threat. Have you had a chance to talk to your people today?"

I peek out from behind my hand. It's almost noon. "No. I've been busy."

"I was worried, and Hercules agreed—"

"*I* didn't agree. I have a security team. I have people here. You didn't need to send anyone to supervise me."

"He's not there to supervise you, Daze, he's there to—"

"Did you call her?" My dad's voice cuts into the conversation, and four words is all it takes to understand why Hercules is here against my express wishes. "I told you not to bother her."

"Daisy, your dad is—*Christ,* Hades, I—"

"I told him not to bother you," my dad says, and my throat closes so tight I can't speak. He hates that I live across the country, and I can hear it in his voice even when he doesn't say the words. It broke his heart when

I moved away. It breaks mine every time he doesn't ask me to come home. I know he wants to. "I'm sorry, Daisy."

"It's okay, Dad."

He takes a sharp breath, like someone punched him. "Are you all right?"

"I'm fine. I'm completely fine. Shane got me into the car and we came home. If you called—I didn't mean to miss your calls. I was tired. I didn't even know where my phone was. I'm okay now. I slept in."

"Good. That's good." It doesn't matter that I've chosen my words as carefully as possible. He knows I'm not telling him the whole truth, but he doesn't press. Part of me wishes he would. Part of me wishes he'd call me on it, but if he did, I'd break down and tell him everything, and that would destroy him. "If you need—if there's anything you need—"

"Daddy, I'm really okay. I don't need anything."

"If you do, you'll tell me?"

No. I won't. "Yes."

"I love you."

"I love you, too." If I say *I miss you*, I really will cry, and then my cover will be blown. I'm barely keeping the tears out of my voice as it is. I'm not sure why I bother. My dad can hear the hidden things, too. He's pretending not to for me.

"We'll leave you to your—*you* motherfucker, I'll—"

"Like he said." Zeus, back on the line. "I wanted to tell you that Hercules should be arriving any second.

I'm the one who sent him, by the way. It was my decision. I'd so appreciate it if—"

"I know it was all three of you. You're saying that so I won't blame my dad."

"Don't! He's innocent. It was all me. If you're angry, I'll accept—"

"I'm not angry. I'm *annoyed*. I'm texting my mom to call you off."

Zeus gasps. "Daisy, please. Don't do that. I promise—we won't interfere with your life, like you asked. Do this one thing for me. Don't bring your mother into this."

"For such a big, scary man, you're super pathetic."

"You think I'm scary? Hades! She says I'm scary. Are you scared?"

My dad's answer is too unkind to repeat.

"We love you, Daisy." Zeus talks over him.

"Hey, is that Daisy?" Poseidon's there too, now, and I miss them all so much I could scream. "Why didn't you assholes tell me you were calling? I wanted to talk to her about—"

The doorbell rings. It's a notification on my phone rather than a tone.

"Daisy," Zeus says. "Tell Hercules—"

"I have to go. He's here, and I don't forgive you for this. Love you, *bye*."

I drop my phone on the bed and cover my eyes with both arms.

This is *not* the day I thought I'd be having. And I'm still in my dress from last night.

I could get changed, but leaving Hercules out on the front porch would be rude.

Not that I *care* about being rude to Hercules. He's always been a hostile asshole, and I'm sure nothing's changed since he joined the Army and I came to California. I ignore the strong urge to go back to sleep and forget about all of this and get out of bed.

Plastic digs into the soft part of my foot. Oh, wonderful. An orange syringe cap. I owe Shane a bonus *and* an apology for putting him through…

…whatever happened last night. Can't have been pretty.

I throw the cap in the mini wastebasket and go to face the enemy.

Sorry. My new security guard.

I am *not* relieved he's here. That's not what this feeling is. I'm not relieved *at all* that I have an excuse to look at him again. In fact, I'm mad about it.

Probably.

In the entryway I tug my dress into place, ignore that I haven't taken a single glance at my hair, and open the door. "I know you're only here because—"

My eyes land on Hercules, standing there in the shaded noontime sun, and every word from the English language disappears from my mind.

Holy shit.

Holy *shit*.

He's always been muscular. It's one of the things I noticed about him the first time we met. It was about the only thing I could notice, since the first time I saw Hercules, he was punching out a guy who'd tried to—

*Well.* Okay. My eyes landed roughly at his waist. He's leaner, and…harder. I've never seen jeans fit like that. My eyes climb involuntarily from his waistband to where tattoos poke out from beneath a fitted black T-shirt, and finally to his face.

Sweet mother of Christ.

The last time I saw Hercules in person was…five years ago?

Roughly five years, one month, and four days. Right before he left for boot camp. He was nineteen and wore a scowl on his face whenever I was in the room. Hercules didn't visit home again for two years after that, and I came to California, and…

And he's not scowling now.

He's watching me, face set in a professional mask, a duffel bag slung over his shoulder. All the light from outside clings to his skin like he's recently bathed in sunshine. Sunbeam droplets catch in his hair.

Jesus, that's *bright.*

He clears his throat. "I'm only here because…?"

I throw the door open wider, pretend I wasn't staring, and wave him inside. "I know you're only here because my dad freaked out last night."

Hercules steps across the threshold, and I am

43

screwed. Because we do not get along. He hates me, and I tolerate him for the sake of my family.

"Wouldn't know. I didn't talk to your dad."

I roll my eyes behind his back. Shut the door. Lock it. "Okay. Then I'd bet all the money in my bank account that you heard him freaking out when your dad called you."

His eyes narrow. "Zeus isn't my father."

This is never going to work. I have the strangest instinct to jump on him. Put my arms around his neck. Test his strength. The second time I saw him, he was handcuffed to a table in jail, and it seemed like a game to him—like he could rip the bolts *and* the table out of the floor.

He looks even stronger now.

He looks like a *man*.

"Listen." I shove my hands over my hair. "I know you didn't come here because you wanted to. I know you're doing my dad a favor."

"He didn't—"

"Doing my uncle a favor, then. I'm sorry."

He raises his eyebrows, golden-brown eyes going wider. "For what?"

"For having to be here. My uncles are a pain in the ass, to say nothing of my dad."

Hercules shrugs one shoulder. His left shoulder. The other one doesn't move. "Zeus offered a job. I took it. Nothing to be sorry about."

"Good. That's—that's good." Great. Fantastic.

Wonderful. I can't think past the pain in my chest, which is complete nonsense. *Of course* it's a job. He can barely stand to be in the same room with me. The paycheck must be worth it. "Anyway, I have to get changed. Make yourself at home."

I don't *flee* to the en suite in my bedroom. I simply go there, leaving Hercules in the entryway.

I do not think of him in the shower.

I don't think of his hands, or his muscles, or his tattoos.

I don't think about him standing guard in the house, ready to put himself between me and a bullet.

"It can't possibly be worth the money," I tell the stream of water.

It doesn't answer.

When I emerge some twenty minutes later, clean and clothed in leggings and a soft, loose top that won't bother my skin—sensitive, after a seizure, because that's convenient for me—Hercules has seated himself at the kitchen island, a tablet in front of him.

He glances up at me. It's a second, maybe two, but I'm overheated by his gaze on my clothes.

A loud, unrelenting siren goes off in the back of my mind. This is a bad idea. This is the worst idea anyone's ever had, and if I could plan on seeing my uncle Zeus again, I'd give him what for.

Because Hercules is both handsome and hot *and* strong. Once, when he was handcuffed to that jailhouse table, he told me he'd met girls like me.

*Girls like me?*

*Ones who get off on a rough fuck with a strange man.*

He's never said anything like that since, but the undeniable truth is that Hercules looks exactly like the kind of strange man I'd like to…

I'd like to…

Do *nothing* with, thanks. He's not a stranger. He's a known entity. We don't like each other, and he's never going to put his hands on me for anything other than his *job*. It would be like Shane, pushing me into the car. Clinical and professional and—

And maybe it wouldn't.

Pressure at my temples says that if it weren't for the painkillers, I'd be on the ground in agony, so I pretend not to notice Hercules looking at me and take out my phone. The tap of a button filters out three-quarters of the light coming through the windows. Even with the special, customized painkillers, it's best to reduce exposure to light well in advance, and more than I think I need to.

It's best, and it's necessary. More necessary with every month that goes by. But then, monsters always live in the dark.

Hercules's eyes are still on me when I lift my head. "Yes?"

"Are you okay?"

"Of course I'm okay." I breeze past the kitchen island to the fridge.

"You made it dark."

"Yes, well, I do most things in the dark. I prefer it this way. Don't be weird."

Air from the fridge is cool on my face, but I can tell he's still watching from the heat on the back of my neck. "You didn't keep it this dark at home."

"I lived with my mom at home. She can't see very well in low light."

Hercules sighs. "You don't have to bullshit me."

"I am certainly not bullshitting you." I take out a carton of eggs and put it on the counter. A slice of cheese from the deli. A pint of milk.

"Anyone who's met your mom knows that she'd live in a pitch-black room for the rest of her life if it meant saving your dad a single headache."

I'm tired. That's why I want to sink down on the floor and cry. Nobody's ever going to love me the way my parents love each other, and that's how it has to be, because I am, in simple terms, a Problem.

One that can't be solved.

"I'm making breakfast," I announce, and go to find a frying pan and a loaf of bread.

"It's past noon."

"How has *your* life been?" I crack eggs into a bowl, careful not to let any shards of shell fall in. "I heard you got out of the Army."

"I didn't get out. I stopped having the necessary physical qualities to serve."

I look at him over my shoulder. Hercules isn't even pretending to do anything with the tablet. His elbows

47

are braced on the countertop, and he's watching me over clasped hands.

"Right. Your…injury."

"My fall out of a helicopter, yes."

"I thought you jumped out of helicopters."

"It becomes a fall if your parachute fails."

"Is that what happened?" I can't explain why my heart beats faster thinking of that scenario. Of Hercules plummeting through thin air and hitting the ground. "A parachute mishap?"

"That was most of it."

The silence gets heavy, and regret crowds into my chest. I don't *have* to be like this. I have my guard up because we never once got along. If he's going to be professional about this situation, then I should at least be…

I should at least be cordial.

"Sorry you had to leave the Army."

"The Special Forces will do fine without me."

"Is that true? I thought you got a lot of awards for bravery. Saving lives. That sort of thing."

Hercules doesn't answer for so long that I glance over my shoulder. He's staring down at the tablet, his face blank. He rolls his right shoulder and stretches out his arm.

"Does it bother you?"

His eyes snap to mine. "Does what bother me?"

"Your shoulder. Isn't that—that's what got hurt, isn't it?"

Hercules cracks a smile that doesn't reach his eyes. "Yes. Permanent damage, as far as the doctors can tell."

"Is there anything—" Jesus, what am I doing? What am I saying? Can't I just cook eggs in silence? "Is there anything I could do to help? Like a massage, or a foam roller?"

He lets out a short *ha*. "Don't worry about it, Daisy. We have more important th ings to talk about."

Oh, God. He read my mind. He read my mind, and he knows the dark sexual thoughts I've had about him, and he's—

"I need to work with your team to find out who was behind the shooting at the gallery." His tablet lights up behind me, throwing my blurred shadow against the wall. "Can you think of anyone you've had a personal problem with in the past?"

"Yes." I can't stop myself. I have zero control. "You."

He blows out a breath. I know he means to keep it quiet, but I hear it anyway.

"We don't have a personal problem now." A brief pause. "Do we?"

"No." My voice goes high and strange, and I stick a fork into the bowl of eggs and stir too hard. "No. Why would we?"

"Because you hated when I lived next door?"

"I did *not*." Some of the egg flies out of the bowl, and I grab for a paper towel and clean it up. "I'm the one who had to convince *you* to leave jail, remember?"

"You weren't happy to see me at Zeus's house."

My face is hot. My chest aches. My *throat* aches. I don't know why a simple discussion about things that happened years ago would have any effect.

I'm tired. That's the only explanation I'll accept.

"When?"

"What?" Hercules asks.

"When wasn't I happy to see you at Zeus's?"

"The first day I got there. You and your parents came over for dinner, and you were pissed."

I laugh out loud and dump the eggs into the frying pan. "What was the weather like that day?"

"Sunny."

"And...what did I do that morning?"

"Came to fight with me in the jail."

"What kind of lights do they have in there?"

"Fluorescent ones."

"I wasn't pissed. I had a headache, asshole. You were pissed at *me*. Because you didn't want to be there. You wanted to be wasting your time handcuffed to various furniture."

"Being handcuffed to furniture isn't always a waste of time."

I wheel around, and he's smiling.

No. He's *smirking*.

"Are you making a sex joke right now?"

"Absolutely not. I'm a professional. I would never."

I walked right into that one, didn't I? I brought up that day in the jail. I brought up the handcuffs. And now he has to be remembering the conversation we had that day.

*Girls like me?*

*Ones who get off on a rough fuck with a strange man.*

Hercules purses his lips and tilts his head down again, scanning the tablet. "Who else? Someone in the art scene?"

"I'm not really in the art scene." I add the slice of cheese to the eggs. Salt. Pepper. Bread in toaster, butter ready to go...

"The shooting happened at an art gallery."

"Yeah. I was there for my friend."

"Does she have a problem with you?"

"She didn't seem to realize we were friends, so no, I can't imagine she'd have a problem that would rise to the level of a contracted shooting."

"Anybody else who's ever taken an instant dislike to you? *Besides* me."

"I don't know." I rattle off a couple of people who have been rude and standoffish at other exhibitions. Comments about how I got where I am because of my father, as though skills can be bought, as though they weren't born into money themselves. Art galleries only exist for rich people. "Like I said, I'm not in the scene very much. I don't sell a lot of pieces."

"Then how did you get well-known enough to be shot at at a gallery opening?"

I turn around and spear him with my best glare. "How do you *think*?"

Hercules laughs. "That face is more intimidating on your dad."

"Everything is more intimidating on a man who's six five and could crush you with his bare hands."

"Is it?" Hercules says it absently. He's...he's tall, too, which I refuse to think about any further. I finish scrambling the eggs as the toaster pops. I butter the toast in five seconds flat, tip the eggs onto the plate, and cover them with a second slice. "This wouldn't have anything to do with before, would it?"

"What do you mean, before?" I pause halfway to the kitchen island, plate in hand. Hercules's eyes are decidedly not unfeeling in this moment. There's heat there. Maybe violence.

"In school. Did anything ever happen in school?"

"I was in school when I met you." He knows what I mean.

Hercules's hands clench around the tablet, highlighting all the muscles in his arms.

I wasn't technically in the school building when a guy from another prep school in the city pushed me into a dark alcove at one of Zeus's fundraisers and kissed me despite my *strong* protest. But I was school-aged when I watched Hercules beat him bloody and go to jail for it.

*That* guy—that rich asshole—had a sister who went to school with me. A sister I had classes with.

"That time at the fundraiser. And there was a time with that guy's sister."

"His *sister?* What time?"

"She went to school with me." It *had* to be unrelated. It was a freak coincidence. *Freak.* I didn't mean to fall asleep in class. "One day, she lost it at me in class. Screaming about how I was a witch. That was it, though. I can't imagine they'd have anything to do with this."

Hercules frowns. "Probably not. It was years ago."

"Right. Here."

I slide the plate over to him, and he blinks like he's never seen a plate before. "What's this?"

"It's scrambled egg sandwiches."

"You make eggs in…sandwiches?"

"That's how my dad taught me to do it. That's how he makes them for Zeus." Hercules flinches back from the plate but catches himself immediately. "Oh, for God's sake, they're eggs. Eat them. They're good."

"I'm nothing like Zeus."

"Whatever. Regardless of how my uncle likes to eat eggs, this is the best way to have them. And I *know* you traveled all night. I know you're hungry, so just, like, shut up and eat them."

I swipe a napkin from the holder and flutter it in front of his face until he takes it. Then I gather a glass with some ice water, and another glass with orange juice, and put them by the plate, ignoring his crossed arms.

"Take a bite. If you really hate it, I'll make you something else."

He glares at me.

I glare back.

Then Hercules picks up one of the sandwiches in his big, strong hands and takes a bite.

I can tell by his eyes that it's *great*, actually.

"See? I knew you'd like it."

"How?" he says around another bite of scrambled egg sandwich. Once he's started eating, he can't stop. He used to eat like that at home, too.

"I already told you. My dad taught me to make them this way."

"Your dad doesn't cook."

"Not that much anymore, but I know Zeus told you they didn't grow up with money. My dad would tell you the same thing. He also told *me* that the only way to have good food with no money is to learn to make it yourself, so he did. Hence the delicious eggs in your mouth right now."

I expect him to scoff at this, but he keeps eating.

"Okay. Great talk. Anyway, bye."

Hercules's eyes follow me around the kitchen island. "...what?"

"I have to work."

"But you—" He stops himself. Shuts his mouth. "I'll come with you."

"Stay where you want, but don't come into my art studio. It's private." I'm not ready to see his face when he sees my work. Nor am I ready to explain why I paint horrors I despise on my good days and abstracts to show my family on my bad ones.

"You got *shot at* less than twelve hours ago, and we still have no idea who did it. I'm not letting you out of my sight."

"It's right there." I point across the living room. "Don't worry. I think I can survive the trip."

I've shut the door of the studio behind me and slumped against it when my phone buzzes again. **Artemis,** the screen reads.

"I can't do this," I tell her the second the call connects. "I. Cannot. Do. This."

"Oh my *God*, Daisy! You can't get shot at, either! Why didn't you call me?"

"I was asleep. I just woke up. And *Hercules* is here," I hiss into the phone. "Your father sent *Hercules* to guard me."

"I don't know what to tell you," she whispers back, though there's probably no need. "He's really good at guarding people. That's what he does. And you *got shot at*."

"Says the girl who once shot an arrow at Apollo? I'm fine. They didn't hit me."

"Daisy. Jesus. You could move home, you know, and then you'd be safer and Hercules wouldn't have to be your in-house bodyguard."

"*No*." I'm way too sharp about it. "Artemis—sorry. *Sorry.* Don't listen to me. I'm tired."

"I get it, but I'm worried about you. And I miss you."

"I miss you too." I want to tell her everything. I

want to stop keeping secrets. I can't find the words. "Please don't worry. I'm fine. But I can't move back there, Artemis."

"But…why?"

"I *can't.*"

"I know, you're forging your own path or whatever, but you could *visit*. You could at least come home until they figure out who was trying to shoot you."

"Please. My dad wouldn't let me leave a second time. *This* is my home now."

It's…my house, at least.

I can never go home again.

# CHAPTER
# FOUR

*Hercules*

THE DOOR TO DAISY'S STUDIO CLOSES, AND I push the plate out of the way and bang my head against the kitchen island.

This is torture.

Looking at her in her soft clothes is torture.

*Not* staring at her ass while she cooked me scrambled egg sandwiches is even worse torture.

Shutting herself in the studio, where I can't see her, is an act of war.

I'm only allowing it because I cleared the entire house this morning before I went to sit on the porch with my phone like a fucking stalker. I exchanged a brisk wave with Shane, who texted me from the gate-house—no updates. Checking the app to see if Daisy had woken up felt like cheating. I did it exactly once. The breathing pattern of the wave changes when she's closer to waking up.

Which is nothing compared to watching her actually breathe.

I have been to war. I have been to fucking *war*. I have been dropped into hostile territory all over the planet, and I'm not going to lose my shit over a girl.

Especially not *this* girl.

I pick up my head like the professional I am and resume eating the scrambled egg sandwich. On the tablet, I tap out a left-handed message to Shane about the art-scene people Daisy mentioned, then go about researching them myself.

Shane reaches his conclusion at the same time I do.

> **Shane:** These people both had public engagements last night. They're weird artist types, not people who hire hit men.
>
> **Hercules:** You think the shooter was hired?
>
> **Shane:** Can't say for sure, but my gut instinct is no. She keeps to herself most of the time. It seems personal.

That's nothing, then. We have no leads, and no idea why somebody would've shot at her, which means…

There's no telling how long this job could last.

I finish the scrambled egg sandwich. These are the best eggs I've ever had. I don't know how to feel about that. I can't picture Hades cooking eggs, anywhere, at any time in his life, but I *can* picture him teaching Daisy how to do it. I'm pretty sure he taught her everything, including that glare.

Picturing her at the stove, her top skimming the curve of her ass, sends a rush of blood to my cock.

"This is a job," I say to the empty kitchen. "It is a *job.*"

> **Hercules:** Is there a shower I could use?

I know there is, but for appearances' sake…

There's a long-ass pause. Dots appear on the screen, then disappear. Appear again. Disappear.

> **Hercules:** A shower is a thing that sprays water so people can get clean
>
> **Daisy:** Guest bedroom. Door to your left

The door in question is at the end of the little hall to the main bedroom. I get my bag and go.

It's a similar setup to Daisy's room, but at the front of the house. I can see the gatehouse through the blinds. Bed's made up with navy sheets, and the room is clean. A watercolor is propped up on the desk, a blue and green tangle framed by dark columns. I lean over and sniff the candle sitting next to it. Something both floral and woodsy wafts straight into my brain's pleasure center. Smells good.

Smells like her.

Fuck.

Stripping off my clothes and getting in the shower does nothing to take my mind off her. According to the rules of engagement—protecting her, at all costs—I'm supposed to be focused on Daisy.

I'm sure as hell not supposed to be focused on how her body looked in that dress she answered the door in. I'm not supposed to focus on how it would feel to take that dress by the hem and tear it off. I am *not supposed to focus* on running my fingers through her white-blonde hair and leaving teeth marks on her neck and—

My fist is on my cock before I can think *inappropriate work behavior.* I spent all night on a plane, thinking about her. I sat by her bedside while the sun rose, making sure she was still breathing. I caught the scent of her shampoo when she came out of the bedroom.

It's this or die.

I brace one hand on the shower wall, shoulder aching, and the world's most depraved shit crowds into my mind. Holding her down. Biting her. Licking her. Making her cry. Making her come. Making her scream.

Making her beg.

Beg *me.*

The thought of my name in her mouth in a broken gasp sends me over the edge. I come so hard I can't hold onto my cock. I use both hands on the tiles to stay upright.

Okay.

Fuck, okay.

That should be enough to get me through the rest of the job.

I laugh out loud, because *look at me.* Both hands on

shower tiles, knees weak from how hard I came thinking about her, light-headed as fuck.

Sure. One orgasm will be enough.

My hair is a fucking mess. I let it grow out after the Army handed me a medal and showed me the door, and now it looks…

It looks like it used to when my mom was still alive. Curly, like hers. Sandy, like hers.

Thinking about her is never good on the job, so I fuck with my hair until it'll at least dry in a presentable way and go in search of Daisy's laundry room.

That's off the kitchen, too. Shelves on one side. A stackable washer and dryer on the other. A folding table.

I find detergent and put my pathetic pile of clothes into the washer, then open the dryer out of habit.

There are clothes inside.

Daisy's clothes.

I make it through cleaning the lint trap before I can no longer ignore the *kind* of clothes.

"She said not to be weird about the dark. I'm not going to be a fucking jackass about her clothes, either."

Except only a jackass would lose his mind about folding a few items of clothing, so I do not lose my mind. I take out a set of pajama pants, worn and soft. Fold. A black tank top, also soft. Fold.

A bra with no underwire. Very fucking soft.

Fold.

A pair of black panties.

Fold.

I'm still having a fucking heart attack over the panties while I fold her socks and leave them on the top of the pile on the folding board.

I'm already hard again.

Jesus fucking Christ. How did I ignore this while I lived next door to her?

I didn't. That's the answer. I didn't ignore it at all. I jacked off in the shower and pretended I hated her and avoided her at every opportunity and now I can't avoid her.

Now I don't want to.

No, fuck, I *do* want to. This is the last place I want to be. But *if* I'm going to be here, I should at least be in the same room. That's the only way I can do my job.

However, she's given me explicit instructions about not going into her studio. I'll have to tell her that it's a one-time thing when she comes out. I don't have to talk to her to protect her, but I do have to be able to see her.

Back in the kitchen, I do a deeper dive into the art scene people. Nothing I find changes my opinion on them. Every article only reinforces my sense that the art scene is the kind of place where people influence each other with gossip and wrinkled noses, not hit men.

Something Daisy said, though…

*That time at the fundraiser. And there was a time with that guy's sister. I can't imagine they'd have anything to do with this.*

It's not likely for that little prick to be involved, but if that's the one incident that sticks out to her from school, it's worth looking into. It's not like I've got any better leads, and Zeus is running down any threats that might have come from her father's business dealings. I don't hold out much hope from his end—no one's foolish enough to go up against Hades with Zeus and Poseidon at his sides. But foolish enough to think Daisy's an easy target? I thought we'd taught Kenneth Coleman well enough years ago.

I never went into detail with Daisy about all the bullshit that followed Zeus bailing me out of jail. Kenny's parents were rich pieces of shit who were more worried about their son's orthodontia than the fact that he'd assaulted a girl. It took them six months to figure out that every refusal to drop the charges against me brought them closer to total ruin.

Zeus made a point of keeping the details mostly between us. An attempt at gaining my trust, maybe. I don't know.

The only other person who knew what a fucking nightmare they were was Hades, who was pressing charges against Kenneth.

I remember the afternoon it ended because I got home from the fancy-ass prep school they enrolled me in to finish high school to find Zeus in the driveway, blocking Hades from getting into one of the many black SUVs that were in the family. There was so much energy in the air that it felt like static, and it still wasn't enough to cover the murderous rage coming off Hades. His dog, Conor, sat perfectly still at his heel, staring at Zeus.

It was frigid. Fucking freezing. Went straight to my core. I'd never been particularly worried about Zeus or his brothers—tall, yes, strong, yes, but able to kill me? Probably not.

That day, I was worried.

"Don't do this," Zeus said.

"I'm going to that motherfucker's office." It shocked me that Hades didn't raise his voice. I didn't know someone so quiet could be so terrifying. "Are you going to come with me and get those animals off your son's neck, or would you like me to handle it for you?"

*Your son* knocked the breath out of me.

"You can't kill him." Zeus smiled, like it was a joke, but I knew it wasn't. "Prison is unlivable for a man such as yourself."

Hades smiled back, and every instinct in my body said *run*. "I won't kill him, Zeus. I'll make him wish he was dead."

They left, Zeus driving the SUV.

The charges were dropped by dinnertime.

He's easy enough to Google, and, I'm seeing now, that was the same year their parents' main business declared bankruptcy. Nobody in Zeus's family ever mentioned a settlement, but I have no doubt Hades was behind it. Who knows? Maybe it was all three of them. I wouldn't put it past their wives, either.

So, what happened to Kenneth?

He took over one of the family's auxiliary businesses after he graduated from…

Stanford.

The asshole was scared enough to run to the op-posite side of the country. No sign he strayed from Stanford during his time here.

What's Daisy scared of?

No—those two things aren't connected. I'm sure that whatever Hades said in Coleman Sr.'s office all but guaranteed that his son would never come near her again. She didn't come to California out of fear.

She came because…

I don't know why. Some vague bullshit about mak-ing her own way. I've made it a point not to ask because hearing her name is like a bullet to the gut for no fuck-ing reason at all.

Maybe I should find out.

Another day.

Regardless, Kenneth didn't linger. He went back to New York to take over the business after his dad died.

After *both* his parents died.

But after she decided to *make her way*. If their paths had crossed, she would have told me. The only red flag here is how gladly I'd stomp him all over again.

The problem with all this research is that it's di-rectly connected to Daisy. I want eyes on her. I want to be sure she's okay.

I don't check the app, but I want to.

Instead, I text Shane about any other possible leads. He has the security footage from the art gallery.

Whoever tried to pick them off did it from a position where they were out of range of the camera.

> **Shane:** About halfway through the list of attendees. Not finding anything.
>
> **Hercules:** Send it over. I'll look too.

Working my way down the list of every person who attended Daisy's friend Marie's exhibition takes me the rest of the afternoon. My shoulder aches, and my back is stiff, and the sun's going down when I text Shane that I came up with nothing.

> **Shane:** We didn't either. No unusual activity on the property today.

I send a thumbs-up emoji like a fucking prick.

> **Shane:** How's she doing?

I have no explanation for the sick jealousy that turns my stomach at that text. Who the fuck does Shane think he is? Obviously, he's been with Daisy long enough to know about her trouble with light and even her seizures, but who does he think he *is*, asking me this?

Pain at my scalp alerts me to the fact that I've taken a fistful of my hair and *pulled.*

He's worried about her, that's all. He's not trying to get in her pants.

He'd better fucking *not* be trying to get in her pants, because she's mine.

She is my…client. My protectee. I haven't discussed payment with Zeus yet. You know what? Fuck it. I'm not taking any money from this. How are we supposed to sit around and put a price on what her life is worth? I won't do it. I'd rather fucking die.

I force myself to remember Shane's face last night. I'm sure he was white as a goddamn sheet. His hands shook. He knew about the seizures, but not about the kit, which means he's not close enough to Daisy for her to have given him one.

I'll have to talk to her about that, too. Her head of security should have that on him always. It's not right that he doesn't.

Unless she's hiding this kind of episode from her security.

> **Hercules:** She's fine, but it's against protocol to give out personal information about a protectee.
>
> **Shane:** Of course
>
> **Shane:** We're on the same team, though! Don't forget

I type out *back the fuck off, prick,* delete it, and send another thumbs-up emoji.

Enough of all that. I leave the phone with the tablet on the countertop and let myself stare at Daisy's studio door.

She hasn't cracked it in hours.

Normal, for artist types.

Right?

Not normal for security types to be fine with hours and hours of separation. There's a case to be made that I'm neglecting my duties by not busting down the door to check on her.

I need an excuse.

Wait—she didn't eat any scrambled eggs. She made me scrambled egg sandwiches, then flitted off to her studio without eating anything. I didn't see a mini-fridge when I looked in last night, just a stool and an easel surrounded by a lot of canvases with their faces to the walls.

Food it is.

A switch near the stove brings the lights up enough to see what I'm doing. Daisy has lots of cupboards, but not many dishes and pots and pans. That tracks. If she keeps to herself most of the time and lives alone, she wouldn't need much.

I find a box of shells in the pantry and put a pot of water on to boil. There's cheese in the fridge. Butter. A little bit of milk.

I'm tipping the shells into the rolling bubbles when it occurs to me that they weren't a random choice.

I'm nothing like Zeus, and he's not my dad, and here I am, cooking his niece shells and cheese because that's what *he* does.

I do *not* love that visual. I was in his house eighteen months, and I can see him at the stove at all hours of the night. He never stabbed the shells this aggressively with a spoon, but he still made them. Sometimes he'd carry the bowl upstairs so one or the other laudable son could keep writing their brilliant college papers. Many times, I'd be sitting out by the pool, hating one thing or another about myself or my life, and see him walk across the yard to Hades's house with the bowl in his palm like shells and cheese has ever fixed anything.

He even made them for me.

I never asked him why he made shells and cheese.

I'm pissed at him, and stuck at the stove, so why the fuck not?

> **Hercules:** Why do you always make shells and cheese for everyone?

He's not going to answer, because I have no right to ask this question. It's his own business.

> **Zeus:** People like shells and cheese

> **Hercules:** Don't fuck around with me

A longer pause.

> **Zeus:** Did something happen?

> **Hercules:** I'm standing here making fucking shells and cheese and I want to know why you do it

Three dots dance on the screen.

> **Zeus:** My sister was afraid to eat during the day in case Cronos came home, but she was also afraid of the stove.

> **Zeus:** She would wake me up when she got too hungry at night

> **Zeus:** Shells and cheese were her favorite

I can't breathe for a minute. It's a fact about his life. It shouldn't mean anything to me.

> **Hercules:** My mom liked peanut butter noodles

This pause feels purposeful, like he's waiting for me to say more. I don't give in.

> **Zeus:** I would have made those for you instead, if you wanted
>
> **Hercules:** No. I can't stand them
>
> **Zeus:** How's Daisy?
>
> **Hercules:** Shells are done, have to go

It's not a lie. They *are* done. I drain the water, add butter, melt the cheese in, add the milk. Find a fork and a napkin.

Time to approach the studio door.

I stand outside for a count of ten. Armed with the fact that the shells are getting cold, I turn the knob and push the door open.

The hinges don't make a sound, and it's *dark* inside.

Daisy sits on a stool at an easel on the ocean side of the room in a bubble of soft light. It's…not much. How can she see to paint?

She doesn't seem to notice that I'm here. Nothing about her posture changes and she moves her brush on the canvas the same way.

She's gorgeous like this.

Which makes no fucking sense, since all I can see is her silhouette in that soft, glowing light. Her hair. The movement of her arm.

Jesus. How *can* she see? Does she seriously live in the dark like this all the time? I know Hades is creepy like this.

It doesn't seem that creepy when it's Daisy, though.

I watch her until *I* feel like the fucking creep, back out of the door, and barge in with louder footsteps.

Daisy drops the paintbrush, her face outlined by the glow. "I told you not to come in here."

"I brought food." I don't stop walking until I'm right next to her, holding out the bowl, feeling very fucking much like my not-Dad. I hate that, but it's better to be close. A lot better.

Daisy's eyes go to the bowl. "I ate."

"No, you didn't. There's no—" I make a show of glancing around the room just in time. "There's no fridge in here. There's no food. You didn't eat eggs."

Her brow furrows. "I forgot, then. I was tired."

She probably felt like shit, since she had five fucking seizures last night. "I didn't forget. Come eat with me in the other room."

"I'm not done working."

"*Be* done working. We have to talk."

"About what?"

About nothing. I want her out of this room. I want to tuck her into bed. From my position next to her seat, I can see how tired she still is. It's all I can do not to pick her up and carry her out.

"Security updates."

She rubs a hand over her eyes, her shoulders dropping, and a quieter alarm goes off in the back of my mind. Daisy's in the dark already. She should be okay.

Aftereffects from last night, maybe.

I put my other hand out. Daisy uncovers her eyes and, with a sigh, puts her hand in mine.

We are not holding hands. I'm helping her up. That's *it*.

She follows me out to the living room and falls into an overstuffed couch. I give her the bowl and the napkin and the fork and take a seat across the room.

Wow—more torture. I want to be on that couch with her. There has to be a security justification for that.

Daisy takes a bite of shells and cheese and exhales like she's been starving for that and *only* that. Then she catches me watching and arches an eyebrow.

"You wanted to talk?"

"I looked into the people you mentioned. None of them seemed like good candidates for hiring a hit man. Shane and I also went through the list of attendees at the exhibition."

"Did you find anything?"

"No." Jesus, she looks so tired. I can't tell her about searching for Kenneth Prickman tonight. Not unless more evidence points to him. "But we should discuss some ground rules."

Amusement is different on a face with enormous black eyes. "You're giving me rules?"

"No, I'm giving myself rules. I have to be able to see you at least once an hour, so I'll be visiting you in your studio. Also, no more forgetting to eat."

Daisy tips a shell onto her tongue. It's not meant to

be provocative. She's not used to anyone watching her eat. "I'm sorry I forgot to eat."

"You are not."

"You're so *worried*." She curls her tongue around the fork, swallows the shell, and almost makes me come in my pants.

What the fuck.

What the *fuck fuck fuck*.

"I might've been worried before, but I'm not now."

"How come?"

"Because I'm watching you eat."

"Mmm. I think you could stand to watch harder." It takes everything in my body and soul not to leap across the room and watch her from six inches away. I'm going to come in my fucking pants. "*If* you're going to be this obsessed with me."

"I'm not obsessed with you. I've been hired to protect you because you got shot at."

She crosses her legs and eats another bite without breaking eye contact. "Okay."

"I'm not."

A shrug. "I said okay."

"If you have any meetings or appointments, I'll go with you. This doesn't look like it's going to be an open-and-shut thing."

"What meetings would I have?"

My fingers. Her hair. I want it so much I can feel it. "About your art, I'd assume."

"No. I don't have any art meetings planned."

"Do you not want to sell your pieces?"

"Selling them won't change anything."

Another alarm bell, this one louder. "Say that again, and a little less cryptic this time."

Daisy shakes her head like she genuinely didn't mean to say it out loud.

"I don't have any meetings planned to sell anything." She stands, and her knees wobble. I see it. I know I see it. The bowl goes on the coffee table. "I'm going to bed. I assume you'll be here in the morning."

"I will be," I say to her back.

*Are you going to be here?*

I don't ask. She's already gone.

# CHAPTER FIVE

*Daisy*

O ne slip-up, and the man your overprotective uncle sent to guard you from a mystery man with a gun gets ultra obsessed.

Hercules is up before me the next morning. When I come out of my bedroom, he's sitting at the kitchen island, tapping away on his tablet.

He gives me a one-second glance. "Morning."

"Good morning, sunshine."

I feel him roll his eyes as I cross to the fridge. "You'd never let the sun in here."

"Touché."

"I don't really think that was a touché-level point."

I take out eggs with what I hope is a casual shrug. "In the interest of keeping the conversation going."

"Oh? You want to talk?"

"You're here. It would be weird not to talk."

The awful truth is that I'm desperate to talk to him and I have no idea why. I don't know if it's his hair—how does a man have such perfect hair, anyway?—or his mouth, or the sound of his voice, or that I really have isolated myself too much over the past few years. I woke up three times last night wanting to go and find him.

For what?

Exactly. For *nothing*. He is my bodyguard, and that's it.

I didn't think about him when he was in the shower yesterday, and I'm not thinking about how his hair is still damp, which means he was in the shower this morning.

"You're making eggs again."

I hold up the carton. "You guessed it."

"I'm not eating unless you eat."

"You drive a hard bargain." I expect more of an argument, but he's gone back to his tablet. I scramble eggs in silence. "Are you...not going to say anything?"

"You're the client. I'm here to talk if *you* want to talk, except if it interferes with protecting you."

"First of all—" I brandish the spatula at him. "I'm not the client. Zeus is. Or my dad. Poseidon probably wanted in on it, too, but it's not me."

"Fine, but—"

"And second of all, since I'm not the client, don't talk to me like one."

Hercules raises his eyebrows. "Why shouldn't I talk to you like the *protectee*?"

"Because we both know this is weird. Acting all haughty and professional isn't going to make it better."

"Haughty?"

"All—*this way, ma'am, step back behind me, there's a shooter out there and we have to secure the perimeter.*"

He bursts out laughing. I've never heard him laugh that hard, ever, and it completely transforms his face. Hercules looks younger when he laughs. More open. Not like the intimidating ex-soldier who showed up on my porch yesterday.

"Is that what you think I sound like?" He swipes tears from the corners of his eyes.

"That's what I *know* you sound like." I turn away in time to rescue the eggs.

"I haven't said anything about securing the perimeter."

"I'm sure you will."

"Okay. Jesus. How *do* you want me to talk to you? Like we're *friends*?"

"Ha!" The toast pops up, startling the hell out of me, and I accidentally stick my fingers too far into the toaster to get it out. "Shit."

Hercules's stool falls over. I drop the toast on the plate and find him halfway around the island, expression set like he's going into battle.

"It's fine." His face doesn't change. He's *breathing* faster. Is this how he was in battle? Way too intense for the situation? That would explain his bazillion medals. "Hercules. It's fine. I, like, *slightly* overheated my fingers on the toaster." I hold my hand out to him, feeling ridiculous. "See?"

He takes my hand. His is a *lot* bigger than mine, and he has fine scars all over the back of his hand. They're hard to see unless you look closely. Hercules examines my fingers for several beats more than necessary—it's really not even a burn—before he drops my hand.

"Be careful."

"Message received, captain."

He rolls his eyes. "I wasn't a captain."

"Stand down, soldier."

His golden-brown irises flash. "Not a chance."

"*Hercules.* We don't even like each other. You can relax."

He takes a deep breath, lets it out, and goes back to his place at the kitchen island. I'm cutting the scrambled egg sandwiches into triangles when he speaks, too soft for me to hear.

"Pardon?" I'm going to put my plate on *this* side of the island, and his plate on the other, but Hercules reaches for both of them. I give them up automatically, like he's allowed to decide where I sit, and Hercules puts my plate next to his.

I'm almost to the other stool, wondering where I went wrong in my life, when he speaks.

"It wasn't you."

"What?" I pretend not to notice that he puts a hand behind me as I slide onto the stool, like he's worried I might fall off.

"It wasn't you that I didn't like."

"Oh?" My face goes hot. Great. He'll notice. Living in the dark most of the time means that any blush is instantly obvious. I can't look at him, but I can't *not* look at him. When I finally get up the courage to steal a glance, Hercules is already looking at me, his scrambled egg sandwiches untouched.

"It was me. I didn't like…" His eyes move to the plate, then back to mine. "I didn't like what I'd become. What my life had become. It wasn't you."

"That's—" Terrible. "Good to know? I think. Because I didn't actually hate you. I thought you hated me and acted accordingly."

"Glad we can put that behind us."

He reaches for napkins, clearly glad to be done with this conversation.

"There's something you should know, though."

"What's that?" Hercules hands me a napkin.

"It would be easier if you *did* hate me. I wouldn't mind if you did."

"What would be easier? The job?"

"Everything." This is why I shouldn't spend so much time alone. I blunder into conversations like *this* without meaning to. "Everything would be easier."

Hercules shrugs. The skin around his eyes tightens

when his right shoulder tries to lift with the left one. "Too late."

The next morning, he takes one look at me and refuses to let me make the scrambled egg sandwiches.

I don't like that.

I *really* don't like that.

"Is there any specific reason you've ordered me to sit here? Or is it for my safety?"

"The second one," he answers, without turning around.

"I've made eggs in front of you twice. You know I can do it."

"You almost burned your hand off yesterday."

"I touched the toaster with my fingertips for less than a second. I was fine."

"Are you fine right now?" He meets my eyes with a glance over his shoulder, and I look away. It's a sign of weakness. I don't usually like to give in to those, but the fact is…

The fact is, I'm not at my best.

"I've never been better." I can't even pretend to look out the window. It's too hard to see through the filters. Hercules goes back to the scrambled eggs with a huff. "You don't get to assume stuff about me because you're here."

"What did I assume?"

"That I'm too fragile to cook eggs."

"When did I say that?"

"When you leaped out of your seat and tied me to this one."

He turns a surprised expression on me. "I would remember tying you to a piece of furniture. Are you making a request?"

My cheeks blaze. "I'm saying I'm *fine.*"

"I believe you."

"No, you don't."

"Does it matter if I believe you?"

"*Yes,*" I snap, and I can't explain why. I don't know whether I want him to argue with me until I admit what's going on or leave it alone.

"Then I fucking believe you. Is that good enough, or do you need me to beg for your forgiveness, too?"

His voice is so sharp, so raw, that I startle in spite of myself. "What? No."

"Go ahead and tell me which thoughts are acceptable to share with you. Do you need me to run them through a rich-asshole filter first? Should I run them by Shane before I open my mouth?"

"Shane doesn't have anything to do with this—"

"You seem *tired.*" Hercules hasn't raised his voice, but the words are like a whip. "If I don't meet your requirements for making eggs, then tell me *that,* and we can find someone who—"

"Jesus Christ, you can make the eggs. What is *wrong* with you?"

"What's wrong with *you*?" He shoots back, and for

the first time in the entire conversation, I get a good look at his face. *He* looks tired. He looks like he hasn't slept. He looks like he might've spent the night trying to find the shooter, or fretting about…

Not about me.

I'd hope it wasn't about me.

I can't tell him what's wrong, and I don't like the feeling I have that he already knows. I do not like being seen that way. *Fucked up.* That's why I'm in California and not New York. I didn't want anyone in my family to witness what I know is coming, and what I can't stop.

He's looking right through me, and it's like standing out in the sun. I can't take it.

"I'm going back to bed."

Hercules tosses the frying pan onto another burner. "Daisy."

"I have a headache. I'm going back to bed."

I go into my bedroom, lie down, and breathe. That was…that was normal. That's what I asked for. I asked for him not to treat me like a *job*, and he went right back to treating me like…

Like he hates me.

"Bullshit," I whisper to the blankets.

Because it's not true. He never hated me like that. He never hated me by insisting I sit down while he cooked. He never hated me by accusing me of hiding, which is essentially what just happened.

And it happened because I'm losing it.

I'm not losing my mind, per se. I'm losing my filter.

I start the day on edge and go to bed exhausted. It's getting harder to recover from the seizures, which is… also my fault.

There's a quiet knock on the door, and it opens.

I keep my eyes closed.

Footsteps cross the floor, and then the side of the bed dips.

He waits.

I wait.

I get sick of waiting and open my eyes. A plate with scrambled egg sandwiches on it hovers in front of my face.

"I'm sorry for being an asshole," I say, mostly to the plate.

Hercules uses the plate to nudge my shoulder, so I sit up and take it from him. He's brought both plates in here. As soon as I have mine situated on my lap, he starts eating like we didn't revert to our previous habits.

I eat, too.

The eggs are good. He made them the way I would.

"I wasn't alone when I jumped out of the helicopter." Hercules mentions this in a way that's so casual it has to hurt.

"Isn't…" I have to swallow a bite of scrambled egg sandwich that suddenly feels dry and unwieldy. "Isn't that usually how it goes? I don't know that much about secret Army stuff, but I thought people usually went with teams."

"I was with a friend. My best…" He puts a section

of his scrambled egg sandwich down on the plate, then picks it back up. "Ollie."

My heart slows down as if it thinks it can slow down time, too. "Yeah?"

"Yeah. His parachute didn't deploy. And his backup one was fucked somehow." Hercules meets my eyes, and it's a shock. He looks how he did when I first met him. Angry and desperate and—and grief-stricken. "Mine wasn't enough to get us both to the ground in one piece. I'd have taken it off midair and put him in it, if I could, but I couldn't."

"God." There are plates. And he probably wouldn't like being hugged, so I don't. "I'm sorry."

"That's what's wrong with me. That's *part* of what's wrong with me."

"You don't have to tell me the rest."

"You don't have to tell me at all. You don't have to tell me anything." Hercules goes back to eating, his shoulders tense. "But you can if you want to."

That night I fall asleep too early. Ridiculously early. Exhaustion comes on fast. One minute I'm eating the best chicken salad I've ever had, and the next I can hardly keep my eyes open.

It means I'm awake too early, too.

That's how I find out when Hercules wakes up.

Before sunrise. Early as *hell*.

I pad out of my room, thinking of the couch, and

almost run into him in the kitchen. The scent of his skin hits me first. He's freshly showered, smelling so warm and clean and good that I could keep walking until my face was pressed to his chest.

His bare chest.

Because he's shirtless.

And he has the lights up enough for me to see his skin.

His right arm, the injured one, is covered in tattoos, but they reach around his collarbone and the opposite bicep, too.

They're covering scars.

The ones on the right side of his body, anyway. The shoulder that didn't survive the Army in one piece has surgical scars crisscrossing the skin. Like the ones on his hand, they're only revealed in *just* the right light.

I can't stop staring.

I know it's rude, I know it's *wrong*, but I'm compelled. How does he look like this? It's not even close to being as bright as the dawn, but *he's* bright, like he has an aura. Like he's lit from within.

Oh, shit.

"Daisy?"

I hear my name from far away. So far away that it takes what seems like hours to have any meaning. In that time, I can't take my eyes off his scars. Are they lighted, too?

Is this a waking dream?

Probably not. This isn't what my dreams are like.

But this feeling of being trapped in one is eerily similar. I actually *will* lose it if my dreams start to involve my actual house. That would make it impossible to tell if I was dreaming, and that would be bad.

Or…would it? I wouldn't mind the dream aspect of my life if Hercules was in them. Shirtless, preferably, because I could look at him like this for the rest of my life and never get bored. Who has muscles like that? Did his tattoo artist take the dips and angles into account?

How much do tattoos hurt, anyway? Do they hurt more if you do them over scars?

I want to know the answers *so* badly. None of them make it to my lips.

This is embarrassing.

This should be embarrassing, but it's not like I can help it. Hercules should know by now.

Would his muscles feel different if he touched me?

"I think you should go back to sleep."

Hercules has his hand on my elbow and has already turned us toward my bedroom door when my brain offers me the answer a century too late.

"Yeah."

"Yep." Sadly, his muscles do *not* feel different when he's guiding me with a gentle touch like I'm a lady out of the past. I'd have to have my body all over his to feel that.

He walks me to the bed, helps me in, and pulls up the blanket. If I could, I'd reach up and pull him down into the bed with me. I'd tell him how flushed my body feels under the sheets. I'd tell him how good he looks, and how I can't understand why I wouldn't admit it to myself before.

*I can't sleep. That's why I was up.*

I don't get a chance to say it before I'm asleep again.

"Are you going to tell me about your painting?" he asks on the fourth day. The fifth day?

I'm so tired.

"No." The problem is, I'm so tired that I can't bicker with him about staying out of the studio. He's been spending more time in here every day, sitting out of my circle of light and being totally unobtrusive. Hercules doesn't push me for answers. It's getting harder not to give them.

I'm painting, and trying not to let it happen.

The thing is.

This is the kind of exhaustion that comes before a nightmare. It's like sleep tries to drag me in. Make it impossible to escape. I'm fighting a losing battle, and I know that.

I fight anyway.

"What are you painting?" It feels like a minute later, but I'm also losing my hold on time.

"A dream."

"I have to say, Daisy, that doesn't look like a dream."

The canvas abruptly comes into focus in front of

me. I haven't been paying much attention while I paint. I never do. The paintings *happen*, same as the nightmares.

It's jagged. Spiky. Thousands of small, sharp brush-strokes, like a legion of claws tearing the canvas apart. Just like fifteen other ones I have stored in built-in shelves on the side of the studio. This is all that comes out no matter what I will my hand to do.

I hate it.

My head swims.

I have to get out of here.

I drop the brush and go. Hercules is on his feet, too, but I don't look back for him. Too tired. I'll lose my balance. What I need is to go outside.

"Daisy."

I have a lovely beachfront property. I wasn't so off about the time, after all. It's midafternoon. Opening the back door lets in blinding light. I'm between painkillers. Perfect timing. Jesus. *Jesus,* that hurts.

The sun is the lesser of two evils, so I walk out into it like I belong there. Out across the strip of grass. Out to warm sand, and stop.

Look up.

My eyes water, but I force them open. It won't take long. It just *feels* like forever. It won't take long, and then—

A hand covers my eyes, and it's blessedly, wretchedly dark. A strong arm goes solidly around my waist, holding me close to an equally solid body. *That's* what his muscles feel like. It's Hercules. I feel like I've always known his hands.

"Daisy." His voice vibrates through his body and mine. "What the fuck are you doing?"

"Uncover my eyes."

"You could not *pay* me to uncover your eyes right now. Answer me. What the fuck are you doing?"

"Listen, it's just—it's not a big deal. Uncover my eyes."

"What happens if I do that?"

"I swear, it won't be a big deal."

A pit of despair opens up underneath me. It feels huge, like all the sand from the beach and from the ocean could fall into it. My eyes are closed underneath Hercules's palm. Everything has a staticky, blurry feeling anyway. It feels so bad. It feels *so bad* to wait.

"Are you…" The note of horror in his voice walks a little shiver down my spine. "Are you *trying* to have a seizure right now?"

"Well…yeah."

He turns me around by the shoulders, his hand lifting only long enough for him to wrap both hands over my eye sockets and lean close. Gold spirals around his pupils, bleeding into honey brown. Lucky guy. My eyes don't do pretty colors anymore. *Freak.* He studies my eyes like there's anything new to see.

"Why?" Hercules is calm now. Steady. Maybe *this* is why he has so many medals. He's calm under pressure.

"It's lesser. It's the lesser."

"The lesser of *what*?"

"Two evils."

"What's the second evil?" His brow furrows, and God, I don't want to tell him about this. I'm already in it, though, and I can't see a way out.

"A nightmare."

"Daisy…there's no fucking way a nightmare is as bad as a seizure."

"You don't know what you're talking about."

"I don't know—I don't *know*?" He takes a breath. Releases it. His hands don't shake at all. "Yes. I do."

"You, like, *really* don't."

"Yes, I do," he bursts out. "I was there the other night. I saw everything."

I'd pull back from him, but that would mean letting the sun in. My body does *not* want to be in the sun. "Which night?"

"The night you got shot at. Shane was still here when I got in. You were having your *fifth* fucking seizure."

"You *lied*."

"Yeah! I lied. I'd have done the same thing for anybody in my—I'd have done the same thing for anyone. Nobody wants to be seen at their worst."

"*That's not my worst.*"

He freezes, his eyes going wide. "So you'd rather do this. Jesus Christ."

Hercules takes his hands away from my eyes so quickly that they squeeze shut on instinct. Then I'm up, in his arms, and he folds my face into his shoulder without asking permission. He swears once for every step he takes all the way back to my house.

He only stops once, his arms tense. "Fuck."

Then we're inside. Hercules deposits me on the couch and takes out his phone. The house goes dark. No light. It feels so good, and it's not right, because I'll fall asleep. A flash almost blinds me again. It's his phone. He's sending a message.

"What are you doing?"

"Texting Shane to get his people on the beach."

"Why? I'm in here."

"Because somebody else is out there, and I want to know who it is. Bad things happen in threes, and I need to know if this is the second."

"Why don't you go—" The couch dips, and then Hercules takes my face in his hands. His legs go on either side of mine. All my nerves spark. We can't do this. But, like…we can. I'm not sure I'm fully awake. "What are you doing?"

"Talk," he demands. "What are you so afraid of?"

"I don't want to have a nightmare. I said that before. I don't want it." Nervousness gathers at the base of my spine. "I don't have nightmares if I have an attack. It's so simple."

"…you know that your brain can *die* from seizures, right?"

"Wow. I never knew. Thank you for telling me. Also, thanks for lying about—"

"I got here when I got here. I should've told you about it, but I didn't. That's my fault. But this?" His hands hint at shaking my face. "This is fucked up. Is this why you're in California? Because of some dreams? I'm pretty sure your family can handle that."

"They can't. And honestly, it's none of your business if I'd rather choose a little pain over a horrendous nightmare."

"It is my fucking business." He leans in so close I can almost feel his lips on mine. I'd barely have to move my head to kiss him. To bite him. To stop *thinking* about his lips and take action. "Jesus, Daisy. If you want pain, there are other ways to get that than killing yourself."

"Like what?"

"Like…" He makes a low sound. Not despair, exactly. Close to it, though. "This is so fucked."

Oh, shoot.

Oh, no.

My head gets heavy in Hercules's hands, and the conversation isn't enough.

The nightmare wins.

It's dark, and then it's not. The space is empty, and then it's not. A cat's eyes glint in the shadows. A kitten. A black kitten.

"Hi." It never comes to me, and I wish it would. "Come here."

The eyes disappear.

I don't have to look for the gates. The dream pulls me to them. The nightmare. Huge, imposing gates.

They're black, and they're not-black, and it doesn't matter because what's *through* them—

Is my family.

My mom. My dad. My cousins. Everybody. Dead. Dead. *Dead.*

I can't stop.

I don't want to go in there, and I do, because where else should I be, if not with them?

I can't—

Stop.

The closer I get, the less clear they are. Less skin, more bone. Less human, more monster. None of them is right, but I know without a doubt it's *them.*

I don't know who I'll be if I go through those gates, and the pull hurts more than the sun. Resisting it turns my stomach. I dig my heels in. Makes no difference on smooth stone.

I put out my hands to stop myself, to grab *anything*, and they're covered in blood.

Both hands. Fingertips to wrist.

Because.

I killed them. I'm the one who killed them. I'm the reason they're through the gates, they're not themselves, I made them that way, I made them—

The kitten screams.

A louder voice taps at the boundary of the dream, then shatters it.

"Daisy. *Daisy.* Daisy. Wake up. Wake *up.*"

It's Hercules.

Resurfacing gives me a pressure headache like you wouldn't believe. My throat feels cut up. And worst of all, the dream's fighting back.

I don't know how I ended up in Hercules's lap, but I lunge for his neck and hang on tight.

"Don't let it happen again." This is supposed to be an order but it comes out desperate. "I don't want to go back in there."

"What do you want me to do?"

"*Anything.*"

"Where's the line? You have to fucking tell me. Where's the line, Daisy?"

"There isn't one."

One of his hands moves over my hair. "Tell me not to hurt you."

I'm going to lose it. "Hercules. *Please.*"

He kisses me hard enough to bruise.

It hurts.

Thank God.

# CHAPTER
## SIX

*Hercules*

THIS IS AGAINST EVERY RULE AND REGULATION in every set of rules and regs ever to exist.

I don't give a fuck.

My brain *tries* to give a fuck, because this is my job. This is my only job now that the Army doesn't want me. This is the only thing left for me to do.

And it's *not* my job, because no money has changed hands. I can do whatever the hell I want.

It's *more* than a job, because my not-Dad asked me to do it, and as soon as my mind comes up with reasons to stick to my professional code of ethics, it shoots them down. Bullets through the heart. They don't matter. If this hinges on *family*, then going above and beyond the call of duty is the only option. It makes no difference if the family isn't mine.

And...

I can't say no to her.

Fuck, I tried, but I can't. I tried to do the responsible thing and ask for her limits. I tried.

I'll try again later.

For now, I kiss Daisy like a feral creature, because that's how she kisses me. Her body stays soft and delicate but her kiss is teeth and claws. Fingernails dig into my neck. One of them meets a pain point from when I hit the ground, and when she finds it, she pushes harder.

It's a battle of a kiss.

At first it feels like me against her. Like every glare and huff and cold shoulder wrapped into a series of bites.

But that's not what it is.

This moment is sharp enough to cut, but that's not all she is. Daisy tastes sweet, like summertime and lemonade and a flower in bloom.

And underneath...

Power.

Like a laugh in the dark. Like razor-sharp nails. Like a nightmare.

Is that her, or the dream? Dreams aren't real. They can't pull people down into them, but that's exactly what happened. Her head drooped in my hands, and her body went with it, and it *pulled*.

What the hell am I saying? I've survived the un-survivable enough times to know that the rules of the world aren't set in stone.

Daisy straddles me and *bites*.

Her teeth hurt like a motherfucker, but it's the hottest thing I've ever felt. My heart beats like I'm actually in a battle.

I am. We are.

But not against each other.

Against the pull in the air behind her.

Fuck whatever *that* is. It can't have her.

Not right now.

I have both hands in her hair before I can think about stopping. It's soft between my fingers and I make fists on instinct. I want to hold it tighter and I want the black hole hovering nearby to have to work for it.

Daisy moans into my mouth.

I break away from her biting kiss. "This the line? Is this too far?"

"Not far enough."

Fingernails streak down the side of my neck and push into my shirt collar. "You don't know what you're asking for."

"Tell me what I'm asking for, then."

She finds my bottom lip in the dark and adds another set of marks to it, so I bite her back. It would be so easy to lose control. Give it all up. Why bother with it? What good did it ever do?

"You tell *me*." Another fistful of her hair. A harder

pull. It tips her chin up so I can skim my teeth over her neck. "You fucking tell me. I'm here for *you*."

"Pretend you're not."

"What does that mean?"

"Pretend you're not here for me. Pretend you're here for whatever big, scary men do in the dark."

"No." Guilt skitters across my consciousness, chased down by regret, and I can't. I can't. "We'd have to—talk. About that shit. Before I—"

"Before you *what*? Tell me what you'd do to me. I know you want to. I can feel it."

Daisy lets her full weight rest across my hips, the heat of her pussy directly over my cock, and my eyes roll back in my head. It's nothing. We're separated by layers of clothing and the last shreds of honor.

I'd fuck her into the bed. I'd make her take my cock down her throat. I'd pinch her nipples and spank her ass and fuck her there, too.

I want to hear *that* scream. Not the nightmare one.

It snaps in the air, and her body jerks backward like a fucking *dream* can take her away.

It can. It is.

I take her chin in my hand and kiss her until she whimpers and grinds down on my jeans. I'd think it was a front, some game she's playing, except her hands are tight fists in my shirt and that fucking thing has its hooks in her.

I don't know how to fight some mysterious pressure in the air. It reminds me of being in the same room as

Hades when his painkillers have run out. That's like a heavy blanket, or high altitude, or being deep underwater. It pops your ears.

This goes one way. I don't know where it ends, but she doesn't want to be there.

"Tell. Me. What. You. Want." My grip might be too tight on her chin, but her body moves with it like she can actually withstand my strength. "I'm not doing this unless you tell me."

"You said—" Her balance tips in my hand. What I *should* do is stand up, cover her eyes, and go after whatever's hurting her, but some part of me understands that it *is* her. That it's coming from her. That her clinging hands and her biting kisses are like climbing hooks. "You said there were other ways to get pain. That's what I want."

"Is that what you were trying to get outside?"

"Yes."

"If this is about the dream and you don't want to do this with me, then you have to fucking say that. You have to say it right now. I'll get another man. I'll have someone brought here."

I wouldn't. I'd rather walk into the sea.

Fuck. I would. If that's what she wanted.

Daisy leans forward with so much force that it has to be hurting her scalp. "If I wanted anyone but you, I'd have *done that by now*. What is it going to take for you to fuck me?"

I can't see her. That's how dark it is. I can only feel

her heat. An explosion goes off in my head. A grenade. A flashbang. Bright, like her, and dangerous as fuck underneath, also like her.

Because.

*Because.*

"You've never fucked anyone before?"

"*No.* If I wanted anyone but you, I'd have—" Daisy gasps. I guess a sudden change in altitude will do that to a person. It takes three full heartbeats to understand that I'm the one who did it. I stood up from the couch, and fuck whatever's in this room with us, whatever's trying to drag her away. "What's happening?"

What's happening is that she lit my blood on fire. Every inch of me is super-sensitive. I can feel every surgical scar and every fucked-up tendon in my shoulder. I can feel where the bones lock together when they're not supposed to. I can feel my cock waging war with my zipper and my heart beating out of my fucking chest.

"If we're doing this, we're doing it on a bed."

"If?" Daisy's arms go around my neck, and her head drops against my shoulder like that thing, that *dark*, has its hand in her hair, too. "You don't want to?"

I find the nearest wall by memory and push her up against it. Her legs wrap around my hips, and I get both hands back in her hair, where they belong. My mouth over hers. Christ, what *is* that taste? How does she taste like that? How does she taste like everything she can't have, and I can't have?

How can I taste her at all?

"Tell me you don't want this."

She arches against the wall, against me. "No."

"Tell me not to hurt you."

"I want you to hurt me."

"Tell me you *hate* me, and you'd rather die than fuck me."

"No, no, *no*." It becomes a chant, her hips rolling against mine, and I'm going to die. This is how I'll die. Stuck between her kitchen and her bedroom in the dark. "No," Daisy whispers, and bites me again.

We make it to the bedroom. It's not easy, because I push her up against every wall I find and mark her neck and her shoulder and her lips. And whatever she was dreaming is a physical tug toward the living room.

It doesn't stop when I kick the door shut.

It doesn't stop when I put her on the bed and strip off her shirt, and her bra, and her leggings.

It doesn't stop when I take the waistband of her panties in my fists.

"How do you want it?"

"Want what?"

"The pain."

A shiver goes through her, and she puts her hand on my wrist. "How can I have it?"

"I could bite you. Put you over my lap. Fuck you like you're not a princess."

"I'm *not* a princess." She's adamant. "But I'm not…"

"Not what?"

"I'm not supposed to want this." *That's* the new

tension in the air, then. Daisy's pure and perfect and *protected,* and she doesn't think she's supposed to like it rough.

I said that to her once, my hands cuffed to a table. *Girls like me?*

*Ones who get off on a rough fuck with a strange man.*

"You think *I'm* supposed to want this? I'm not." Another flood of guilt, up to my eyeballs, to the top of my head. "I'm not supposed to want to fuck you like an animal."

A short, delighted gasp. "That's what you want?"

"That's what I've always wanted. Why the fuck do you think I stayed away from you? I couldn't have this."

"You can have it now. Take it. Take it, please. Make it hurt."

Her panties come apart in my hands. I wasn't aware of starting to rip them. There's no missing her nails digging into my shirt, though. No missing how she tries to rip it off me, too.

I help the cause and shed all my clothes.

Daisy pulls me into the bed. On top of her. She moves at the right moment so we're centered, safe from falling.

Time stops.

It's an illusion, but I only know that because my heart still beats. Daisy's hands slow on my chest. She's trembling.

"It's okay to want this," I tell her. "However you want it."

"You sound…" I don't like the way she says that. It's the same way her *father* says it, and he hears all the pathetic things you'd never say out loud. I do *not* want to think about him in this moment. "Worried."

"That's not what it is. It's just memories. You don't want to get into that right now, I swear."

"You're not worried about me?"

"I'm so worried about you I can hardly stand it. But not because you want a certain kind of sex. Because I don't want you to hate me for it later. I don't want you to be ashamed of it later."

"That guy at the gala," she says, so softly I could pretend not to hear, if I was an asshole. "I didn't like that."

"This isn't the same thing. You're *asking* me to do this. And you can change your mind whenever you want."

"I hated what he did."

"I know."

"I want you to do more." Daisy's entire body tenses, and I guess doors don't matter at *all,* because the pressure is in here now. "I want you to do it *now.*"

"Does it need to be pain? Only pain?"

Her hands go to my hair, and she threads her fingers through the same way I did to her. She'll take me with her like this. We'll both be dragged in.

I can't say I mind.

"What else is there?" she asks, her voice tight.

Part of her snaps into focus. When Daisy thinks of intensity, she thinks of pain, because that's her life.

That's her body. The brightest things hurt the most. For her, the opposite of pain is only its absence.

Nobody's taught her pleasure.

Even my mother knew about that.

Goose bumps race over my skin as the pressure gets closer, stronger. I'm not letting it have her. If I have to fuck it out of her, then I will.

"Do you trust me?"

"Yes." More tension. "Hurry. *Hurry.*"

I dip my head to one of her nipples and bite. Daisy lets out a sob, and the pressure recoils.

It doesn't leave.

I bite until her body tries to escape and lick over the marks, then repeat it on her other nipple. Her hands clench at my hair. She's not gentle.

It feels so fucking good.

So good.

Just to touch her.

Fuck.

I can hurt her all she wants, but I can't do *only* that. Daisy makes tiny begging noises while I kiss down over her belly, down and down and down until I'm forced by raw need to push her thighs apart.

Her legs tense, and I pat at one of her hands, locked in my hair.

"Don't let go," I tell her.

I think she says *okay*, but all I care about is that her fingers stay in my hair while I lick her clit.

*I didn't know,* Daisy says from a million miles away. *Oh my God. I didn't know.*

I take that as an invitation to lick her everywhere. The dream—the tension, the thing, whatever the hell it is—*hates* that. Her hips buck up into my hands and she pulls me closer to her cunt by the hair. I could get away if I tried, but fuck that.

I'm not going anywhere.

Not when she tastes this good, this sweet, fuck, how did I live next door to her for a year and a half and never eat her out? I could've climbed in her bedroom window. I could've taken her into any of the bedrooms. I could've—

I could've—

Who cares?

I eat her like a madman, and Daisy fucks my face like she doesn't care if it hurts.

Right—she wants it to hurt.

I test my teeth over her clit as an experiment and she shoves my face into her pussy and comes, wild, slick, *everywhere.* I lick it all off her, then drag her to the edge of the bed.

Daisy lets out a frustrated growl when I take my mouth away. Before she has any more time to complain, I put her over my lap and take her throat in my left hand. She gets one good kick in. Then my right palm connects with her ass.

My shoulder screams, but it's drowned out by Daisy's howl.

That's the hottest sound I've ever heard.

The dark pull of the nightmare, if *that's* what it is, shrinks back. I laugh out loud and spank her again.

"Is that what you like? Is that why your pussy was so wet? You like being punished?"

Holy fuck, she's not trying to get away. She's trying to push her ass into my hand. I wish it wouldn't hurt her to have the lights on. I wish I could see this.

I settle for spanking her again, twice, four times, six.

"You're fucking filthy. You pretend to be a little princess, untouched, untouchable, but all you wanted was me. You wanted a red ass and somebody to hold you down and hurt you."

"Mmm." The sound goes through my palm. "Yes. *Yes.*"

I run my hand over the hot curve of her ass. "You sure this is what you want? You don't want some rich prick to be sweet to you?"

"No—no, I don't, I don't—"

"Be a slut for it, then. A good slut knows how to beg. Hasn't anyone taught you how to beg?"

"Please."

I laugh again, and the heat of her body skyrockets. Or maybe it's in my imagination. Either way, she's soaked. I can smell her. Daisy has no idea how much restraint it takes not to pin her down again and lick her until she screams.

"That was pathetic. You can do better."

"Please. Please. Please, hurt me."

"Who should hurt you?"

"You. Please. Hercules, please. I need it. I need you to—*please*." She's not crying, she's desperate. Daisy *would* have a ridiculous threshold for pain. She looks breakable, but she's not.

"Need me to *what*? Use your words, or I'll gag you and take them away."

"Hit me again."

"I'm not hitting you."

"*Spank* me again. Do it harder. Please, please—I can't, please—"

I give her ten, all in a row, and her wounded howl is better than any medal I ever won in the Army.

"Don't stop, don't, don't—"

I don't stop.

Her body tenses, then curves over my lap, and then she gives in completely.

I know what that is.

It's trust.

I don't deserve it, and way in the back of my mind, doubt creeps in. A sense of humanity. I shouldn't be doing this. Not to her. Not to anyone. It makes me like the men who fucked my mother. It makes me like the men who hurt her, and—

Pressure. My ears. Hers. It's that fucking dream. A last-ditch attempt. That's what it feels like.

I pull her off my lap and bend her over a pillow on the bed, pinning her hard to the covers. My hand knows the way to her face in the dark and I shove two fingers into her mouth hard enough that she *does* gag.

"Suck. *Better* than that."

Daisy recovers, her tongue curling around my fingers. I want that tongue wrapped around my cock, but that's not going to beat this thing in her mind, this thing trying to get at her. At both of us. In the field, you don't stand around waiting for the enemy to get stronger. You shoot it between the eyes.

That's what I'm doing.

For *her*.

She wants it. She *wants* me.

My fingers leave her mouth with a wet *pop* and I push them into her slick hole because I want to feel her heat, feel the clench. I get what I wanted. Daisy tries to fuck them, so I pin her more solidly against my body. My thumb and index finger are enough to spread her cheeks.

She makes a wordless, questioning sound when my soaked fingers make contact with a *much* tighter hole.

"You wanted it to hurt, didn't you?"

"I—I—"

"Did you change your mind, sweetheart? Want me to be nice? Want me to put you on your back and let you get used to me and fuck you slow?"

Her sounds get desperate.

I deliver two hard slaps to her ass. "Words, Daisy."

"No, that's not—that's not—that's not what I want."

"You're shaking. Are you scared?"

"Yes."

"Do you like it when I scare you?"

*Yes.* A whisper into the mattress. I put my fingers to her hole and push.

"I've never felt anything tighter than you. Does it hurt?"

She gasps. Gasps again. I'm two knuckles deep. Not particularly gentle.

"Can you take it? Answer me, princess."

"Good—" She *just* manages it. I'm going to have to give up on coherent sentences soon, and I don't mind that at all. That feels like victory. That's *real* victory. "Job. Good job. Say—"

"You want me to tell you you're doing a good job? You want me to tell you you're such a good girl?"

"Yes." High. Embarrassed. Perfect.

"Then take my fingers *better* than that. You were a whore for my mouth on your pussy, but I don't believe you like this. Fuck my fingers like you mean it."

Daisy doesn't miss a beat. She pushes back on me, taking the rest of my fingers, and I hold still.

"*Move,*" I snap. "That's not fucking my fingers. You're sitting there. That's not what I told you to do, is it?"

She moves, and I fuck her deeper with my fingers. This *has* to be painful. I'm an animal right now. I didn't bother to ask about lube. To hell with stopping. Even her body is sweet like sunshine. Even the way she fucks herself on my fingers is bright and warm.

"Good. That's a good girl. I knew you could do it. Princess-types like you always take some time to learn. It's not your fault, baby. Nobody taught you a damn thing. You're so brave, being such a slut for me. Fuck— your asshole tried to keep my fingers. Should I put my cock there instead?"

"No. No. Fuck me. Instead. Please? Fuck me now. Please?"

"Who should fuck you now?"

"Hercules, please, please, please. Please."

I drive my fingers in deep, stretching her around two knuckles, spreading them wide so she feels the stretch, and lean down over her. Daisy shakes head to toe. My breath on her ear sends a shiver down the full length of her spine. So do my teeth on her earlobe.

"You can still change your mind," I whisper.

She turns and throws her arms around my neck, an upside-down tackle that lands me on top of her. Daisy's legs find my waist, her sweet, soaked cunt sliding help- lessly against my cock until I take it in my hand and give her the right angle.

Daisy exhales on the first inch, her entire body puls- ing around me along with her cunt.

I've succeeded.

I've worked her up past the point where she can think, and well past the point where that fucking night- mare's going to touch her.

And I don't want to always hurt her. I don't want her to only think of pain when she thinks of me.

So I smooth a hand over her hair. Brush my lips over her cheek. Kiss her bottom lip with no teeth.

"Shh. There's no rush."

A panicked whimper.

"The dream is gone. You don't have to rush. Can't you feel it?"

"No." Her voice trembles with the rest of her. "I can't feel anything but you."

"That's good. Can you take me, or do you want help?"

The silence is like a penny falling into a well, almost audible.

"You can ask for help. I won't tell anybody."

"Help," she whispers. "You. Do it. You do it."

"Okay. Hold on."

Her arms curve around my neck and find my hair, and I find...

Not restraint. Not humanity. It's whatever she needs.

I stay close enough to kiss her while I rock my hips. Not too slow, because she's too keyed up for that. Not so fast it hurts.

This shouldn't hurt. Not this time. If she wants me to fuck her pussy so hard she cries, we can do that another day.

Daisy's body melts around me, letting me in like she was born to do this. I'm halfway inside her when her mouth meets the side of my neck and she kisses as soft as I did.

Maybe she wants this, too.

No, she *does* want this, too. That's what all those sounds mean. They're wondering, almost floating, and it makes me both furious and fiercely happy that nobody's ever given her this before.

I'm three-quarters of the way in when she rocks her hips up to meet me, taking me deeper and deeper until there's nowhere left to go.

Daisy doesn't want to let go of me, but she doesn't resist when I push her down to the pillows and lift her hips with my left hand. It angles her body so I can reach her clit, and I circle it light and quick while she clenches around me, all her weight in my palm.

"Come on my cock. That's so good. You feel fucking incredible. Good girl. Oh, you're so fucking close. Do it. Yes—*there,* yes—"

I fall into her arms and fuck her while she comes, fuck her while *I* come, saying her name into the curve of her shoulder.

She's not the only one who forgot about pleasure.

If it wasn't already dark, I'd be blind with it.

When it's over, I put her on the side of the bed closer to the door, curve my body around hers, and watch her while she falls asleep.

Nothing's getting to her now.

# CHAPTER
# SEVEN

*Daisy*

**W**HAT AM I SUPPOSED TO DO?

*Not* fuck Hercules constantly?

Exactly. There's no way around it. The sex is for health reasons, and for sanity reasons, and because I can't breathe without wanting it.

I realize that within about five minutes of waking up the next morning, no signs of the nightmare, a naked Hercules in my bed.

The one *single* problem is that I can feel it starting to come on again. The next nightmare is distant, waiting in the wings, but it's still there.

He opens his eyes as I climb on top of him.

The windows are set to let a little light in during the morning so I don't lose track of my days, so there's enough to see the shadows and lines of his face, enough to see the pink flush in his cheeks, enough to see the gold streaks in his eyes.

Hercules arches an eyebrow at me, sleepy, wary. "You don't want to discuss last night first?"

"You're already hard. Do *you* want to discuss last night?"

He purses his lips like he thinks we should, which would be honorable and totally unnecessary. It had to be done. I had to be fucked. He had to do it.

There's a huge part of me that's relieved to the point of breathlessness that it *worked*. There's another part of me that wants to do it again for any reason whatsoever because it felt *that good.*

I slide my pussy over his cock in case that helps him decide.

"No." His sleep-rough voice is definitive, and then his hands are on my hips, and nobody discusses a damn thing for the better part of an hour.

Hercules forces me to put on a robe and dresses himself in jeans, then sits me at the kitchen island and makes pancakes. It's all very off-script. The light is only as bright as he needs it to be.

Still hurts.

Not a great sign, but it's easy enough to ignore while he's shirtless in the kitchen.

"Talk." Hercules doesn't turn away from the bowl where he's stirring pancake mix.

"Why should I?"

He looks at me over his shoulder, his eyes bigger than I've ever seen them. "Daisy. Talk."

A flash of heat moves over my body. Did my soul depart my mortal coil several times last night? Yes. Yes, it did. Do I want to leap on top of him even now? Of *course* I do. But I want more, too.

Maybe it's the seizures. They've changed my brain forever, and I want all the things I can never have with Hercules. Not permanently, anyway.

A kitten mewls.

I whip my head toward the sound. Hercules is around the island, his body between me and the not-real kitten, before I can say anything. "What is it?"

"Nothing."

He narrows his eyes. "What did you see?"

I scrub my hands over my face. "I thought I heard a kitten. There's definitely no kitten in here, though. You can stand down."

He moves back to the opposite counter.

"If I'm standing down, then you need to start talking." The thing is, hearing a kitten is not a good sign, either. I stare down at my hands until Hercules *thunks* the bowl on the island. His eyes are narrowed. Fiery. I couldn't see him last night, but I bet he looked like this.

"What?"

He holds my gaze, and my lungs shrink. They can't

take in as much air as before. Nobody looks at me like this. Nobody outside my family can make eye contact with me for a normal amount of time without getting uncomfortable.

Hercules isn't uncomfortable. He's making a decision. I can almost hear his thoughts spinning in his head.

Then he leans down, his hands cupped around the bowl, veins in his arms showing under his tattoos. This man knows *exactly* what he looks like. He knows he looks rough and beautiful and strong, like the world broke him and put him back together again for me.

God. Another *ridiculous* thought.

"Baby." His voice is low and warm and teasing, and that's it. I'm done. I'm ruined. I don't even like being called *baby*. I don't like it at all. "Tell me what the fuck has been going on. And be careful with your hands."

He goes back to cooking pancakes, leaving me in relative privacy to discover that I'm gripping the countertop on the kitchen island for dear life.

"I was born on a mountain in New York."

Hercules waves a spatula in a hurry-up circle. "Skip to the relevant parts."

"I moved here because the nightmares were getting worse, and I was worried I wouldn't be able to hide them."

"How long have you been trying to kill yourself?"

He's so blunt about it that my face freezes like a

cartoon. It takes a beat to unfreeze it. "I'm not trying to kill myself."

Hercules's eye-roll is mostly in the set of his shoulders. "You were weird for several days, and then you walked out into direct sunlight in the middle of the afternoon. That doesn't sound dangerous to you? Not at all?"

I begged him to fuck me last night, so there's not much point in hiding anymore. At least…not from him.

"I've survived every seizure I've had so far."

"You've survived every nightmare, too."

"Yeah, but I can't feel my impending death once I black out from a seizure. I feel it the whole time I'm in the nightmares."

His eyes meet mine, a pancake sizzling in the frying pan, and I wonder if he's seeing *me* or a memory.

"Is that what they're about, then?"

"Pretty much, and—" And talking about it summoned one. I can almost see it. I *can* see it. There's the gates, the black stone floor, and the kitten's eyes glowing in the dark.

I don't know I'm on my feet, standing there with nowhere to run, until Hercules takes my chin in his hand and kisses me.

Hard. With teeth.

I bite him back on instinct, my entire body lighting up in a way that feels both foreign and perfect.

"You don't do that anymore." *This* is how he sounded in the Army. This. Right here. There's no room for argument in his tone. "You tell me the second it starts to happen. And you don't walk out in the fucking sun. I'll fuck you all day and all night if I have to. I don't care. Is that understood?"

"Yes."

"Tell me not to hurt you."

"*No.*"

The pancake in the frying pan burns to a crisp while he fucks me over the kitchen island.

"How has the situation gotten worse?"

Hercules asks the question when he's inside me. His handprints burn on the skin of my ass, and I am bent as unceremoniously as possible over a stack of pillows. He fucks me with agonizing patience.

"You were right. It doesn't—it doesn't always have to hurt." I didn't actually realize, on a practical level, that intensity doesn't always mean *pain.*

"I know. How has it gotten worse?"

Hercules tiptoes around the question, because describing the nightmares makes it feel like there's one in the room. That makes no sense. They exist in my head. I am the alpha and the omega of the nightmares. They shouldn't feel like a separate entity.

He slides his hand between me and the pillows and strokes my clit with his fingertips. "Talk."

"Don't want to talk."

"Baby."

"I feel them all the time, now. It used to happen when I'd—" How does any of this matter when he's tilted his hips to push himself as deep as he can get and he's winding me up with a gentle touch I never thought I'd like? "When I'd be asleep for a while. Late at night. Now it's all the—the—the—"

"Fuck, that feels good. You have such a tight little cunt, Daisy. Good. That's nice. Finish talking to me when you're done. You don't want to be done? Here. Go again. You can come as many times as you want, as long as it's on my cock."

I'm a panting mess by the end of the third orgasm. Hercules resumes fucking me at the same pace, like nothing happened, and it's mind-altering.

Which is the whole point.

Or maybe it's not the whole point. I don't know.

"Finish your sentence."

"What sentence?"

"It's all the time, now?"

"Yeah. I can feel it coming. All the…" His fingers are back on my clit. "All the time."

He kisses my nape, then drags his mouth down to my shoulder. Nips with his teeth. "Feel this instead."

I have bruises on my collarbone from where he's bitten me. Hercules spends an entire afternoon pretending to be sorry about it. He kisses all his bite marks, then kisses them again, then kisses his way down between my legs and doesn't resurface until I beg him to stop.

That day, the person on the beach comes back.

Maybe he *is* Hercules's second thing.

Shane chases him down but doesn't catch him.

"Talk," Hercules orders, his hand around my throat, his other hand under my ass. I'm riding him in bed in the lowest possible light.

It still hurts.

I shake my head *no*, and he pulses inside me.

"Tell me not to hurt you."

I shake my head harder, letting him feel it in his palm.

"I won't spank you unless you talk."

I make myself heavy in his hand and rock on his hips. I love the impact and the burn and the way he always, *always* says I have to do better if I want anything from him. Hercules doesn't know that I can hear the pain in his voice when he says it. He doesn't know that *I* know it's a caustic, self-deprecating joke. He thinks he's the lesser one, and he's not.

He saves people. I hurt people. That's the difference.

"What do you want me to say?"

"Did your painkillers stop working?"

"No."

"Don't lie to me."

"They didn't."

"Baby," he whispers. "Don't lie."

I come on his cock instead of saying anything at all.

A person shouldn't be sex-obsessed just because the man living in her house to protect her is basically a god.

Actually, I'm not sure what the rules are about that. My parents have never said anything to make me believe that they'd mind if I was sex-obsessed. My dad, however, has said plenty to make me believe that he would murder any man who hurt me, which presents…a bit of a conflict.

I have not yet sat down with my father to chat about consensual hurting, because I think that discussion might kill him.

Then again, maybe he'd be cool about it.

I laugh into my canvas. My dad is cool about a lot of things, but I don't think the mental imagery would work in my favor.

I'm not done laughing when my heart breaks.

The thing I haven't told Hercules—the thing I haven't told anyone—is that I don't think I'll ever be home to have an awkward conversation with my dad, and all at once, I desperately want to.

It's just that the nightmares feel like dying. They feel more like death every time I have one. When I seize, I can feel my brain powering down, but I'm still there, minimized. In front of the gates, it's more like I feel a tug on my very soul.

Hercules's voice filters in from the living room. He took a shower without me, which I teased him about until he went so far as to forbid me to come with him.

That felt unfair.

It's easy to hear him, though, because I keep the studio door open now. For a long time, I kept it closed out of habit. Shane was in and out of my house. Sometimes other people from my security team. I didn't want them to know I worked in the dark, so I left the rest of the house light.

Hercules hates when any door is closed between us, so it's dark all the time now.

"No." He uses a clipped, guarded voice on the phone with Zeus. "*No.* Three people went after him. I was—I was otherwise occupied, Zeus. I'm not leaving her anywhere alone while I chase some asshole down the beach."

There's a heavy silence.

"Do you think I'm not frustrated? Do you think I'm not searching? This isn't any of your business. *Please.* If you want somebody better to guard your niece, then I can recommend—no, that *is* what you said."

A few more beats.

"Are you so sure that this isn't about you? Or your brother? She's your weak spot. It wouldn't be hard for some asshole to find that out."

I don't see the brush move over the canvas. I don't feel it. I might as well be in the other room with Hercules. As soon as that thought registers, my hand grips the brush like I'm going to throw it. I could be naked with him right now instead of painting nightmares.

I close my eyes against the low pool of light around my easel.

"I'm going to fix this," Hercules barks. "And I'm not doing it for *you*, I'm doing it for her, so why don't you fuck off?" A shorter pause. "I'm fine," he insists, and my heart aches again. "I'm *fine*. Nothing's wrong inside the house."

He's lying for me, and that feels worse than lying on my own behalf.

"No, I do not need *help*. I'm ending the call now. Have a great night."

I pry my eyes open as his lips meet the curve of my neck. Hercules wraps himself around me like we've been fucking for years instead of days. Frustration heats the air around him, or maybe that's the strength of his pulse.

"Talk." The word is barely more than a breath on my skin.

I shake my head, a new habit, anticipation warm and dark in my chest.

"Baby." Hercules's hand goes between my legs as he says it, his palm cupping me through the panties I'm wearing with one of his T-shirts. "When did the painkillers stop working?"

"They didn't stop," I insist. He's been on this for two days now. "They work like they always did."

He uses his other hand to take the paintbrush out of my hand. Hercules lays it gently on the easel's tray, then wraps that hand around my chin.

"Don't lie."

"I'm not lying."

"*Look.*"

I squeeze my eyes shut and shake my head, my pulse ticking up like a jump scare is coming, like he's going to *make* me see.

He wouldn't.

Hercules wouldn't do that.

"Baby." Teeth graze my earlobe. "Look."

I open my eyes. "Oh."

"Your colors are bleeding."

The whole canvas is bleeding. Not with blood red, but the sharp strokes I normally use are gone. It's a nightmare, but it's blurred, as if...

"It doesn't hurt, I just can't stand to be in the light. My eyes want to close. I can't keep them open."

"I'll fix it."

"Hercules, if there was a way, I'd have already—"

"I'll *fix* it." He bends me over the stool and yanks my clothes down, fingers stroking lightly over where I'm already wet. He finds my opening and steals my breath with three of them, pushing in hard.

"You're—you're frustrated."

"Yes. I'm fucking frustrated."

He unzips his jeans, and all of me is ready for him. I've been ready since he walked into the room. I want him, even if it can't stop what's happening to me. Even if the pain and the nightmares are coming anyway.

"Wait." His hand goes still on my lower back, and I stand up from the stool and turn into his arms. "Does this make you feel better?"

"Does what make me feel better?"

"Fucking me hard over a stool. Fucking me like you're mean."

His eyes change. Hercules is more open to me, though he hasn't moved an inch. "Sometimes."

"Is that what you want right now?"

"It doesn't—" His honey eyes go wider when I cover his mouth with my hand.

"Tell me," I demand. It's a play from his book, and I feel him smile under my palm.

Slowly, so slowly, he shakes his head.

"I don't always have to bite you," I say. "We could start off soft."

I replace my hand with my mouth and kiss him like I might have if we'd both lived different lives. If we'd both been sweet, normal people who led normal lives with the normal amount of pain.

Hercules takes me to bed and fucks me softly until he can't stand it anymore.

He leaves deep bite marks.

I like them that way.

# CHAPTER EIGHT

*Hercules*

I DIDN'T EXPECT HER TO LET ME SLEEP IN HER BED. I'd thought she'd want some distance, despite the relentless fucking. I thought Daisy would maintain power by kicking me out of the bed when I'm not sucking her clit or spanking her ass or fitting my cock to her tight, wet pussy.

She doesn't.

She's like a kitten that way. Curls up on my chest and goes to sleep, every time, and what would be the *point* of putting up a fuss? It's not a job. Nobody's paying me. I'm here of my own free will. She hasn't kicked me out yet.

I don't care. I don't care. I don't care.

It's been ten days when I make her come so many times in a row that she cries herself to sleep, hot tears on my chest.

The last thing I think before I drift off is *it should be enough.*

That's when the dream comes.

I feel it in the room, but I'm too far gone to do a damn thing about it. Or I could already be dreaming. It's impossible to tell.

The apartment's a crumbling place on a corner nobody wants to visit, all the way on the edge of one of the outer boroughs, cheap and shitty with a door that doesn't lock. My stomach turns at the sight of stained carpet and the plywood coffee table with a chunk missing along one edge and the kitchen with a busted microwave door. I fixed it with packing tape. The stove's not connected. It's all we have.

I'm out on the couch, bouncing my foot against the floor, waiting with a quarter in my palm. I've been waiting so long that the metal's warm.

Quiet, so I don't ruin the asshole's fuck.

*He's* not quiet about it. He grunts like a pig, and there's not a single inch of insulation in any wall in this room, so I hear everything.

I hate everything.

I hate the nervous adrenaline and the sick, bitter fear and the overwhelming anticipation.

More than half the time, my mother's clients don't

leave without encouragement. They have to be dragged out by the shirt collar, and they sure as hell don't like that. Not from somebody who looks as young as me. Not somebody who can kick their ass anyway.

It wouldn't be so bad if they never got any hits in, but an angry motherfucker almost always gets lucky. They never seem to understand that they got enough. That they got more than they deserved by being in the bedroom with her for thirty minutes, or forty-five, or an hour, depending on how much they're willing to pay. They never understand that they're lucky to be alive. The reason I don't kill every single one of them is that I've taken enough direct hits to the skull, I've had my neck stomped into enough curbs, I've taken enough knives to the kidneys to be pretty sure I'll live forever.

I don't want to do that in jail.

But Jesus, they deserve it. My mother's crying, begging the asshole to be done, be done, she's given him all she can, and my fists clench tight.

That's the debate. Step in too early, and they take it out on her before they go for me. Step in too late, and she's got new bruises on her neck or a stubborn black eye. That's a problem, because that's how we pay the bills, and they don't want to buy time with a prostitute who's been beat to shit.

Five minutes. That'll get us to one minute past the thirty he's paid for, and I can drag his ass onto the street.

I picture the cottage.

I'll never get to take my mother to the cottage she

dreams about if we can't pay the bills. If we can't put away a little money. It was easier when she worked at the old place, and sometimes we fight about it. I feel like a jackass, fighting with her. It doesn't make any sense. There was money there. That's what she says. It was safer there.

She got pregnant there. It could've been okay, if she stayed, except she didn't, and she won't tell me why.

The cottage. It'll be in the countryside. Neither of us cares very much where we end up, as long as there's a lake or a pond or a river. She wants running water. That reminds her that life never stays still. It's always changing. Something better is always coming.

*Always* sticks in my mind like a curse. I've been on the edge so many times, vision fading, bloodied all to hell, and I keep coming back. Nobody's ever managed to knock any of my teeth out. I'm a fucking wonder of the world, and it never helps anything. My body doesn't feel thirteen, but I know that's how old I am. Not old enough to get a job that pays enough to cover us both. Under the table shit. Beating people up. Delivering packages. Nobody pays what they say they will.

Last guy I worked for said I was too pretty, and drew too much attention.

Is *that* why she left the old place? Because I'm too fucking pretty? I can't help that. I wish one of these assholes would turn me ugly so she could go back.

The cottage is going to have a door that locks and wood floors and fresh air. Nobody's ever going to come there looking for a quick fuck. Nobody's going to leave money on the bedside table and a bruise under my mother's eye.

We have to make it to the cottage.

A *crack* from the bedroom has me on my feet, running before I can decide if it's been five minutes. I crash through the hollow door, splintering it in half.

No. No. *No*.

"What did you do? What did you *do*?" I howl it at the bastard, but I already know the answer, because I can see.

He broke her neck.

He fucks with it a little, like he's making sure it's well and truly broken, and spits in her face.

"You're dead. You're fucking dead."

The man doesn't look at me. He shrugs his pants up to his hips, buttons his fly, and takes the crumpled bills off the bedside table.

I want to kill him, *need* to kill him, and I can't move.

He swipes his thumb under his nose and brushes by me like I'm not fucking there.

"No. You're not leaving."

It takes all my willpower to swing my arm around and grab for him. My fingers lock around his wrist, and his other hand shoots out, a fist to my shoulder.

Shouldn't be a big deal. I've been hit harder before, but the bone shatters. All the bones shatter. He grins, gleeful, and somebody's screaming. It might be me. I'll never be able to bury her like this. I'll be fucked forever.

"Finish it, then. Finish it." I'd rather die than stay here like this.

He shakes me off. "Places to be."

"You motherfucker. How fucking—how dare you—"

The asshole doesn't look at me. He turns his back and goes, stepping around—

Daisy.

"You're not here. You're not supposed to be here. Don't go in the bedroom."

"What bedroom?"

One blink, and the apartment's gone. Daisy's standing in a stone cavern. Not a cavern—a room. Black stone. Gold striations. I try to move my shoulder, and it hurts so badly it steals my breath.

Now that she's here, I can feel it.

That pull.

Irresistible.

Relentless.

It's so strong that I don't know how she's withstanding it. I stumble toward her against my will and she stops me with a hand on my chest.

"What room?" she says again.

Her voice sounds too real, and she's too solid for this to be a dream. Is this fucking real? Invisible power radiates off her.

It's like…

Like a laugh in the dark. Like razor-sharp nails. Like a nightmare.

Ice washes down through my veins. Somewhere behind me, there should be a bedroom door, and in that bedroom is my mother, dead.

"Didn't you see it?" I ask her. "Behind me. The door."

Daisy tilts her head. "There's no door."

She winces, and the pull gets stronger. It sets my teeth on edge. It makes my muscles want to fight and never stop fighting.

"What's wrong? What's hurting you?"

Her face calms, her eyes going huge and innocent. "Nothing hurts here."

I'm not doing my job. I haven't checked for security flaws. I haven't checked for anything.

I tear my eyes from Daisy.

That's when I see the gates.

They're fucking massive, and as soon as I'm aware of them, the pull turns painful. The gates are huge. *Gates.* I can only see one, but I know there's more. I don't know how I know, only that I do. Heavy black stones outline darkness. Nothing but darkness. It's pitch-dark, like Daisy's bedroom.

And then it's not.

Then I can see the apartment, and the broken door, and my mother's staring, lifeless body. My shoulder shatters again. Shatters and shatters and shatters. There's nothing left to break, but it doesn't stop.

Daisy frowns up at me. "Hercules?"

I can't speak.

"What are you looking at?"

*Don't don't don't don't don't.*

I can't stop her. Daisy turns, her hand dropping away from my chest, and I can't lift either hand to stop her. Pain radiates down to my wrist, and my fingertips, and my toes. It hurts more than hitting the ground ever did, and that's not right. This isn't real. It's not real.

It feels real.

Daisy looks at the gates.

There's a moment of terrible, pressurized silence.

"Daisy." My mouth doesn't work, but I *make* it work, because fuck this. "Daisy, close your eyes."

She screams.

It's the worst sound I've ever heard, and it vibrates into all the stone. It shudders around her.

We're closer to the gates.

Closer still.

She hasn't taken a step, but whatever the fuck this place is moves toward her. It wants her in there. My mom stares, dead, dead, dead, and through obliterating pain I sling an arm around Daisy's chest to stop her.

It doesn't work.

It's not working.

The pull is strong enough to burst my eardrums and the pain, Christ, holy fuck, it hurts.

Her scream splits in two.

It's coming from two places at once.

A shadow streaks past in the corner of my eye.

It's a kitten.

Daisy thrusts one hand toward it, and her hand is bloody. Covered in blood. So covered I can't see her skin. Is it her screaming or the kitten? Is it both of them?

"Don't." The razor-sharp power expands her voice, but it doesn't stop the kitten. Why the fuck is there a kitten? "Come *here*."

The kitten pauses. It's so tiny. It's shaking, and that scream from its tiny mouth won't stop.

"Please?" Daisy's voice drops to normal.

It turns and runs through the gates.

The second it crosses the threshold, the stone room judders, the entire space jumping like an earthquake. A high-pitched whine cuts into my ears. Stone shears. The room tears apart. No—darkness tears into the room. Thin ribbons of darkness that spread like cracks in glass, ripping through solid rock.

It gets darker and darker and darker, pushing at my temples, ringing in my ears, until Daisy goes rigid in my arms.

I get a single glimpse of her face. Eyes wide. Staring. Nothing there.

"Wake up," I shout at her. "Wake up. Wake *up*." I stomp one foot on the floor, pain be damned, and stomp harder. "Wake the fuck up, wake—"

My foot crunches through the stone and lands on the mattress. The pressure in Daisy's bedroom is so intense that I could be sick. She's tense against me, the way she was—

The way she was in the dream.

"Daisy. *Daisy.*" I shake her face, my heart out of control. "Daisy."

Nothing.

My hand slams down on the bedside table, and thank fuck, there's my phone. I don't have time to adjust the brightness on the screen before I shine it at her. "Fuck."

This is exactly how she looked that first night, during that seizure. It started happening in that dream. In that *nightmare.* I saw it. I saw it happen. I felt it happen.

I open the app, and that blue wave is a storm, way above the red line. Fuck. *Fuck.*

The phone rings in my hand.

Shane.

I gather Daisy up in one arm and answer it with my free hand, shocked I can hold my phone at all. The broken bones felt real.

"What's going—"

"—*away from the windows,*" he shouts, and a bullet hits the side of the house. I would know that sound anywhere. Another one slams against the siding. "Hercules. Tell me where you are. Get away from the windows. Get away from the fucking windows."

I'm already on the floor, Daisy in my lap, no memory of having gone there.

"What the fuck is happening?"

"Guy on the beach. He ran a speedboat up onto the sand."

"He got two shots into the siding. You know the windows are bulletproof, right?"

"I don't want either of you in sight. He's—fuck. Fleeing on foot."

"Are you *fucking* kidding? *Shoot him.* Put a bullet in his head."

The call cuts out for a second or two. "—cars on the street. Might be more than one person. The house is surrounded, but—"

"We have to go."

"What?"

"Daisy can't stay here. She's seizing again. Some motherfucker is *shooting at the house*. We have to fucking go."

"Hercules. Stay in the—"

"Does the SUV have bulletproof windows?"

Stunned silence. "Yes."

"Drive it onto the porch. We're leaving. We're leaving right now."

"There could be an active—"

"Shane, I don't give a fuck who's out there. If there's traffic, if there's chaos, we'll use it as cover. I'm not waiting until every asshole with a sniper rifle has a clear shot to pick us off."

"I—"

"That includes *you*, prick. If you can't drive the SUV over here, then get your ass inside so I can go get it. We have to go."

"I can't recommend that, given the—"

"Shane." I shout his name at the top of my voice. "The seizure started *while she was asleep.*"

He lets out a long string of curses, because the man is stubborn, but he's not foolish. Anybody who's spent more than a week with Daisy can't help but know that it's *light* that sets off pain, which sets off seizures.

We're in a dark room. She was *asleep.*

She was having a nightmare.

We were having a nightmare?

"I have her. I need you on the porch, ready to drive, in three minutes."

I don't need three minutes to get my bag. The kit goes in it. Daisy's phone. I leave the pistol in the bottom of the duffel bag and carry Daisy into the laundry room.

She's not the first unconscious person I've had to transport and dress. Our laundry is mixed together on the folding table. I drop my phone on the floor, flashlight facing up, and get her into one of my sweatshirts. Panties. A pair of her sweatpants. I get myself into jeans and a T-shirt.

It's been three minutes exactly when I stick my feet into my shoes at the front door. The bag's slung over my shoulder. Phone in my pocket. Daisy's in my arms.

Her SUV rolls up onto the porch, taking out part of the railing. Shane shoves the door open, pistol out, and rushes toward the door.

"Give me the code if it's clear right now," I call to him.

"Midnight blooms," he calls back. "Three, two—"

Shane opens the door with his free hand, and I get the fuck out of the house that's now a target for every kind of nightmare. I put Daisy in the front seat. Her head lolls, body slumping, and I go for the back.

I slam the door shut behind me at the same time Shane jumps into the front seat and reverses hard away from the house. I have to lean up over the center console to gather Daisy and pull her back into my lap.

"Where?" Shane asks, his eyes pinning me in the rearview mirror.

"To her plane."

I dial Zeus, wedge the phone between my face and my shoulder, and get the kit. This has to stop before we get on the plane, because we're not landing for *anything* until we're home.

A *bump* gets my attention.

It's pandemonium on the street. Too much traffic. It's never this busy. Red and blue lights from cop cars. Three men in dark suits are briefly lit up in Shane's headlights, running for Daisy's house.

"Hercules?"

"Is the plane ready to go?"

I hear Brigit gasp *Zeus* in the background of the call, then quick footsteps. "It can take off in fifteen minutes."

"It needs to take off in ten." Take the cap off the bottle. Swab the top. Syringe. Check for bubbles. "We're on the way to the airstrip now."

"Okay." Muffled *thudthudthuds* on the call says

Zeus is texting at the speed of light. "Hercules. Is Daisy okay?"

"No."

"What happened?"

"Guy drove a boat up on the beach and shot at the house. There might be more than one person."

"Her house is secure. You can stay in the house. We'll send more teams to—"

The meds go up to *that* line. I turn Daisy in my arms, push up her sleeve, and tear an alcohol wipe open with my teeth. She doesn't flinch at the cool, or the needle going in.

"She had a seizure while she was asleep."

Something crunches, like an enormous fist made direct contact. Like Zeus's fist made contact. "When?"

"Now."

"Did you—"

"I gave it to her. It should be working by the time we get to the airstrip."

"Hercules—"

"Is it going to work? Is it going to fucking work? Because she was asleep, Zeus. She was dreaming. What happens if this is every night? What happens if this is every time she falls asleep? Do you even know?"

"It will work for now."

"How the *fuck* do you know?"

"I *don't* know." I've never heard ice in his voice like this before. I've never heard him sound so much like Hades. "I can't say anything for sure, and if you think

I've had the luxury of being *sure* all my life, then you're a fucking fool. You wait and you hope, Hercules, that's all there is to do."

It has to be rage making my muscles tremble.

It's not fear. It can't be fear. I won't let it.

"Has this ever happened before?"

Zeus's struggle to regain control is palpable over the phone. It feels like a cocktail party that can't hold its shape.

"Yes."

"To her?"

"No."

To his brother, then. "I have to be sure. Promise me it'll work."

It's a ridiculous, childish thing to ask for. It's the kind of thing you ask your dad for. I hate myself for asking.

"I promise, Hercules, it'll work."

I hate myself even more for believing him.

"Okay."

"We'll be here when you get home."

For the first four hours, Daisy's out cold. The first time she wakes up, her eyes get huge.

"Why are we on the plane?"

"Our second bad thing. A guy shot at your house. We weren't waiting around for the third thing to happen."

Her eyes get bigger. "How'd they get close enough to shoot at the house?"

"I mean, first, bullets can travel a long distance. Second, they drove a speedboat onto the beach."

"Did Shane get him?"

"Not as far as I know."

"Hmm." She purses her lips. My adrenaline has faded enough that I'm ready to argue against whatever she says next. That *Shane always* or *is Shane okay?* or *why didn't you go after him?* "Whatever," she says, and goes back to sleep.

I check the app while she's resting. The blue wave is below the red line, but it looks restless. Not normal.

I fucking hate that.

The next time Daisy wakes up, she frowns at the plane's interior. "We're here because someone shot at the house?"

"Yeah."

"Did Shane get him?"

"No."

She sits up and stares into my eyes, her hair a blonde cloud under the hood of my hoodie. "You were in my dream. Do you remember?"

My stomach falls out the bottom of the plane. "You were in *my* dream."

Daisy puts her head down on my shoulder and goes back to sleep.

She wakes up again after an hour. "Did they catch the guy?"

"I haven't heard anything since we took off."

Daisy's quiet for a minute. She doesn't put any space between us. Not an inch. "The windows in the house are bulletproof. Why are we on the plane?"

"What do you remember from your dream? Also—here."

She uses her yawn to swallow one of her painkillers. "It was the same nightmare as always, but it…" She scrunches her nose. "Broke, because…"

"Because you had a seizure in the middle of it."

"Fuck," she says softly.

"I know."

It's after sunrise when the plane touches down at LaGuardia. I rub Daisy's arm until she wakes up. Three identical SUVs wait on the tarmac for us, and Daisy sighs.

"Did they at least catch the guy?"

At that very moment, I receive a text.

**Shane**: Nothing yet.

I show it to her.

"I hope he doesn't feel too bad." Her tone is absent, like she knows it's the kind thing to care about Shane's feelings, but either she doesn't or she's too tired to worry about it right now.

"I'm sure he'll be fine."

The plane trundles to a stop next to the line of SUVs, and Daisy presses herself tight to my side. "Hercules."

"Yeah?"

"Who knows I'm coming home?"

"Everybody."

A few beats of silence. My stomach doesn't have anywhere to fall. If she's pissed at me over this, kicks me out before we get there, then I'll accept it. She'll be safe with her family, at least, and that's where they want her, anyway. Now that I've got her here, that's where she'll want to stay.

She lifts a hand to touch my cheek. "It's okay."

"If I thought there was another option—"

"We'd be in my bedroom right now. I know."

We get into the second SUV without incident. One of Zeus's people drives us through the city to the fancy, quiet neighborhood where Daisy's dad and his brothers have built their houses all in a row. The entire super-property is fenced, but not the individual yards. She should be safe anywhere inside that fence.

Daisy doesn't say much. The closer we get to the houses, the more reserved she seems. She's not a very loud person in general, but…

This is weird.

"Do you…not want to be here? Because I'll have them take us somewhere else. I don't care what Zeus wants."

"You don't?"

"No. I only care what you want."

Her black eyes search my face. The SUV can't get as dark as her house, so she can see me, and she should be okay for a little while. Long enough to get inside.

*Let's run away.*

*Let's disappear.*

*I'll go with you.*

That's what I want for her to say.

"I've been homesick," is what she says instead.

Which…hurts. Which has no reason to hurt.

We get to the street. The houses. The gates. The SUV drives through. It's taken us to Zeus's house, not Hades's, probably because the bastard has told everyone in his family that Daisy's coming home and he has the most room. All three houses use the same glass with the same filters, so they can all be as dark as necessary, but we're here, at what's never going to be my house.

"Oh, Jesus," Daisy breathes.

"Zeus threw you a party. What the fuck."

I said *everyone* in the event that Zeus actually told every member of what he considers to be his family, and he did. Zeus and Brigit are there with Calliope, Artemis's younger sister. Poseidon and Ashley are there with Orion, who stands as close as he can to Calliope, and their twins, Castor and Pollux, who'd look identical if they weren't always wearing opposite expressions. Castor looks impatient. Bored. Pollux looks affable. I'm not sure either one is true. Ares and Apollo have wedged themselves in next to Artemis.

They all stand slightly behind Hades and Persephone, who has her arm on his elbow as if she could ever hold him back from anything.

Daisy's chin wobbles. She covers her eyes with her

hand, dropping it only when the SUV comes to a complete stop.

Then she throws the door open without waiting for the driver and hops out of the car. It's been a long night, and her knees aren't quite steady, but she does her damndest to jog.

She's already reached her parents by the time I have my feet on the ground and my bag over my shoulder. Hades gets down on one knee, like she's still little. I guess, all things considered, she is. Persephone puts her arm around Daisy's shoulders and hugs her tight while Hades's hands go to Daisy's face.

Which is when she brushes the hood of the sweatshirt back.

Everything stops.

Zeus freezes, halfway between the welcoming party and me, Brigit at his side. Daisy and her parents are statues.

I don't know why they've stopped, or whether I'm hallucinating it, until Hades moves his hand to touch the side of her neck.

It's my sweatshirt, so it's too big. Taking the hood off has exposed the curve of her shoulder.

And the teeth marks there.

And the bruise.

I can see from here that Daisy's forgotten about it. She looks down at her dad, tired, confused, and then she's looking up and up and up, because he's risen to his full height.

His eyes meet mine.

They're her eyes, only they're cold and sharp and violent. He wears all black, like his eyes, and it cuts him out from the house behind him, from all the scenery. He'd be an obvious threat even if his clothes weren't a contrast. He's always been an obvious threat. The first day I met Daisy, he held me by the collar with zero effort until the cops took me away. Nobody else has ever been able to do that.

Well.

This is it, I guess. This is when we find out if I can die.

My chest hurts so much already that I don't care.

"Hades," Poseidon calls.

That seems to remind Hades that he hasn't yet started killing me. He runs the pad of his thumb over Daisy's cheekbone without looking at her and moves.

He doesn't run. He doesn't bluster. The absolute calm reminds me of a sniper picking off shots. He doesn't have to run, because he knows he'll catch me, and he knows he'll kill me. It reminds me of the gates in Daisy's dream. Inexorable. Unavoidable.

"Dad," Daisy says. "*Dad.*"

No reaction.

My heart beats harder like the damn thing's worried I might die. I'm worried I might *live.*

"Dad, *stop.*" Both Persephone's arms go around Daisy, and then Brigit's stepping in to hold her, too. I can't see Poseidon because Hades is too close. He tilts his head on a slight angle, his hands still at his sides, and I know that once he lifts them, it's over.

Fifteen feet.

Ten.

Eight.

Six.

He's only a foot or so out of arm's reach when Poseidon tackles him.

Everybody's shouting over each other, Daisy loudest of all. "Just *stop*. Stop. Can you hear me? Stop, Dad!"

Hades doesn't fall. The full weight of his brother barely rocks him. He pulls against Poseidon like Poseidon is a testy breeze and not a grown man. One of Poseidon's arms goes across Hades's chest, a human seat belt, and then I can't see either of them.

Because Zeus shoves himself in front of me.

This close, I can feel that however he calms a room, however he makes it feel better, it's not *light*. It only seems light to the people he's affecting. It's power like a lightning storm, coiled close to his skin.

"Hades." He sounds like they're at a party, having a friendly disagreement over sports or drinks or whatever the fuck else people argue about over cocktails. "I won't let you kill my son."

# CHAPTER NINE

*Daisy*

THIS ISN'T A PARTY, THIS IS HELL BREAKING loose.

All I catch from Zeus is *my son,* and Hercules puts a hand on his shoulder and tosses him out of the way. Well—*tries* to toss him. Zeus bolts forward instead. Takes a second in all the flying limbs to understand that's because my dad got away from Poseidon and attacked.

It's a real blunt-force situation, because Poseidon tries to break it up and blocks one punch from going straight into Zeus's face. This gives Zeus enough time to grab my dad's face and hold on tight.

Ares and Apollo sprint past and collide with Hercules, who's winding up to come after my dad. It's a crowd of tall people and muscle. Brigit calls over the fray. Ashley holds Castor and Pollux back from running into it just for kicks. A hand slips into mine.

It's Artemis.

"This is a shitshow," I tell her.

"I know." Zeus says this at the top of his voice, but he's not shouting, not exactly. It's the way you'd talk to someone who's having a breakdown, which...maybe my dad is. "I know. I know. Okay? I know. I get it. You can't kill him."

My dad doesn't say anything. His free arm, the one Poseidon's not holding, darts in. He takes Zeus's wrist in his hand and squeezes so hard I'm surprised the bone doesn't crack.

"He wouldn't hurt her. I can't let you hurt him. I'm not going to. He's my son, and I trust—"

"I'm not your fucking *son*," Hercules spits. Ares and Apollo hold him back. "Let him do whatever he wants. I don't give a fuck. You want to kill me? Try. Right now. *Let him do it.*"

Zeus closes his eyes.

It's a flinch, like he's heard this before, and then a weighted sensation comes down over us. Heavy. Invisible. Almost like syrup. It's not happiness. It's not peace. It's like a blanket over my feelings. The terror doesn't feel so close. The disappointment feels manageable. The guilt is still the worst.

Artemis sighs next to me and squeezes my hand.

My mom hugs me tighter. "I'm sorry, sweetheart." she murmurs. "He's tired."

The words make no sense at first. I've never heard Mom describe Dad that way. It's such a simple word, but it doesn't match with anything I know about him. He's the one who stayed up with me as a kid. He's the one who played with me in dark rooms when the light made me sick. He was always, *always* the one to get up first, whispering *we should let Mama sleep.*

It's full sunlight, the broad, bright part of the morning, so I see my dad's shoulders shake.

Just once.

He doesn't make a sound, or else it's covered up by Hercules bickering with Ares and Apollo, so *that* doesn't make any sense, either. It's like we've landed in another world and are surrounded by strangers who look like people I love.

My mind takes it in pieces. Zeus, still holding my dad's face, only it looks less like fighting and more like he's holding him up. Poseidon, his arm around my dad's back, only he's not dragging him away from Hercules. He's patting him, like...

Like my dad might be exceptionally fragile.

That has never been true a day in my life, unless it's been true every day of my life, and he and his brothers have been perpetrating an effortless conspiracy along with my mom and my aunts to hide the truth from me.

Unless I'm not the only one who's used distance to pretend.

His shoulders shake again.

My mom doesn't startle when I whip my head around to stare at her. The movement's too much for my faulty brain, but I'm *not* getting dizzy right now. Silver eyes look back at me. Her hair shines, the color of a copper penny but darker, richer. Pieces click into place. Pressure hangs in the air. I'm used to that. It only goes away when the painkillers are fully kicked in, and my dad likes to push them to the limit. *In case,* he always said. I never understood what he was planning for, and I don't understand it now, but I can feel the difference.

The quality of the pressure isn't straightforward. It feels…torn, like the ragged edge of cloth, or paper. It feels like it's hanging on by a thread.

His shaking shoulders. *He's tired.* The way my dad walked toward Hercules like murder was nothing to him.

The way he hasn't thrown his brothers off, hasn't slapped their hands away, hasn't done anything but hang on.

"How long has he been like this?"

My mom's face falls, her eyes soft and sympathetic. "Daisy."

"How *long*?"

She shakes her head.

"Don't—no. Don't say this isn't your secret to tell. Just tell me. *Tell* me. Has it been the whole time?"

Artemis lets go of my hand, and she and Brigit move in to the trembling sculpture garden of half the family. I expect Brigit to go to Zeus, but she doesn't. She walks straight into the huddle of her sons and puts her arms around Hercules's neck.

It looks real. Like a real hug. Like her brother-in-law and her son didn't almost rip out each other's throats. Artemis goes to Apollo and tugs him gently away from Hercules. He stays close, but he watches Ares, not Hercules.

Ares doesn't let go. His eyes stay on Hercules, who stands up straight, as rigid as if Brigit isn't touching him. The set of his jaw says *rage*. The look in his eyes says *help*.

Brigit's persistent. She keeps hugging him despite the fact that he's become a statue. I can't hear what she's telling him. Hercules stares into the middle distance.

Until I take a step away from my mom.

His eyes snap to mine, and it's like that day at the jail. He expected me to pick everyone else over him. He expected me to give up. Hercules was so sure that I would that he made it easier to do it. The dickish behavior and his complete resistance to getting any help were designed to make me turn my back on him.

I'm not going to do that.

I wave to him instead.

It feels ridiculous, and my mom makes a tiny huffing sound, like a laugh she didn't mean to let out.

I do it again. A circle, toward the house. I add in a gesture at the sky, then my eyes.

As in, *it's bright as hell out here. Come inside with me. Hurry up.*

He's absolutely still for a few more heartbeats, and then he rolls his eyes and hugs Brigit back. I can tell by the way his arms go around her that his shoulder's stiff. It probably hurts.

Castor starts a slow clap.

"Oh my *God*." Calliope covers her face.

"Are you serious?" Orion reaches over and slaps Castor lightly on the back of the head.

Poseidon laughs. "Why are you all still standing here? Go the hell inside."

"Aren't we going to sing?" Castor asks. "I thought there was going to be singing."

Poseidon shoots his son a look over his shoulder. "Go. Inside."

Brigit's the one to drag her sons toward the house, Artemis with Apollo. Calliope and Orion shoo the twins in the direction of the front door.

I turn around and give my mom a hug. I'm so *mad* at her. I missed her so much. "You should have told me."

"Yes, well, I was forbidden."

"*Please*. Men can't forbid anything. That's the rule."

"Sometimes I can't say no to him."

I squeeze her tighter. Hercules is the one who never says *no* to me. "You should go in."

"*You* should go in." My mom pulls back and brushes my hair away from my face. "You're tired, too."

"Mom. I can't stay out here forever. I'll be right there."

She purses her lips. "Will you?"

"*Yes.*" On second thought, it might not be my dad who's impossible to get away from. I might've had that one wrong, too. "I'll be inside in a minute. And I'm starving."

And additional pressure is starting to build at my temples already. I really can't be out here. Not if I don't want everyone to crowd around and have a firsthand view of how dicey things are.

My mom kisses my forehead, then goes to the front door. "Zeus. Poseidon."

Their heads both turn to her like she's a queen and not their sister-in-law.

"What?" Poseidon calls.

"Let go of my husband and come into the house."

"Persephone," Zeus begins, reasonable as ever. "I don't think—"

"What did I say that wasn't clear? Do you need me to rephrase? Let go of him and come inside. Daisy's hungry."

She doesn't say anything about my dad.

"We have a *cook.*" A tiny hint of exasperation enters Zeus's voice. "He's been cooking all morning. His name is Cook, if you haven't—"

"Zeus, get the fuck inside." Wow. *Wow.* This, from my *Mom*?

"Christ." Poseidon disentangles himself from my

dad, grabs Zeus by the shirt, and *drags*. "I'm not going up against her over this. I want to be able to f—"

Zeus claps a hand over Poseidon's mouth before he can finish his sentence.

My mom wriggles her fingers at me, opens the door, and ushers Zeus and Poseidon through it.

I have a very limited amount of time left to stand in the sun, and this is heartbreaking, so I go over to my dad at top speed.

The SUV drives away, and then he's alone in the driveway, his hands over his face. He's wearing his soft clothes, the ones he wears when everything irritates him, and he doesn't uncover his face when I get close.

"Dad." I tug at his wrist. His hands don't move. "Daddy."

He drops his hands to look at me, and I get the shock of my life.

He's crying.

I can remember him crying maybe…five or six times in my entire life, and most of those happened when I was very young. I assumed he was stopping it when his shoulders shook, but he hasn't.

My heart dies a little more.

Because he doesn't cry like a normal person. I don't think he actually *has* a crying-face. Tears just run down his cheeks, and he blinks and blinks, but it doesn't do anything to stop them.

I feel like a mega-asshole, because I also didn't notice what my mom meant by *tired* before. The sun was too bright, and her hair was in my face, and I felt extremely witnessed by a crowd in a way that I've avoided for years. My parents have flown out to visit me a handful of times since I moved to California, and only when I felt confident enough to let them, and that…

That was a mistake.

Because my dad doesn't look *tired,* he looks too thin, too pale, too haunted. That's saying something, because neither of us spend very long in the sun.

*You should have told me,* I want to say, but I know where that conversation will go. He wouldn't have said a word. He'd have died of worrying about me before he made me feel the slightest pressure to move home.

"Daddy." My voice shakes. It's not what I was going for, but I can't help it. Not now that the pressure is getting worse and I don't want him to have to carry me inside and perish from stress in front of everyone. "I asked Hercules to do it. He wouldn't have touched me otherwise."

His eyes go to the bruise, and for the very first time in my entire life, his expression matches the tears. My dad's forehead creases, and his eyebrows draw together, and his eyes get wider.

I *don't* flinch. I don't say anything else. I don't rush to give more details.

I didn't lie. I wouldn't. He'll know that, in…

In a minute.

His eyes come back to mine.

It hurts to be out here now. Not real pain, not yet,

only the precursor. My brain is screwed up. All the nightmares and the seizures and the cross-country flight have done some damage. They've at least depleted some crucial energy.

"Daddy…"

"Okay."

"If you want to go in, we can talk about—what?"

"Okay. I heard you."

"So you're…not mad?"

He smiles, more tears sliding out of his eyes at the same time, and I'm so relieved I almost fall over. Not that I thought he *would* be mad at me. I didn't refrain from sleeping with any guys before Hercules because my dad gave the impression that I wasn't in charge of my body. I'm not even sure I meant the word *mad.* I don't want him to be disappointed because I like teeth marks and bruises in addition to…everything else.

"No, I'm not mad." He swipes both palms over his face, which isn't enough to banish the tears. "I'm tired."

"Oh my God!" I burst out laughing. "You're such a liar. You look terrible. Why didn't you tell me to come home if you were going to worry yourself sick?"

"Why didn't you tell me you needed help?"

"I don't! I didn't. I didn't need anything."

"Checkmate."

"You did not just *checkmate* me, Dad. We don't even play chess."

"I did, and I'd do it again."

"For the record?" I hold up one finger like I'm

making a point in court, and he arches an eyebrow. "It's not that big of a deal."

"Okay."

My mouth drops open. "You're not going to argue with me?"

"Why would I argue with you?"

"Because you think I'm lying."

"Are you lying?"

*Yes. It's a huge deal. I don't know how to stop it. I don't want you to see this. I don't want anyone to see this. I thought Hercules could stop it, but he can't, and that's the end of the line.*

"No."

"Okay."

"*Fine.* Yes."

"I know." Of course he does.

I throw myself into him like I'm five years old again, my arms wrapping tight around his waist, and bury my face in his shirt. His hands move up and down on my back, and neither of us say anything for a little while.

"I don't think I can do this," I whisper into his shirt.

"Now that you're home, it won't be so bad."

"I might die." I say this part so softly that my dad could ignore it, if he wanted.

He doesn't. "I won't let that happen."

*This* is a lie, and we both know it. People die from stuff. People whose brains like to freak out and screw around with electrical impulses are even more likely to die.

I don't call him on it, because I'd rather believe it, at least for a little while.

"Also." Tears sting the corners of my eyes, so I wipe them on my dad's shirt. "You can't murder Hercules."

"Because you're in love with him?"

"I am *not* in love with him."

"Okay."

"Who gave you this habit? I don't like it."

"What habit?" My dad smooths my hair.

"This habit of agreeing with everything I say."

The sound he makes could be a laugh, but it could be a miniature sob, too. "Why would I argue when you're here?"

"Checkmate."

"That was not a checkmate."

"Can we go inside? We have all day to do bad chess jokes."

"I'm wounded." I'm off the ground the next second, in his arms.

"Dad. I'm way too old for this." I'm *also* too old to hide my face in his neck. I stopped doing that when I was five. Six, at max. But I'm exhausted, and it's painfully bright, and I might die.

"Okay."

His voice is back to normal. No sign that he was ever crying. That having me live across the country was slowly killing him.

Still. My dad doesn't put me down.

I'm never going back to California.

But it's not because I think I have to stay for my parents, or for my cousins, or for anyone else. It's because I don't think this ends with me being able to go anywhere on account of being dead.

I just...I didn't plan on dying here, where it would be burned into everyone's memory.

# CHAPTER
# TEN

*Hercules*

**T**HIS IS FUCKING AWKWARD.

Everyone pretends not to be looking out the window the entire time Daisy is out there with her dad, but that's not the only thing they're faking. Persephone keeps exchanging weighted glances with Brigit and Ashley. Orion and Calliope carry on a whispered conversation in the corner of the room like two government spies. Castor and Pollux switch personalities for no reason at all, Pollux putting on a broody, impatient expression and Castor making his face blank and innocent.

They're all pretending this isn't an emergency situation.

I told Zeus we were coming home, but I didn't mean to give the impression that she was on the verge of death.

From the way everyone's acting, that's the logical progression. *Seizures while asleep* to death.

For my part, I pretend to be engrossed in the painting behind the settee, one of the series she was working on just before she left for California and they got spooky. I don't really understand this one. It somehow manages to avoid committing to either a color or a form. If a Rorschach test could be printed in the dirty-greige shades of snow clouds, it would be this picture. Tilt your head to the left and there's a suggestion of a dog. To the right, and it hints at a smiling mouth. As soon as I start to pick out a shape, it blends back in.

Everyone avoids talking to me as long as I stare at it, though, so I keep trying.

Meanwhile, Zeus and Poseidon bicker loudly in the kitchen until Cook kicks them out.

"—seriously think you were going to tackle him? For fuck's sake, Poseidon, the man's on the verge of a nervous breakdown," Zeus says as they come back into the enormous family room, his voice barely hushed.

"So? He's always on the verge of a nervous breakdown. I *know* you know this."

"Next time, do it *sooner*, is what I'm saying, I can't have one of my—"

Poseidon slaps Zeus open-handed on the chest. "Shut the fuck up. They're back."

"Jesus. Was breaking a rib truly necessary?"

"Zeus, I say this with all the affection in the world, but don't be a little b—"

The door opens, and Hades comes in carrying Daisy in his arms. I almost turn away, because it feels wrong to watch, like it's a private moment in a private space, but nobody else does.

"Hungry?" Zeus asks.

"No," Hades answers. "Turn down the lights."

Zeus takes out his phone, and within seconds, the house is dark.

I expect complaints from Castor at minimum, but he and Pollux go into the dining room and come back with a bunch of balls. They're small lamps, with soft light, in the shape of the moon. It's like what Daisy has in her studio.

Pollux comes over to where I'm standing with Ares and Apollo, feeling like an intruder, and offers me one with a flourish. "Lighted ball?"

"Thanks."

"I have more balls available, if you'd like to cup—"

Ares smacks two of the balls out of his hands.

"If you'd like to cup one in your palm so you can *see*," Pollux says in a breathless, offended tone. "You are not setting a good example for the youth."

"How old are you again?" Ares swipes one of the

balls from the floor and tosses it in the air. Catches. Tosses. Catches.

Apollo steals it from him. "He's twelve."

"I'm *fourteen*." Pollux says. "Asshole."

"Me?" Apollo looks genuinely hurt, except for the laughter in his eyes. "You're the one making jokes about balls and *I'm* the asshole?"

"Yes. You're supposed to have higher standards. You're the pretty one *and* the smart one."

Apollo flinches for a fraction of a second, his smile faltering, and laughs. He seems to notice Ares's glower at the same time I do and elbows him in the side.

"Pollux called you ugly."

Ares recovers. "Beauty is in the eye of the beholder. Maybe he can't see."

"Pollux," calls Poseidon.

"Come over here. I need one of those balls."

Pollux leaves, throwing a glare over his shoulder. In the less-crowded part of the family room, the one with more furniture, Hades has taken a seat with Daisy in his lap. She hasn't moved since they came in, and I'd bet anything she's asleep.

That's not what scares the fuck out of me.

It's that Hades leans his head against the couch, turns his face away, and goes to sleep.

One of the twins put one of the ball-lights on a nearby chair. That's the only reason I can see them. It happens as fast as a person would pass out. He keeps his arms around Daisy, but the tension goes out of the rest of him like somebody cut through the thread connecting him to life.

On the other side of the room, Persephone puts a hand to her chest and breathes deep, trying her best to keep a smile on her face. Brigit steps over and puts her arms around Persephone, then Ashley joins in, and I hear one wobbly *I'm fine* before Persephone's being whisked into the dining room.

These are not the signs of a situation improving. This is the kind of thing people do when there's not much time left.

I knew this was a life-or-death situation. I knew when she walked onto the beach that it would take drastic measures to fix this.

I knew, but I didn't *know*. Not at the front of my mind, with words and images and visions of standing at another graveside.

"Hey." Ares reaches over Apollo and pushes at my shoulder. "Let's go."

"Go where?"

"To another room," whispers Apollo. "Everybody's too busy crying. Makes it awkward to eat brunch."

"Alcohol," Ares says. "You look like you need alcohol. Immediately."

Zeus approaches the couch with soft footsteps and covers Hades and Daisy with a huge-ass throw blanket. He has about a million of them. They're big enough for the tallest people. Zeus tucks it in around them, then slides his arm neatly under Hades's calves and sweeps his feet up onto the ottoman. He takes off both Hades's shoes, adjusts the blanket so his toes are covered, and leans down to kiss Daisy's cheek.

I can't fucking breathe.

I don't belong here. I should go. Because this *is* a private space. A guy like that doesn't go to sleep anywhere that's not home.

To *him*. It's not my home, and it never will be, and there's no point entertaining the fantasy now that my job is over. There are no more—

"Alcohol," Ares repeats, and this time he and Apollo team up to herd me to a den off a long hallway. Apollo hits a switch on the wall and the windows let the morning in. Then he gestures at me.

"What?"

"Sit down."

It only takes one not-very-hard push on my chest to send me backward into an overstuffed sofa. The second my ass hits it, a weight comes down. I'm heavier. The air is heavier. It crushes my shoulder. Ares claps his hand over the broken bones, and the breath goes out of me.

Then he's peering into my face like I burst through a wormhole to get here.

"Bro." He squeezes my shoulder. You know what? I can die. I can die from the splintering pain. Except nothing should hurt. The nightmare wasn't real, and the bones aren't broken, because if they were, he'd be able to feel them crunching under his hand. "You look like shit."

"Really? I feel great."

He rolls his eyes and pushes a glass into my hand. "Drink."

"I thought you meant beer."

"I thought I meant beer, too, but you look like *shit*."

"So you think..." I lift the glass, my shoulder screaming. "A seven and seven is going to make me all better?"

"No." He stands up, finally letting go. "I'm not a dumbass. No amount of alcohol fixes anything, but it'll make it harder to think about."

My plan is to sip at it, since the glass is three-quarters full, but as soon as I get it to my mouth, I know I'm not going to lift it a second time. Ares and Apollo watch while I drink what is *way* too much Seagram's in one go.

Apollo whistles. "Wow. You know you're not actually going to die, right?"

I burst out laughing so hard that the glass falls to the floor. Fuck. I can't stop. I laugh so hard I can't breathe. I laugh so hard my eyes fill with tears. I laugh so hard I have to push my fist into my gut to keep the damn thing together.

Ares sprawls on the floor in front of the opposite armchair and laughs at me. Apollo follows along like he's seen this happen a million times. A man losing his shit because of one sentence.

At some point, Ares hands me a second drink, and I tip that one back, too.

I'm drunk.

"Well, actually, this *is* better," I admit. The reality of the situation still exists. It's much worse than I thought. The danger isn't hypothetical or in the future. It's imminent. She could die. She could *die*. Why didn't I let myself know this before? "I can't save her."

I admit it in a sober, terse tone to Ares and Apollo.

Apollo narrows his eyes. "Who?"

"Daisy. Can't save her. Can't make the trade."

Ares watches me. "When's the last time you slept?"

"You guys know. You know what's happening, right? You know all about it. Zeus said."

"He said her house got shot at. And they have to readjust her painkillers," Apollo says, cutting a glance at Ares.

"Oh." I make my eyes big and surprised. "Is that all? Good, then. That's great. I'm wrong, then. Don't listen to me."

"You think she's going to die?" Ares asks. "Here? Or at the hospital?"

Next to him, Apollo's gone pale. "They wouldn't take her to a place like that."

"That's where you go to save people," I point out. "If that helps."

"They wouldn't let her die in there." Apollo gets louder, which is strange, coming from him. "They wouldn't," he insists, like Ares was arguing with him.

Ares gets to his feet, expression open and calm. He's not always like that. Apollo's the one who can shrug on nice manners, like he was raised rich, at the drop of a fucking hat. Ares is the angry one. The one who doesn't mind putting his body on the line for a cause.

Right now, though, he's the fucking—

The *picture* of serenity.

"They wouldn't," he reassures Apollo.

"What are you talking about?" I'm interested, because half the conversation is missing and I'm drunk.

"Mmm. No." Apollo says that like he's declining a refill of his water glass and leaves the room.

Ares slides back down to the floor. His eyes trace a path along the carpeting. My heart's going fast and hard, but there's no fucking way I'm getting off the couch. I doubt I could sleep, either.

"He was talking about our mom," Ares says into my drunken silence. "The hospital upset him."

"Wait." I close my eyes to see if it makes me less drunk. When was the last time I had a drink before this? Before the Army, I think. "What hospital?"

"The one she died in."

My stomach lurches. "Why didn't you say before?"

"I don't know, man. There was never a good time. You were pissed as hell when you got here, and Apollo doesn't like to talk about it. Was he supposed to challenge you to a duel? Force you to sit down with him?"

"A duel?"

"You're actually drunk, aren't you?"

"Yeah, because of *you*."

"To be fair, you look like you need to be drunk. A least for a while. Take the edge off."

"The edge of what?"

"Of almost getting into a fight with Hades. Nobody walks away from those."

"I wouldn't have minded."

He's quiet for a long time, watching.

"I think everybody else would mind if he took you out. If anybody took you out."

I shake my head, dismissing it. "They'd be fine."

"No," he says slowly. Pointedly. "We wouldn't."

"I wasn't here long enough for anyone to get attached."

"Just out of curiosity, how long do you think it takes?" He blinks, his dark eyes unreadable.

"A lifetime, probably." That makes me laugh, but I get a handle on it before it gets out of control. "Longer than any of you motherfuckers have."

"Do you…think some of us are going to die?"

"Not soon, since we're surrounded by a bunch of teen parents, all grown up."

Ares gives me a look. "Nobody here was a teen parent."

"The point is—"

Saved by a knock on the door. I don't have any idea how that sentence was going to end. Ares gets to his feet, nods to Zeus, and goes out.

"You okay?" Zeus says into the hall.

Ares makes an affirmative noise.

Zeus closes the door behind him. He crosses to the armchair, sits, and runs both hands over his face. "Hi."

"Hey," I say back.

He peers at me. "Are you drunk?"

"Yep. Your sons made me do it."

His eyes narrow. "My sons?"

"Yes. Your real sons. Your *first* sons. What happened to their mom? You didn't tell me about any of that shit."

"From what I understand, she was a sex worker who was attacked on the job one night and died in the hospital."

The nightmare elbows its way back into my skull. It's not a tough job, because it was mostly a memory. It was a memory of the way my mother died. The only difference was that I found her later, after it was too late to stop anything.

I only discover I'm replaying the whole damn thing again when I become aware of Zeus's hand on my non-fucked shoulder. He's crouched in front of me, and has been talking to me for...

No idea how long.

"—thinking about? Hercules. Talk to me."

"Why didn't you tell me you collected the sons of whores?"

He doesn't flinch. "I left it to them to talk about it, if they wanted. I left it to you."

"Fuck that. *You* tell them."

"Hercules." Zeus's voice is even softer now, like I'm some fragile bastard who has to be coddled. "I don't know what happened to your mother."

"I—" I did. Didn't I? "I told you."

"Remind me what happened."

I never fucking told him. I never told anyone.

"One of the men killed her." I could spit at him. I could be sick. "When I was thirteen. Snapped her neck. I found her in the bed. He didn't bother to cover her. She never got her cottage."

"*Fuck.*" Zeus squeezes my shoulder, so gentle I want to punch him. "I'm sorry."

"If you're that sorry, stop being a fucking liar."

His eyes widen. "I didn't lie."

"You told me to bring her home, and that was bullshit, wasn't it? You told me to bring her here, but you can't save her."

"Hercules—"

"You *promised.*" Now I sound like a fucking kid, and there's fuck all I can do about it. "You promised it would work. Why did you lie to me?"

"It *did* work. You got her here. She's okay right now, and she—"

Horror crashes into me. I fumble in my pocket for my phone, and bring up the app.

The blue line is fuzzy. It's not quite right. But it's not jagged, and it's not above the red line, like a seizure.

"She's okay," Zeus says. "We have time to fix this."

"You mean *you.* All of you." A wild anger claws its way through my lungs, and through my chest, and through every soft part of me. I'd kill Zeus if I could punch him with my good hand, but I can't.

"I mean that we'll consult with whoever we need

to consult with. This problem is too big for one person to solve."

"You mean because *I* couldn't do it. I wasn't enough. God, you're a bastard. You wanted me to bring her home because you knew I'd fuck it up."

"Hercules, that's not—"

"That's *exactly* what you meant." I shove at his chest hard enough to lay anybody else out, but Zeus only readjusts his position, like he was planning to do it anyway. "And you know what? You're fucking right."

He shakes his head. "I don't understand."

"I wasn't enough for my mother, either. I wasn't enough for Ollie. They needed more than I could give them."

"Your friend from the Army? What could you have—"

"My *life*," I snap. The words feel dirty in my mouth. "That's what I could've given. I could've traded with either one of them, and it would've been better that way. I'm right back where I fucking started. I can't do enough for her. And you *knew* that."

"You did everything you could for her, and then some. You did everything I asked—"

"I can't die."

His grip tightens on my shoulder. "Nobody in this house wants you to die."

"Don't *lie* to me. Don't look at me and say that shit. You'd pick her over me any day." It's an ugly, curdled truth, and I've carried it around with me for so long that it's calcified. "You'd be right to do it, too. She's always going to be worth more. She's not some street orphan with a criminal record. You *love* her."

"I—"

"Hate me," I demand. "Hate me starting now, because you're sure as fuck going to hate me when she dies."

"No."

Zeus denies me so lightly that I take a swing at him. A big, drunken swing with all my strength behind it. It's no small amount. I watch from a distance, outside my body, to see whether I'll break his nose. Whether I'll kill him, too.

He bats my hand away before I can touch him.

My balance is fucked from going after him like this, and from being drunk, and I fall forward into him.

Into a hug.

I don't want it. I don't want it. Don't touch me.

"Nobody wants you to die," he says, his palms warm on my back. Fuck. I was saying all that shit out loud. "Nobody would be happier without you. I wouldn't be happier. Daisy wouldn't be happier. We're keeping both of you. It's okay."

"I can't make her happy if she's dead." My voice sounds tight and miserable, and I can't tell if I'm bleeding from the eyes or crying.

"We're not going to let her die," he promises.

"You're a liar. Why didn't you say this would happen?"

"Listen. *Listen.* Because I hoped it wouldn't. This didn't happen to Hades until he was older, and the circumstances—I thought we had it under control."

"This one's not under control, you bastard."

"It will be." Another promise. "It will be. It'll be fine. We figured it out once, and we can figure it out again. Okay? It's fine."

My drunk ass keeps arguing with him until my eyes close. I'm not sure if it's him or me who rolls me onto the couch. The last thing I feel before I'm out is a blanket. It lands softly, and gets tucked in tight.

# CHAPTER ELEVEN

*Daisy*

EVERYONE THINKS I'M GOING TO DIE.

They're probably not wrong. It's what I've been coming to terms with in California, in relative solitude. Having the entire family gather 'round like I might bite it at any second is a change of pace, to say the least.

Being at home doesn't make me any less tired. It makes me *more* tired. I can't stay awake for most of the first day, and most of the morning on the second.

And when I wake up, I can't immediately have sex with Hercules.

Which is a major problem.

That, I'm pretty sure, was the only thing stopping my imminent death.

Funny, right? Sex for survival? Ha, ha.

Plus, at home, there's a certain pressure to act like I'm *not* dying. Otherwise, everyone gets very morbid and sad about it and there are a lot of tears in everyone's eyes, and I can't with that. This is the entire reason I moved to California. I didn't want them to see me like this, and I didn't want to see *them* like this, tense and worried and making secret battle plans when they think I can't hear.

On the second afternoon, Artemis cuddles next to me on the couch, and we watch the drama of our family play out in all the little globes of light. Artemis has brought one over and shoved it in the corner of the couch.

"Those things are hilarious," I whisper. "I only have one of them in California."

"They're kind of nice, though," she whispers back. "Although given the circumstances, I'm not sure it's helping the atmosphere." My cousin makes big, sad eyes at me.

I slap her lightly, which is about all I have the energy for.

"I could die," I point out. Hurts my chest to say it like a joke, but…I could. That's why I'm here. And if I'm going to be here, I might as well say it. "And you're making jokes about the lighting."

"Pollux was the one who started the jokes, not me."

"He was making jokes about balls, not the lighting at my living funeral."

Artemis rolls her eyes. "This is *not* a living funeral. Look."

She points across the living room, through the dining room and into the kitchen, where Uncle Zeus is arguing with Uncle Poseidon. They think they're being quiet, but their voices carry. They always do.

"—go there with some rope, put her on the train, and—"

"I am *not* going to the mountain with rope. Jesus, Poseidon. You've had days to think about this, and the best you can come up with is a kidnapping?"

Poseidon raises both hands in the air. "Sometimes it works out for the best."

"With Demeter? You think kidnapping our sister, Demeter, would work out for the best?"

"There's only one way to find out."

"*That's* never going to happen," I tell Artemis.

"I don't know." She eats an apple slice from the bowl she brought. "Uncle Poseidon seems pretty convincing."

"You're not looking at the whole space. It's not going to happen." I point at my mom and dad, who are sitting at the end of the table in the dining room. The lights get progressively brighter on the way to the kitchen. Zeus and Poseidon are brightest. Mom and Dad in half-shadow. It's enough to see that my dad is looking at my mom like he has never heard two more foolish people speak in his entire life.

My mom shrugs.

My dad pretends to die.

Artemis chokes on her apple. "Oh my God. How are you not funnier when your dad is a comedian?"

"How are you not more charming when *your* dad is—"

I don't finish the sentence because Hercules walks into the room with Ares and Apollo, and I have no brain cells for anything but him. I have no energy for anything but him. He's carrying one of the little glow-lamps in his palm, and the shadows on his face are so beautiful that I'd keep my eyes open forever, even if it killed me.

Whoops. It might kill me.

Hercules holds out the lamp like he's offering it to me. Ares makes a face at him. Nobody here should be offering me a ball of light if they want me to survive.

But Hercules would, because he's not actually offering me a tiny ball shaped like the moon to stick in my face. He's saying *here, destroy this, and we can go be somewhere in the dark.*

That would be extremely preferable to this.

Not to mention…it's necessary.

I didn't think through the consequences of coming home. I didn't have a choice about getting on the plane due to being unconscious. But if I *had* been conscious, I'd have pointed out the sex problem. Namely, that coming home is a guarantee that we'll have to find the limit of the sex boundary.

It was working, for a while. The longer I go without it, without him, the more likely I'll have a nightmare.

In fact…

There's one in the room right now.

I started feeling it about an hour ago. The dark, gravitational pull. Increasing fatigue, though I've spent hours and hours sleeping.

Hercules feels it, too. He narrows his eyes and glances over his shoulder, like it might be visible.

It's not. It never is. But the fact that everyone's walking around with small lamps in their hands makes it seem like it could be lurking in any one of the pockets of darkness.

It *pulls*.

Hercules whips the lamp in his hand at Ares, who barely manages to catch it before it hits him in the eye.

"What the fuck, man?"

*Horny,* mouths Apollo. Hercules doesn't see, because he's moving across the room like he's on a battlefield somewhere. The only part of him that's not all fluid grace is his shoulder, which is hurting him. It's a recognizable stiffness.

"Um," says Artemis. "Should we…give you guys the room?"

"We're in a mansion. There are tons of rooms. And anyway—"

Anyway, Hercules is here, and he bends down over me like this isn't a family room full of our family and picks me up from the couch.

Artemis covers her eyes with one hand.

"You can look," Hercules says. "I don't care."

"I don't know the *rules*," Artemis shoots back. "What are the rules for this?"

"Doesn't matter." His voice drops so I'm the only one who can hear. "Your house or this one?"

"This one." I run my nose along the side of his neck and honestly, truthfully can't resist biting him. Softly. A little bite. "It's closer."

So, being home means that Hercules occasionally has to whisk me upstairs to fuck.

It would be more awkward, I think, if it wasn't the general consensus that the sex is keeping me alive. As it stands, it's still pretty awkward. At my house in California, nobody could hear what went on unless a member of my security team happened to be walking nearby, and I pay them to keep their mouths closed as well as to protect my safety.

And, actually, it's nice that we have to leave every so often. It gives everyone else the chance to argue. With each other. With, from what I can tell, various doctors. With Demeter and her husband.

I'm naked under the sheets in Hercules's old bedroom when voices rise downstairs. His heart is slow to settle, and I put my hand over it to feel the beat.

"You'd think they'd find something better to talk about."

He runs his fingers through my hair. "There's nothing better to talk about than saving you."

"That's a little dramatic, don't you think? I mean…I'm not actively dying. I haven't had a seizure in two days."

He huffs. "It could be better. And those fucking things are creeping into every room."

Even this one. I can feel the nightmare at the door. The growing dark. I'd think it was definitely a hallucination if Hercules couldn't feel them, too.

"There's nothing I can do about those."

"How do you *know* that?" Frustration edges into his voice. "Have you ever tried to control them?"

"Yes? Obviously. I've read every book about lucid dreaming ever published in, like, three different languages. I had to learn basic Latin for one of them. I can't do anything about it."

"So we're waiting, then. We're waiting for the next one to come."

I don't say anything.

Eventually, he sighs. "You're always waiting for the next one."

"I live between them." It sounds sad when I say it like that. "That's what I've always done."

"Baby," he says.

"I know."

We spend two days at Zeus's house, and two nights at mine. Hercules carries me across the yard like an invalid. I am *not* an invalid, but everyone seems to have agreed that I shouldn't spend energy on unnecessary things like walking on my own two feet until they can teamwork their way into a solution.

On the third night, I wake up a little before three.

The thing about sleeping all the time is that I'm also, bizarrely, awake all the time. I have to work at keeping my sense of night and day.

And…why? It's a lot of work, and I'm tired.

But here I am, three in the morning, wide awake.

So far, Hercules has been staying in a guest room. Frankly, I don't think that's going to work out, but I'm willing to try it for appearances' sake.

A very reasonable voice in the back of my mind says *what appearances? He takes you upstairs to fuck, like, twice a day at Zeus's house.*

I don't know. An appearance, maybe. The idea of appearances.

I get out of bed and go to find him.

His bed's empty.

The house is quiet, which doesn't mean anything. He could be sitting downstairs in silence. He could be sitting anywhere. I stop in the hall and listen. My parents are asleep in their bedroom. Conor sleeps close to their bed. I can see his eyes in the dark when he shuffles around to look at me.

"It's fine," I tell him, and he lays his head down. His eyes disappear.

I go to find Hercules.

It's as dark and quiet downstairs as it is upstairs. No bright exterior lights. Nothing except the moonlight, and a muted glow from the pool by Zeus's house.

Hercules sits at the side of the pool, his feet in the water, looking up at the stars.

I don't bother with a blanket. It's warm enough outside, even at night, and it feels good to go outside without any armor. Hercules keeps looking up at the sky while I cross the yard. He must be deep in thought, because any other time he'd be rushing over here to make sure I don't over-exert myself by strolling on soft grass.

I'm about ten feet away when he turns his head, eyes going wide.

"Don't get up." I wave him down, but he's pulled his feet halfway out of the water.

"You shouldn't be walking around."

"I can still walk around. I don't know why everyone thinks I shouldn't walk around."

"Conservation of energy. You have more important things to do."

Fine. He's right. The walk *was* slightly draining, but that seems like a mindset issue, really. I take a seat next to him and stick my feet in the pool. Hercules puts his arm around me with zero hesitation and holds me closer to his body, like he's afraid I might tumble into the water and drown. That's a nonsense fear. My uncle Poseidon taught me to swim. I don't think I could drown if I wanted to.

"You know," I mention, trying to keep it casual.

"Seizures are an excess of energy in the brain. It would be better if I walked around more."

"Bullshit," he says.

"Yeah. Maybe. Or *maybe*, if I walked in the dark…"

He doesn't say anything. The sky is clear, at least over these houses. It must be some kind of optical illusion. The sky over the city is never this visible. Tonight, I can see constellations.

"Why are you out here instead of in bed?"

"Why are *you* out here?" His hand moves up and down on my arm. Up. Down. Up. Down. It's a smooth, soothing movement.

"I woke up."

"So did I."

"*What* woke you up?"

A sigh. "Same things that always do."

"Like what?"

"It feels like bad luck to talk about it." He seems to make a decision. "I'll tell you when this is over."

My throat gets tight against my will. That's what everyone keeps saying. *When this is over.* It might not *be* over. Or—when it's over, I might not be here to talk about anything.

Thinking about it makes the nightmare seem closer, like it's lurking in the foliage at the property line.

"Let's talk about something else, then."

"Do you think…" He sounds like he's casting about for a less death-oriented topic. "Do you think Apollo is ever going to bring somebody home?"

I kick my feet in the water, a slow slide under the surface. "What do you mean, bring somebody home?"

"A girlfriend. A boyfriend. *Somebody.*"

His arm gets tighter around me. The silence turns thoughtful, and then it's gently broken by the burble of the pool filters. The answer feels obvious to me.

"He brings Artemis home. I thought that would change when he went to college without her, but it didn't."

"Like…a date?" It's the first time Hercules has brought up the idea of dating. The idea of two people being normal together. Dinner. Movies. That kind of thing. We haven't had to talk about it. Our situation was never *normal,* what with the shooting and my apparent inability to keep my brain in check.

"Like a chauffeur. Like…a bodyguard."

"Uh-oh." He sounds so worried about it that a laugh bursts out of me, echoing across the surface of the water and bouncing off the pool house. Hercules slides his hand around to my mouth and covers it with his huge palm. "Baby," he whispers, and every nerve in my body echoes it back at him. It doesn't make any sense that my nerves should light up at the sound of his voice when the rest of me can't bear brightness, but it happens anyway. "Don't wake up the whole fucking house."

"Would you be mad if I did?"

"Why would I be mad?" He presses his hand closer so I can't say more. "They'd see us sitting by the pool."

I pull his wrist away and kiss his open palm. "What if they didn't see us sitting by the pool?"

"The hell else would they see us doing?"

"I don't know." I kiss the tip of his index finger, then close my lips around the first knuckle. "Something... else?"

He shivers. Everything about him is stronger than a normal person, even his shivers. "I didn't think you were the type."

"The type to what?"

"To want to get caught fucking by your own family. There are places you can go for this."

"I am *not* the type. I can't believe you'd say that." I suck his finger into my mouth to the second knuckle, and his arm tenses.

"Baby." He turns his head so his breath brushes the shell of my ear, followed by his lips. He's *mean* like this. Mean, because by now I want a lot more than a soft kiss, and so does he. And—look. We could get caught making love by the pool. It probably wouldn't be that big of a deal. But the things running through my mind—his fist in my hair, his teeth digging into the bruise on my shoulder, my cheek pressed into the patio tiles—would probably not go over well. "Don't lie."

"Fine." I turn into his neck and dart my tongue out to lick the soft skin there. "Maybe I am the type. I guess I wouldn't know."

"What *do* you know?"

I know that if I turn like *this,* if I reach like *this,* I can feel how hard he is under his shorts.

*Hard.*

I take him in my hand through the cloth and Hercules tips his head back like he is in awe of the constellations.

"We're in full view of three houses," he points out. "Anyone could be watching."

"Would you like that?" He can't help turning his face toward mine, and his teeth sink into my lower lip. A sharp bite. A sharper kiss. "If some stranger was watching?"

He takes in a breath that's definitely meant to sound offended. "I'm not the type."

"You're a liar. I bet you liked winning all those medals. I bet you liked when everybody looked at you."

His other hand is in my hair now, his fist clenching in steady increments. He's the one who taught me that it's possible to pull someone's hair in slow motion. It probably looks romantic from a distance. And it *is* romantic, because it's what I want, because it hurts, because the thing I can't stand about being here is being away from him *way* too much. I can't think when he's kissing me like this. I don't want to think. We could sit here by the pool forever with his mouth on mine. Would that be so bad?

No.

"You're wrong."

I'm too busy planning a strategy to climb on top of him to keep track of the conversation. "About what?"

If I throw myself directly on top of him, we'll probably both fall into the pool. It's harder to sneak back inside if we're both soaking wet. Then again, we'd have to take off all our clothes, so maybe it's a wash.

"I never cared about winning any medals. I never cared about those assholes looking at me."

"You didn't?"

"The only person—" He nips my earlobe. "—I've ever wanted to look at me—" His mouth moves over mine, all heat and softness, no teeth this time. "—is you."

That's when it happens.

The nightmare pounces, tackling me from behind. It's dark and terrifying and horror steals the air from my lungs. Horror, and certainty, because that's the worst possible thing, isn't it? He only wants me to look at him, and I'll be dead. Who's going to look at him then?

My gasp interrupts the kiss. Hercules doesn't hesitate. His hand curves around my chin, his arm around my back, and he yanks me away from that *thing*, that fear, scrambling to his feet at the poolside.

Maybe I *can* drown. This feels like drowning. This feels like being pulled under into deep, black water.

The breeze rushes through my hair, because he's running.

Like any door in the world could keep it out.

Like any wall could keep it out.

Like *anything* could keep it out.

Hercules runs anyway, straight across the yard to my parents' house. To *my* house. He leans down to open the door with his mouth on mine, kissing hard enough to draw blood, and throws us inside.

I can't keep my eyes open.

It gets clearer and more real every second. The stone. The gates. A kitten's eyes, flashing in the dark.

"*No.*" My back meets the wall, and his hands are vicious on my sleep pants. Those panties won't ever regain their former shape. "Daisy. *Baby.*"

I focus all my energy on keeping my arms around his neck. I'm half here, half there, my body hot and flushed and wanting, my soul somewhere else.

"Fight," he orders, and at first I can't, because there's nothing *to* fight. It's in my head. Then his hand is in my hair, pulling harder, *yanking,* and of course, of course, I'll fight to stay with him. To anybody else, this would look like an attack. He pinches and bites, digs half-moons into my skin, wraps my legs around his waist. Hercules holds me so tight that he can hardly get his zipper undone.

But he manages.

He always does.

Then both hands go to my hips, and he uses the wall to balance me while he pulls me down onto his cock. He's not gentle about it. He doesn't care what it takes to get this *thing* off me.

It feels so good.

His teeth meet the fading bruise at the curve of my neck, and he makes a new one. The nightmare hisses. It's not happy about being dismissed. I can't think of victory now. I can't feel superior, because it's still so close, because it could come back any time, because these waking attacks are the scariest thing. I was tired. I wasn't asleep, and it's here, it's here, it's here—

My head knocks against the wall and Hercules puts a hand behind it to cushion me while he fucks me like no one could possibly watch. As if my parents aren't sleeping upstairs. As if we're not standing by a door that's made entirely of glass.

He doesn't care, and neither do I.

It's not all pain. That fades into a heated, intense pleasure, partly from the way he handles me and partly from the way I don't feel fragile right now. Not at all. Never again.

"Baby," he breathes, low into my neck, and then I fly over the peak. Came out of nowhere. But it didn't, did it? It was always Hercules. He was always carrying me up to the ledge and pushing me over. He comes with me, hips powerful enough to knock through the wall. "Fuck."

When it's over, when he's spilled every bit of himself into me, he keeps me pressed to the wall, his forearms braced on either side of my head.

I don't understand what he's doing until I *do* understand.

He's trying to block it. To hide me from what was coming.

It's not here now.

It'll be back, but it's not here now.

Exhaustion sweeps in like dark water. One minute, I'm coming down from the high. The next, I'm too tired to speak. I lay my head on his shoulder instead.

Hercules doesn't say a word.

He gathers my destroyed clothes from the floor and carries me upstairs.

He sleeps with his back to the door, curled around me, standing guard.

# CHAPTER
# TWELVE

*Hercules*

**W**HAT I WANT IS TO BE ALONE WITH DAISY. In this house. In *any house.* That's impossible, because her family won't stop hovering.

I get it. I really do. This situation is worrying. Except I only have one tool, and it's to dick her down whenever possible. That's hard to do when a bunch of people are standing around with sad, worried faces or else gathering in rooms to have secret strategy meetings.

This doctor or that doctor?

Kidnap their sister or bribe her?

Take *everyone* to the mountain?

It's an endless round of questions and endless people coming in and out of Zeus's house. Hundreds of questions. Thousands of questions. No, she won't go to the hospital. Yes, she's had this condition since childhood. No, there is no other drug regimen that's helped. Even this process is a pain in the ass, because everyone who sits with her has to talk around her custom, unapproved by the FDA painkillers.

After the incident at the pool—which, what the fuck—I start sleeping in her bedroom. Nobody says a word to me about it. Hades watches me when we come downstairs in the morning, like he's trying to decide if he has to do some stealth-murder, but he never makes any veiled comments.

Every day is a weird combination of family time and extended naps. Daisy keeps trying to paint, but her attention slips away from the canvas. The blue wave on the app stays fuzzy. I feel like it could forget its shape at any time.

Everybody else thinks so, too. I catch Zeus frowning down at his phone at least six times a day. Hades doesn't need an app. He takes one look at Daisy, and the corners of his mouth turn down.

I can't sleep.

I *should* sleep, but I don't know when the nightmare is going to come again and fuck everything up. It would make sense for it to come when she's already asleep, but I've seen what it does. I've seen how it can drag her in if she's tired.

Or…is that changing, too? She didn't seem tired out by the pool. She said she was wide awake.

I catch her staring into space.

It's totally understandable, given that she's the one who's most sensitive to light. There's not a ton of stuff to look at when you're sitting in the dark. But during conversations, she'll trail off, looking at…

Nothing.

It's been three or four days when she rolls over in the middle of the night. I fucked her slow and quiet for an hour when we got into bed. I thought she'd be out for the night, but I feel her turn, and then:

"Tell me about your friend."

My heart tries to jump straight over the memory. It trips and falls instead, ending up right in the center of the damn thing. It's instinct to buy time.

"What friend?"

"Ollie."

"What do you want to know?"

"Where did you meet him?"

"At boot camp." I still remember him from that very first day at processing, when we spent eight hours waiting around to fill out forms and talk to different people in the Army's finest display of wasting time on bureaucracy. "He had a big smile. And he didn't care if everything took forever, which it always did."

"A big smile?"

"Yeah. Like a happier version of Ares. Dark hair.

Dark eyes. Always laughing, unless he was taking some-body out."

"And he was your friend?"

"He was my best friend."

"Was Ollie short for Oliver?"

"No. His name was Iolaus. He only told you that if he really liked you, because people had given him shit about it when he was a kid."

"People are assholes."

"Yeah."

Daisy sighs. She's quiet for so long I think she's fallen asleep.

"What happened?"

"The day with the helicopter?"

"Yeah."

There are details I could give her. The whole inci-dent was documented all to hell. Plenty of paperwork. I could give her the sequence of events. The probable equipment failures. The overall outcome. Ollie, dead. Me, alive.

Always alive.

"What happened was that I couldn't save him." This is the only part of the story that matters. This is what it comes down to, again and again. "I tried to give him my parachute. I tried to…I tried to make the trade."

"The trade?" She stretches out next to me, her body curling around mine. Daisy *fits*. Like nobody else ever has. Like nobody else ever will.

"I'd have traded my life for his. I tried to. I tried everything I could to soften the landing, but I couldn't."

"Hercules..." Daisy reaches across my chest and traces the scars underneath my tattoos with a fingertip. "That wasn't your fault. If somebody's falling, you can't—you can't always save them."

"Maybe I could have. If I'd been different."

"Different how?"

"I should've died." I can still feel the wind in my hair. It was surreal, the way the ground rose so slowly, then so fast. We had so much time. Then we didn't have any. "But I don't think I can."

Her hand stills. "You can't die? Why—how would you know that?"

"I can't tell you how many times I've been..." Daisy already has nightmares. She doesn't need the rest of this in her brain, too. "I've been hurt. Stabbed. Shot. Crushed. Beat to hell. And it never kills me. I should've died with Ollie, but I walked away with a fucked-up shoulder."

"Your shoulder isn't nothing." She traces the scars again. "It hurts you all the time."

"It doesn't hurt as much as not being able to make the trade." It's late, and I've been up for the past few nights. I wouldn't admit this under normal circumstances.

"But you can't actually do that." Daisy's voice is so soft. "You can't trade yourself for somebody else."

"That's not the only time I've tried."

"It's not?"

"I tried to trade myself for my mom, too. It didn't work. She died anyway."

Her short, sharp breath sounds like a memory coming back. "How did she die?"

"Murdered by one of her clients. He snapped her neck. I told him he could kill me instead, but he didn't have it in him to do the job. Or…he couldn't. But he could kill her, so he did."

She inches over until she's practically on top of me. "When?"

"When I was thirteen."

"No," she whispers. "I'm sorry."

Daisy *is* sorry. I can feel that in every line of her body. I can also feel, from how her head gets heavy on my shoulder, that she can't stay awake to prove how sorry she is. I don't need her to, anyway.

I run my fingers through her hair.

"Baby."

"Yeah?"

"Go to sleep."

She does. Out like a light, breathing deep and slow.

"You're the third one," I tell her when I'm sure she can't hear. "You're the last one. I can't do it again. So you can't die, okay? You can't die."

"Hercules."

I must've dozed off. I meant to keep watch, but she

was warm and relaxed and there was nothing in the room with us.

"Yeah?"

"It's coming."

Daisy's right. It's weird this time, though. Not a presence in the room, but a looming thing in the distance. Like chasing us through the yard didn't work, so it's going to try by air.

The last of the sleep fog dissipates. Daisy trembles at my side, her fingernails light on my chest.

I kiss her forehead. "Are you afraid?"

"No," she whispers.

It clarifies the trembling in her body. On some level, she is scared. We're all scared. But it's not fear that has her so wound up. It's need. It's bloodlust. Daisy wants to fight.

I pull her on top of me, and both her hands slide into my hair and *hold*. She leans down, her teeth gentle on my lip. A flash of pain, then she pulls back. Her cunt is hot over my cock in her sleep shorts. Everywhere she touches me is amplified by adrenaline. Daisy's touch is the clearest thing in the dark, dark room, but the rush is the same as it was in the field. Our job is to stay alive, keep each other alive, like I've done in countless enemy territories. Deserts. Mountains. Rolling plains. The breeze from all of them touches my face when she does. Daisy lowers her hips, centering herself over my cock and adding weight until I could come from the contact alone.

"Tell me what you want."

"I want it to be soft and gentle and careful." Her voice has a laugh curled into it. Not that nightmare laugh, but a tease that's meant only for me.

"Baby." I push my fingers through her hair and pull her down for a kiss that's twice as hard as the one she gave me. "Don't lie."

"I would never."

"Tell me not to hurt you."

"No. But..." A little sigh.

"You know I can't spank you. It would be too loud. I can't turn your ass so red you beg me to stop."

She shivers. "You're mean, saying that to me when you won't do it."

"Tell me to do it, and to hell with the consequences."

"No..." That's too far in the other direction. I want her to know that I *would* spank her until she cried. I'd do anything. I don't care who hears. But there are other factors in play, like the tension around her seizures and the worry that's palpable in both houses. "Do you have a quieter way?"

Of course I do. "Tell me not to put you over my lap."

"I won't."

"Tell me not to make you take my thick fingers in your tiniest, tightest hole."

She sucks in a breath.

"Tell me not to let you touch yourself until you've stretched around my cock."

"No. No—"

"Baby. Tell me not to do it. Beg me not to do it. It'll hurt. You're so tight, and you're so small, and you'd have to take it *silently*."

"*No.*"

"Last chance."

Daisy rolls her hips into mine and kisses me, vicious. I kiss her back until I can't stand it. Until neither of us can stand it. I'm not careful with her clothes. A few seams pop, but all that matters is we're both naked in seconds.

I'm so hard I'm already leaking, but it's like any scenario where I might encounter a hostile. I have to be the one to keep my presence of mind. So I'm the one to gather lube and a towel while she whines, scratching at me. I'd love to let her bait me into losing control. I'd love to have the kind of life with her where I *could* lose control, completely, and not worry that she'd be dead on the other side.

Daisy has her teeth deep into my shoulder when I take a seat on the edge of the bed. I have to pull her head away by her hair, which she loves, and I get her attention with a bite to her bottom lip.

"Can you stay quiet or do you need a gag?"

She makes a soft, low noise.

"Baby. Answer." I give her hair a shake, then tip her head back and lick her neck. "Answer me *now.*"

"I can stay quiet."

"If I have to, I'll put you on your knees and gag you with my cock. Tell me not to teach you that lesson."

"No."

One more taste of her sweet, hot mouth, and I put her over my lap, one hand around her throat to keep her in place. Daisy was made for this. I half-remember ordering her to brace her toes on the floor, but she does it now without any prompting, arching her back and spreading herself open for me.

The urge to spank her is so strong that my shoulder aches. Tension runs up my arm over and over. She'd love the heat and the sting. I'd love it, too. I want my palm to ache, but I settle for running my fingertips over her sit spot. Daisy trembles, but she doesn't break. I feel her swallow under my palm. Her elbows reach my thighs, and she digs them in for balance.

I have to reach close to her head to lube up my fingers. She wants pain, not torture, and I won't damage her. Daisy stays perfectly still, waiting.

I touch her pussy first. She's already soaked. What the hell am I supposed to do? Keep my hands to myself? *Fuck* no. I push three fingers inside of her to feel her clench around me. Her sweetness mixes with the lube. She leans back, wanting more, but I pull them away. I'm not about her cunt yet.

Daisy whimpers at the loss of my fingers, which is cute. I soothe her with a few light circles over her clit, then drag them all the way back to her hole.

Jesus, she's tight.

I make a mess of her with the lube, with her own wetness.

"Spread your thighs. No—wider than that."

Daisy does, her breathing picking up.

"Tilt your hips so I know which part of you to hurt."

It's a subtle shift, but the movement pushes her asshole more firmly against my fingers. I put two against her hole. Just a touch. No pressure.

"You can still change your mind. I'll fuck you however you want. Tell me not to hurt you."

"No," she whispers.

I lean over so I'm closer to her ear, so the sound has less of a chance to carry, and push my fingers inside her. It's a tight fit.

"How bad do you want it to hurt? You're tense, baby. I can hurt you without a fight. Don't fight me. Relax, and I'll hurt you how you want. I'm only in to the knuckle. You've done this before. Do you need to fuck my fingers to make it happen, or can you be good and let me stretch you?"

She braces herself on the carpet, trying her damndest to stay still.

"Good. Take my fingers. I'm not going to stop, because I know how much you need this. I know you need it to hurt. I know you can take it. Fuck, Daisy, you're so tight. Does it hurt?"

A shallow nod.

"Want it to hurt more?"

She nods again, breathing shallow and unsteady.

I let go of her throat, add more lube to her asshole, and push my fingers in the rest of the way. They're in deep, and as soon as my palm is at her neck again, Daisy gives up her weight. Puts more pressure on my fingers. She hides a moan behind closed lips.

I scissor my fingers, stretching her, and she struggles. Not enough to get away, but her hips try to escape. She forces them back onto my fingers again and again.

"Good girl. You're taking this so well, and I know it's hard. It hurts your hole to get fucked by my fingers. No, no—don't fight. Don't fight. There. Let me in. *There.* I felt that." I start to slide them out, far slower than I pushed in. "You know I have to fuck you with three fingers now, don't you? Tell me not to put three thick fingers into your asshole."

"N—no."

"Then I need your help. Lean into it. Stretch your asshole around my fingers. Oh—I felt your tears. That's okay, baby. Don't spend any energy trying not to cry. Don't make any noise. Good job. There's one knuckle. I'll help *you* now. I won't stop. You don't have to think, just take it. Breathe. *Breathe.* There. A little more…a little bit more, baby, you can do this."

Her body shakes, and I could swear the room gets darker. It's not a nightmare. It's her, or it's me. I push my fingers in as deep as they can go.

"*Now* you can fuck my fingers, princess. Show me how much you want this."

"Can't." A breathless whisper. "I'll fall."

"I would never let you fall. Move your hips. Fuck my fingers."

"Hurts."

"Tell me to stop."

"No."

It's an awkward position, over my lap, and it takes Daisy a few tries to figure it out. Fucking my fingers means letting more of her balance settle over them, pushing them even deeper.

"Good. So good, baby. You're almost ready for me to hurt you with my cock, and then I'll touch you how you want. Do you still want that?"

She nods, her hair brushing my naked skin. My cock twitches on her hip. Too much more of this, and I'll be forced to put her on her knees and come down her throat.

I lean over and kiss her temple. "When you're ready, ask for my cock."

Her muscles clench around my fingers, and Daisy hisses. "I'm ready. Please, Hercules. Your cock. Please. Please."

The hovering approach of the nightmare has faded. Drawn back, like it realized it was overpowered.

"Hands and knees, baby."

I pull my fingers out of her and help her do it. Hands and knees on the bed. Daisy curls herself into the ideal position to fuck her any way I want, and I climb on behind her. The head of my cock brushes against her cunt. *This* is the thing that'll kill me. Not fucking her sweet pussy. So I give myself one, slow stroke. Daisy lets out a high, desperate whine.

"Baby." I roll my hips into her because *fuck me.* "What did I say about making noise?"

She fucks me back, so I pin her to the bed with one hand.

"Show me the hole you want me to hurt."

Daisy can't stay silent while she repositions, covers rustling while she reaches back to spread her ass even while her hips move impatiently against mine. We're in the faintest possible moonlight, a bare hint of gray, so I have to put my hands over hers to get the full picture.

I add more lube and sink three fingers back in. Daisy's pussy grips me tight, then tighter, and her fingernails scratch on the sheets.

Why can't it be like this all the time? Why couldn't we have met under normal circumstances, without violence as the first thing she ever saw me do? It's a question that circles like the nightmare.

Fuck that.

Not now.

I pull out of her and notch myself to her hole. She's wild as a person can be without actually running away, but I can feel from the air, from the energy, that running is the last thing she wants to do.

"Shh," I say, out of habit more than anything. Warning her as much as myself. Her parents are forty feet away at maximum, and the last thing I want on the fucking planet is to be interrupted by a Hades who thinks I'm killing his daughter. Irony of ironies, I'm doing this to keep her alive. "Lean into it, baby."

She takes a deep breath, steeling herself. Far, far in the distance, I hear a sound that reminds me of a roll of thunder. A storm that might miss us entirely if I can pull this off.

"Good. This way. Here." I put my hands on her hips and guide her back and back and back. Daisy pushes her face into the mattress and helps me give her the first few inches. If it wasn't already dark, my vision would be blacked out from how tight her ass is. It doesn't matter that I've been getting her ready for as long as we both could stand it. "Good job. Good girl. Does it hurt?"

"Mmm," she says, muffled by the mattress.

"Tell me it hurts too much."

"No." She lifts her head, and when she speaks, her voice trembles like it's an effort to whisper instead of screaming. "Not. Not. Not enough."

Not enough, but intensity doesn't always mean pain. It means *intensity.* I can give her that.

So I fold myself over her, freeing both hands to give her more of what she wants. I make her take the rest of me too fast, too hard, and all I get for that is a stifled moan. This is *exactly* what she wanted, exactly what she asked for, and all I can do to make it better is blow her mind.

Literally.

I pinch her nipples. Bite the curve of her neck. Daisy turns her face toward mine when I do it, and it's not the easiest thing, kissing her while I'm fucking her ass like an animal. But I'm a man of many talents.

One of them is survival. One of them is violence. One of them is being able to do more than one thing at a time.

I'm not sure how it happens. One second I've got her crowded against the mattress, fucking her into the sheets, and the next she's arched up into my arms, on her knees, almost upright. I can't breathe. It's like there's too much oxygen, too much energy. It would be blinding, if it were made into light. Daisy trusts me to keep her upright, to keep her in place, and there's nothing I'd rather do.

She's flexible and soft and small in my arms, and it feels like an act of war to fuck her like this.

But not against her.

It's never been against her, has it? It's always been against this thing. Her nightmares, and the truth that haunts me. The rotten core at the center of me. The part of me that makes me inhuman, that makes me worthless.

I'm worth something to her.

She whispers my name, over and over, until I remember the promise I made.

"Baby. Yes." One hand between her legs. My fingers, her clit. That's the promise I made. Her body gets hotter around me, tighter, and she must have been close before I touched her because her head knocks against my chest and she comes hard, like the pressure at the center of a black hole, strong enough to crush anything, but she doesn't, she doesn't. "Yes. Good. Yes. *Yes.*"

And then I can't say a fucking thing, because all her pleasure and intensity backfire onto me and pulls me over, too. We've fucked a lot since I went to California, and no release has been as powerful as this one. I lose control of my hips. It drains me. There's nothing left when it's done.

Nothing but her.

A small, soft voice whispers in the back of my mind. I think it's her at first, but Daisy's not saying anything. She's breathing, spent, burrowed into my arms like she never wants me to leave.

*What if it was on purpose?*

What if it was good on purpose? What if I'm tired on purpose?

She wouldn't have done that.

The nightmare would. But that would mean it's farther inside her head than either of us know.

No. That's not what it is. I ignore the misfiring neurons from a hard fuck and carry her into the bathroom. Clean the both of us up. Dressed enough for an emergency. Then, because I'm a fucking gentleman, I tuck her into a chair and cover her with a blanket while I change the sheets. They're clean and dry when I put her in bed.

"I think it's coming back," she murmurs, sleepy. She sounds like she's already dreaming.

"I won't let it happen."

It's half lie, half hope.

I hold onto it for as long as I can.

The night wind gusts through the open side panel of the helicopter. A constant *whump-whump-whump* from the rotors hurts my ears. We're high above the ground, hidden by cloud cover, flying over a country we're ostensibly not at war with.

Ollie pats my arm and gives me a thumbs-up. His smile is big in the dark, white teeth flashing, and one of his dark curls has escaped his helmet.

"No."

He motions by his ear and shrugs. Then he punches me lightly on the bicep and mouths *calm down, motherfucker.*

I can't calm down. Usually, our helmets have radios. For this mission, we're using a simpler version so if any one of us is caught, the hostiles won't be able to listen in.

"Ollie."

I grab him above his elbow, but the rotors are so fucking loud. I might only have a few words to explain the situation and stop it from happening.

But I can't open my mouth.

I can't think of what to say.

He pats my hand and laughs at me, saying something else I can't hear. It ends with *seriously.* It's one of our oldest jokes. He says I take things too seriously, but that's how you get into the Special Forces in the first place. You take things seriously.

"Ollie." It takes an unreal amount of energy to get his name out of my mouth. "Don't."

"Don't what?" he shouts. Then he grips my arm easily, so fucking easily, like he's sure we'll both make it to the ground.

"Thirty seconds," the commander calls. I can't see him. His voice came from somewhere behind us, but I can't turn my head.

"Thirty seconds," Ollie calls back. He gives me a little shake and pulls me to sit beside him, our legs dangling out over thousands of feet of open air. I stare into his eyes. They're still dark, still dancing, still alive.

"Fifteen seconds," the commander calls. "Final checks."

Ollie's hands move over his parachute pack. I do the same thing with my left hand and take his elbow in my right. His pack *isn't there.* There are no straps to check, no buckles to snug down. It's not there, but his hands move like it is.

"You don't have a chute."

This isn't—fuck. This isn't how it happened. He had one, but it didn't work.

This is not how it happened.

"Five," the commander calls. "Four. Three."

"Ollie, you don't have a fucking chute."

He doesn't hear me. When the commander gets

to one, he tips himself out into the clouds, and I go with him.

It's a count of ten until we're supposed to deploy the chutes. Ollie does his count out loud. I'm already trying to get out of mine, but the damn thing won't release. It has its claws in.

He still hasn't let go of me.

"My chute. *Fuck.*" It's a terror-laced shout in the wind, and I shove aside the certainty that this has already happened, that it's already over, and grab his uniform jacket. Grip his front straps with fists.

"I've got it," I promise him. "I've got it."

His smile flashes in the dark. "It's okay."

"Take—take it off. Take it."

We're past the point where the chute will do the job it's supposed to, but there's a chance. He still has a chance.

Ollie frowns, reaches up toward my shoulder, and yanks.

The parachute deploys like a punch to the chest. It's like being hit with a bomb in reverse. Shakes us both, but it doesn't—

It doesn't slow down.

We don't slow down.

Not enough. Because my parachute isn't rated for two people. It's rated for me, and I'm heavy enough to need all of its strength. Too much fucking muscle. I'm too strong for the parachute.

"Let go," shouts Ollie.

"Not a fucking chance."

Because the ground is coming up. There are lights down there, dotting the countryside. It's slow, the world a vast shape below us, until it's not.

Until it's screaming up at us.

The parachute keeps trying to drag me up toward the sky, but I can't let that happen. I have to get *below* him. It takes all my strength to twist us. We're not at the right angle for a safe landing, for either of us, but it's the only landing.

I feel Ollie hit the ground.

I'm on the ground, too, but the shattering, splintering pain in my shoulder is nothing compared to the limp set of his body. The impact knocked him out. That's all it did. It knocked him out. My shoulder hurts so much that I can't move him off me. I do it anyway through a haze of pain and the taste of blood in my mouth.

He doesn't have a pulse.

I tear the glove off my left hand and turn my head to throw up from the pain. Don't know how I'm still using the right one.

But he doesn't have a pulse.

I know before I touch him, because his dark, laughing eyes are staring up at the sky, empty, empty, empty.

"Ollie, fuck. Ollie—no. No—"

A massive shape knocks into me. It's so big that I end up on my back. A soldier. The enemy. I roll over onto my hands and knees, scramble up, because I'll fight any motherfucker if it saves Ollie—

213

Daisy looks at me, her forehead creased with confusion. The sprawling countryside's gone. It's that stone room. The stone gates.

"You fell," she says.

"Ollie—" I throw my hand behind me, wrenching my shoulder in the process.

He's gone.

The night's gone, and the ground, and everything else. There's more stone tile, and—is that a door? The outline of a door. It's not the gates. It's the opposite of the gates, directly across from it, and if it's a door, maybe it goes somewhere else. Maybe—

I don't know, because a dog starts barking.

*Howling.*

There's nothing but Conor barking and a feeling like a laugh in the dark. Like razor-sharp nails. Like a nightmare.

"Conor?" Daisy blinks, and Conor streaks back into view. He's the shape that knocked me over. It was Hades's dog, in Daisy's dream, in this godforsaken room. "Conor, it's okay."

Conor barrels toward me, his barks so loud they could tear my skull apart. His teeth dig into my broken shoulder. My vision dims. I don't know what I'm yelling at him. Takes too long to figure out that he's not trying to bite me, he's trying to drag me.

To Daisy.

Because—

The whole scene stutters. Conor drags me a few feet toward her, but then the gate *pulls*.

It's stronger than the huge dog, stronger than me, stronger than anyone.

And *through* the gate, there's Ollie. He's on the ground how I left him, staring, dead—

Off to my left, the kitten mewls.

"Daisy. Wake up. Wake up."

The kitten runs past, circles Daisy's feet, and heads for the gates.

"Come here," Daisy calls to it. "Come—oh, come here."

"Daisy—"

Conor releases me like there's nothing wrong, nothing happening, and turns his head toward the gates.

For a second, everything's perfectly still.

Then Conor and the kitten both move. Daisy grabs for the kitten, but it slips through her hands. Her face is a mask of horror.

"Stop him!" she screams. "Hercules, stop him. Stop him—"

I throw my arms around Conor's neck and hold on. He's a huge fucking dog, and my shoulder's broken, and there's no way I can do this, but I do. Now the pain *is* blinding.

But not so blinding that I don't see the kitten.

It jumps through the gates, toward Ollie's body, and that's when it happens.

Just like last time.

The stone cracks first, ribbons of black slicing through like deadly acid oil. The floor shatters. Everything is screaming static, because this is what a seizure looks like from the inside of Daisy's mind, and there's nothing I can do to stop it.

Nothing.

Nothing.

Nothing.

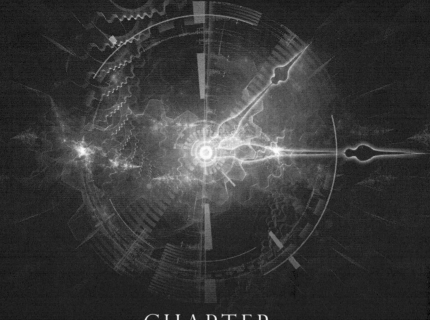

# CHAPTER
# THIRTEEN

*Daisy*

I WAKE UP IN MY DAD'S LAP.

Not a good sign.

An even less-good sign is that the room is pitch black, no light *at all,* and there's already a conversation in progress.

Also, Hercules is holding my hand.

I squeeze, because for the first little while, that's all I can do.

"Daisy," he says, and he sounds terrible, like he's been awake for days and days and days. I hope he hasn't.

Another hand—my dad's—brushes my hair off my temple. He puts the pad of his thumb gently at the corner of my eye, and when he discovers that my eyes are open, his whole body sags underneath me.

"Daisy." My dad sounds worse than Hercules.

I clear my throat. "Hi." Then there's hair in my face and a light, flowery scent, and feathery kisses. One of them almost goes into my eyeball. "Hi, Mom."

"Fuck," Uncle Zeus says from an unknown place in the room.

"Hold it together," Uncle Poseidon says, and then there's a *slap*.

"Jesus, Poseidon, that was my *neck*."

"I was trying to clap you on the shoulder. Brotherly shit."

"Go slap Hades in the face, then." Even Uncle Zeus, who is the king of sounding like he's at a party at all times, sounds like he's filling out paperwork at the DMV.

"I don't want to die," Poseidon chokes, and…

It's starting to sink in that this was, maybe, really, really bad.

I mean…Hercules is sitting next to my dad on a couch somewhere in one of our houses *and* holding my hand, so…

My lips feel clumsy, like my brain doesn't want to connect. "Does someone want to tell me why you're all in here, talking about me?"

Mom keeps running her fingers through my hair, arranging it as much as she can without making me pick up my head. My dad's heart is *racing* in his chest, which doesn't seem right. He's sitting down. His heart should be resting.

"Do you remember the dream?" Hercules runs the pad of his thumb over my knuckles.

"It was the same as always."

"No." A heavy sigh. "It wasn't. Tell me what was different."

"Nobody likes to remember bad dreams."

My dad takes a breath. "Was Conor in it?"

The entire thing, start to finish, comes back in frightening clarity. Usually, I try not to dwell on the nightmare. It's always been the same one, as long as I can remember. The only thing that's changed over the years is the kitten, and lately, the kitten going through those gates.

"Yes," I admit.

"He wasn't in it before," Hercules says. "It was only the kitten."

There's a soft sound, like Zeus rubbing his hands over his face. "Take us through it again."

"The first dream that made her have a seizure—"

"Wait." I try to get up, get out of my dad's arms, but I can't. I'm too tired. Even attempting to lift my head makes me dizzy. "You're giving out my personal information?"

"Yeah. We're kind of past that being personal infor-mation," Hercules answers.

"Why?"

An awkward silence.

"Should we…leave?" Poseidon asks.

There's a knock at the door. "I have lunch," Brigit calls. "Can I bring it in? There's no light on in the hall."

"Daisy's awake," Zeus answers.

They must break the door down, because Brigit and Ashley burst in, talking over one another, and my mom laughs a little bit and moves out of the way so they can kiss my temples, too.

"Artemis is going to be so happy," Brigit says. "Should I—"

"She's been awake for five minutes," my dad says. "Let's wait at least twenty to crowd her."

"Of course, of course. Daisy, what do you want to eat? Cook made sandwiches, but if you'd rather have an easier lunch, like a burrito—"

"How is a burrito easier than a sandwich?" Poseidon asks.

"It's all wrapped up in a tortilla, so there's less chance of the insides falling out." I can't see Ashley roll her eyes, but I can hear it in her voice. "Which might be handy if you're eating in complete darkness."

"I don't have to eat in complete darkness," I say.

Another awkward silence.

"Yeah, you do," Hercules says finally.

"What?"

"You woke up once before. One of those balls almost took you out."

My dad actually flinches.

"And the screaming," continues Hercules, "almost

took out the rest of us. I'd say, until this is...resolved, there's no light for you. At all."

"Is that why you told them about the dreams?"

"Yes."

His pause goes on long enough that it's obvious he's hiding something.

"...and what?"

Hercules squeezes my hand. "The important thing is, you're safe. We've secured the perimeter."

"Oh my God." This conversation already hurts. It's already tiring, and I don't know how long I've been out. "You did not say that to me right now. Why would it matter? The perimeter here is always secure."

"Two nights ago—"

"*Two*?"

"Yeah, Daisy. Two nights ago is when you had that dream. And when somebody blew up the mailbox."

"The...mailbox? What mailbox?"

My dad is tense again. Not good. *Really* not good. And I don't know if it's because of the nightmares or the seizures or the general tension of the moment, but I can't remember if we *have* a mailbox.

"The one on the outside of the front gate," Hercules says. "An unidentified man left an explosive inside. It went off while I was trying to get the seizure to stop."

My stomach sinks. It's empty and hollow, which is how it always is after a seizure as a result of the part where I throw up. But it's worse this time. Worse, because whoever was after me in California followed me here.

"Does that mean they're after you?" Nobody answers. "Dad?"

"I don't know," he says.

"How could you have enemies?" Poseidon huffs. "You're a recluse whether you live on a mountain or not."

"I have friends," my dad says, indignant.

"You have friends who have enemies," Zeus puts in. "How you *have* so many powerful friends when Poseidon is, in fact, correct is a matter of—"

"I haven't gotten into it with anyone since that Coleman motherfucker. That was years ago, and he's dead." My dad's voice is cold and quiet, with only a hint of anger. I probably shouldn't find it so comforting, but I do. "That bastard is dead."

"A member of his family, then?" My mom asks. She kisses my temple one more time and leans back. I think she's sitting by my dad's knee.

"There's only the son left," Zeus says. "And he seemed pretty spineless back then."

"No. No. Go back to the dream thing first." Metal *clinks* like Poseidon's uncovering a tray. "We need to do this in order."

"The first dream that she seized in the middle of was the night we came home. There was a stone room, and these enormous stone gates—"

Poseidon shudders audibly. "Black, right? Fucking huge?"

My dad turns his head, though I know he can't actually see Poseidon. "How do *you* know what he's talking about?"

"I saw them once."

There's rustling. I bet Ashley's sitting on Poseidon's lap.

"When?" My dad asks flatly.

"That day on the beach."

Zeus makes a sound like he's in pain.

"Jesus." It doesn't matter if I want a burrito or a sandwich. All I can do is lie here. "*What* day on the beach?"

"When you were a little baby," Poseidon answers. "We went to France."

"Where your mom lived?"

"Yeah. I thought she was dead. Then there was a headstone for her at the church, so I—"

"So you tried to drown yourself in the ocean." I can't describe my dad's tone now. "There were no gates."

"There were no gates that *you* saw. But I did."

"Big, black gates in the water?" I can't tell if my dad's skeptical or afraid. Could be both, or neither, or a third option.

"Yes?"

"They're not in the water in Daisy's dream," Hercules says. "But they're unmistakably huge, black gates."

"*Thank* you." Poseidon's hand slaps something, probably his thigh. "It looks peaceful through there."

"It's not peace through the gates. It's death. I saw—" Hercules cuts himself off. "I came into it sideways."

"Sideways?" Brigit. "What does that mean?"

"It was my dream first." Hercules is holding my hand tighter, but I don't think he notices. "I was dreaming about my mother. I was dreaming about the night she died. It was a nightmare, and then it wasn't mine anymore."

"What the fuck," Poseidon says, under his breath.

"Then, two days ago, it was a dream about being in the field with—" Hercules takes a deep breath, his grip so tight on my fingers that it hurts. I don't want him to let go. Not for anything. "With Ollie. About the night he died. And then it wasn't my dream anymore. We were in that stone room. The difference was—"

"That Conor was in it." This, my dad says with no emotion, all of it hidden, tucked away.

"*And* the kitten. The kitten has a thing for the gates. It goes through them every time. And when it goes through, Daisy has a seizure."

"I don't want to be the one to say this," Poseidon starts.

"Don't," Ashley says.

"But is there a case for—"

"*Poseidon.*"

"Taking out the kitten? For fuck's sake. One dream kitten shouldn't be this much of a problem."

"You think Daisy should go into her dream and kill a kitten?" Zeus is horrified.

"*No*. I think she should…you know. Take it out. Take it…somewhere else. Away from this stone room. You can't negotiate with cats. That's why we don't have one. If this cat has a death wish—"

"How do you know it's death through the gates?" My mom's soft, and thoughtful, and her question sends a bolt of ice down my spine.

"Because it is," I tell her. It's a weight off my shoulders, and it's awful, because this is the one thing I won't tell her. I won't tell any of them. "It is."

"The gates show the nightmares," Hercules answers, his hold softer on my hand, thumb moving over my knuckles. "I saw my mom through them, after she was dead. And Ollie."

A tear leaks out of the corner of my eye and lands on my dad's shirt. "I never saw that."

"What do you see?" My dad asks.

I shake my head, which hurts, then shake it harder.

"Okay," he says. "Okay."

"So." Poseidon says around what must be a mouthful of sandwich. "This is fucked."

Zeus sighs. "If only two people have ever seen the dreams—"

"It's more than two," I say, at the same time as my dad.

I put my hand on his chest. Is he *kidding*? He has to be kidding. "What?"

"I didn't see the room." His heart speeds up again. "That's not what I dreamed about."

Somehow, my mom's touching both of us now. "Was it Rosie?"

It's such a gentle question, but my dad's chest hitches. He's quiet for way too long before he clears his throat.

"No. It was Conor. But the scenario was the same."

"How did it end for you?" Hercules is the most tentative I've ever heard him.

"He came back," my dad says simply. "Was that you?"

"Daisy asked me to stop him from going through the gates, so I did."

There's a *thud*.

"Poseidon, get up off the floor," chides Ashley.

"I can't." He sounds miserable. "I can't. You want me to shoot somebody from the bow of a moving ship? Fine. You want me to beat up an asshole? Any day of my life. If it's both of them, then—*ouch*. You motherfucker, you can't *kick* me when I'm on the floor."

"This is a mindset issue," Zeus announces. "There is a solution to this, and we're going to find it. Shut your obstinate mouth."

"Who did you mean?" My dad asks. "Who else has seen one of your dreams?"

"That guy who—who—" It feels gross to talk about him. So gross that I start to fall asleep in the middle. "The guy Hercules beat up at the charity thing."

My mom gasps. "How would *he* have—"

"His sister. Not him. His sister was in class with me at school. I was tired one day, and I fell asleep. Woke up to her screaming her head off about how I was a freak, a witch who put visions in her head."

"In a *Catholic* school," my dad practically spits. "Give me a fucking break."

"She said I wanted to kill her parents. Obviously, I didn't. I don't. But she dreamed it."

"Maybe it wasn't you, sweetheart." My mom pats my knee.

"Well, given what's happened with Hercules and Dad, I have to assume—"

"Why didn't you say?" My dad whispers. It's not a question he's really asking, and the answer doesn't matter. It can't help us now. Besides, I'd heard that *she* died last year.

"It *could* be the brother," Poseidon says, thoughtful, from the floor.

"Or it could be some other unhinged motherfucker attacking the house," my dad counters. "It could be anyone, and I can't go looking."

"Why not?" I ask.

He laughs, soft, more of a breath than anything, and—oh. It's because of me. He might leave the room, but he won't leave the house until he's sure I'll be okay.

And…I won't, if somebody blows up the house because of my dreams.

Except we're not sure if it *is* because of my dreams,

or if it's because of my dad, or if it's because some people are evil at the core and there's nothing we can do about that.

Eventually, my dad hands me off to Hercules without saying anything. I'd be mad about it if I wasn't half-asleep.

"Where are we going?" I say into his neck.

"Don't open your eyes."

"Did you turn *lights* on?"

"No. They're on the emergency setting. Whatever you call it. It's barely a glow. *Don't* open your eyes."

I make an annoyed sound into his skin. Hercules goes up a flight of stairs.

"Baby," he says, and it heats me up from the inside. "Don't open your eyes."

I don't, because part of me knows what'll happen if I do. It doesn't matter that the minimal glow of the lights is meant for a true emergency, like seizure sensitivity or a complete failure of the painkillers. It'll hurt me anyway.

"How many shots did you have to give me?"

Hercules's body moves like he's kicking at something. A *thud* proves it. "Zeus gave you one. I gave you two."

"What are you not saying?"

He cradles me in one arm and reaches with the other. A pile of cloth lands on me. Towels. Hercules reaches again. Water runs.

"You don't have to do anything," he comments.

"Just sit there while I wash your hair and get you cleaned up. I have clothes in here already."

My skin tingles, the heat from his voice dissipating. "I asked you a question."

"Does it really help you to know, or are you insisting because you're a stubborn princess?"

"Wow. Does it really help you to keep secrets, or is it because you're a stubborn asshole?"

"Aren't *we* a match made in heaven?" His voice is breaking down, getting rougher, and the strain of all this—having to sit next to my dad on a couch for two days, probably, the nightmares, being here at all— breaks through like the sun through clouds. I want to flounce away from him, but if he puts me down, my legs will give out. I settle for taking my arm from around his neck and tucking it into my belly. Hercules stands by the shower, the humidity billowing out to wrap around us, and holds me tighter. "None of it worked."

"What—that's—what do you *mean*, none of it worked?"

"The benzos that normally stop your seizures didn't work. And then you woke up—"

"I don't remember waking up."

"I'm fucking glad, because it was the worst—the worst thing—" This is a man who's been to war, who watched his mom and his best friend die, and his heart pounds, having to say this to me. I don't want to be his third bad thing, but I'm afraid it's too late. "You fought it, Daisy, but you couldn't fight. I'd be okay if I never had to watch your dad put a pill on your tongue and hold his hand over your mouth to make you swallow it while you screamed so hard your voice gave out, and the tears—"

"Hey." Forget all of it. Forget being annoyed at him. Forget being irritated that I can't walk by myself, that my brain is being slowly wrecked by some mysterious nightmares that I've never been able to fix. "I'm sorry."

"I'm fine," Hercules insists, his voice cracking. "It's your dad you should apologize to. I thought he was going to have a heart attack. All that, and it didn't even work."

"The painkillers didn't work?"

"No. Zeus has some emergency injectable version of those, too, and it was like we hadn't done anything. You didn't stop screaming until you'd been in the family room for ten minutes."

That hurts him more than anything else. "What did I do?"

"Like I said." A tension in his voice says he's getting ready to lie. "You fought. And kicked. Got me in a bad spot on my shoulder. Your dad had to take you into the room and…and sit with you."

"And hold me in one place."

"Yeah."

"I'm *so* sorry."

"It's nothing you need to be sorry about. I'm the weakass motherfucker who couldn't handle it." He reaches out, movement jerky. The knob in the shower squeaks.

"You're…" That's not the whole story. "You're used to your shoulder hurting you. We have pretty athletic sex, and we have it a *lot*." My heart already aches, but it feels like it's on the verge of breaking. Hercules doesn't like to talk about things that hurt him. I hate to press the issue, but…I have to know. "What did I do, Hercules?"

He sets me down on the shower's outer ledge, makes sure I'm balanced on the glass, and tugs my shirt over my head. My bra. His fingers go into the waistband of my leggings in a brisk, impersonal manner that says even more about how he feels. He can't touch me the way he wants to, because he'll break down. The thick silence is proof of that.

Hercules eases me down onto the bench, puts one of my hands on the edge, and steps back to strip off his own clothes. I hear them land in the hamper.

Then I'm in his arms again.

He steps into the shower with the unanswered question hanging between us.

I can tell from how his body feels, all tense, his breathing deliberately slow, that he's working up to answering.

In the meantime, I let him hold me under the stream until every inch of me is covered in warm water. I let him put me on the inner ledge and wash my hair, his big hands gentle, untangling every knot he finds. I let him balance me against him and run a washcloth all over my skin.

"Sit down," I tell him when he's finished.

Hercules tenses. "Why?"

"Just do it." He sits, both of us in the hot water. I move so I'm straddling him. It's less sexy than I'd hope for, because I keep having to catch my balance on him, but Hercules puts his hands on my hips and steadies me. I concentrate hard on washing *his* hair. Adding shampoo and rinsing the curls. I let them form around my finger as I go.

Hercules sits up straight for the first few minutes, but then his shoulders let down. He lets his head rest on my shoulder and keeps his breathing slow while I add conditioner and let it rest, stroking his nape with my fingertips.

I rinse the conditioner, too. "Did you bring an extra washcloth?"

He leans over, my body secure against his, and gets it. The soft square presses into my palm a second later.

I'm not sure I do as thorough a job on him, but I move it over his skin with the most care I've ever given anything. He makes a small, pained sound when the washcloth touches his injured shoulder.

"Did I kick you that hard?" I lean down, nudge his head out of the way with mine, and kiss it. I'll let the water take care of that, then. "I'm sorry."

"It hurts more since the nightmares."

"Because you're…tense? Or…"

"Because in the first one, I dreamed the man who killed my mom crushed it with his hand. I felt the bones break. I've been getting flashes of the pain ever since. And two days ago, I—I hit the ground with Ollie. And broke it again."

I lift my head and kiss his lips, soft as I can, sorry as I can. My entire torso is heavy with horror. I only break away so I can breathe.

"I'm sorry." I can't afford to cry. It'll steal the rest of my energy, and if all the things that keep me alive are failing, then I need it. But my lungs feel too big for my aching, constricted chest. "This is why I went to California. I knew this hurt people, or—I knew it would. I knew it would come to this. I tried to stay away."

"This is nothing."

"It's not nothing because it happened to you. That doesn't make it lesser, and I won't—"

"You begged your dad to kill you."

My hands find Hercules's face. Water from the shower runs down his cheeks, but some of the streaks are hotter than the others. His voice is tight, though, and his hands tremble at my waist.

"I...I didn't. I couldn't have."

"You did. You begged to die. You wanted him to do it. You said his name."

I fold forward, then, my forehead landing on his shoulder, my arms going around his neck. My throat hurts like there's a rock-sized diamond in it. I let the tears out slowly as I can. I can't afford to sob, so I don't. I breathe through each one, letting it out on an exhale.

Hercules's hands move to my back, rising and falling, the slide smooth from the water. Every time I think I've gotten a handle on it, more tears come. Fighting it takes more energy than stopping it, so I don't.

It's the most tiring thing I've ever done, but I'll be damned if I fall asleep. All I can do is let the waves go through and out. Through and out. I'm not going to die from *this*, at least. I'll make it through this.

And I'll make it through because Hercules still smells like himself, even though I've run a soapy washcloth all over him, even though we've been inside for days. He smells…bright. His skin has a wonderful scent, like strength and adventure and something woodsy, like being in a forest nobody's ever been in.

Either that, or my brain's making it up.

I don't care.

I inhale that heated scent until the tears stop.

My head is so heavy that I can't pick it up no matter how hard I try.

"This is embarrassing." I get a mouthful of shower water. "I can't move my head."

"Don't worry about it." Hercules detangles my hair with his fingers a bit more. "Ready to get out?"

My arm is roughly as heavy as my head, but I put my palm flat on his nape and hold on. "I don't want to die."

The first sound he makes is so broken that it doesn't mean anything. His effort to make this okay, too, actually *could* kill me. Hercules clears his throat once, then twice.

"Baby," he says.

I turn my head to kiss his neck. He's so warm like this. So solid. It's impossible to believe that he couldn't win any battle he stepped into.

I don't want to tell him that he can't save me.

So I don't.

"Yeah?"

"I wouldn't blame you if you did."

"No." I can't catch my breath at first. "You can't say that to me."

"I said it to you, and I mean it."

"You really—you feel like that about me? You want me to have what I want even if I'm dead?"

"Baby," he says, and doesn't say anything else.

That's a *yes*.

I want to tell him I love him, that whatever else has happened, I love him, that he's the only one I want in my bed or in my dreams, but I don't want to say it here. Not when it's under duress. Not from him, but from my own damn brain.

But then…there might not be another chance.

Still. Saying it feels like resigning myself to the worst possible outcome, and I can't.

Hercules stands and turns off the water. He makes it seem easy to get a useless person out of the shower along with him and dry both of us off. We're dressed before I know it. He's even brought a chair in so I can sit while he works a wide-toothed comb through my hair. It's starting to dry by the time he sets the comb aside.

"Time to go back to your special room."

"It's a family room." He picks me up, ignoring my argument. "There's nothing special about it."

"You should sell tickets to people to let them experience absolute darkness, like they do at national parks."

"Which national parks?"

"The ones with caves. That's what that room is like."

"It's just a room."

"Yeah," he says with a laugh. "A room with the fanciest furniture known to mankind, and a bed that pulls out of the wall, and absolutely nothing that might suddenly light up."

"Are you...okay in there?" I'm probably an asshole, because it didn't occur to me that the darkness might not be comforting for him. Like...not at all. "Some people can't handle the dark like that. If it's bothering you—"

"Baby." Heat. Every time he says it. I never in my life imagined being called *baby,* or letting a man say it so many times. "Fuck that."

"I could sit with you instead," I offer. He's moving at a steady pace, and then we're at the stairs.

"No, you can't."

"Um...what?"

"You can't sit with me. You have to sit with your dad. But I'll hold your hand. Obviously."

"It's…not obvious? Why would I have to sit with him and not you?"

"I'd show you, but I think—and I'm not being a callous bastard—that looking at a phone screen would kill you. So I won't be doing that."

"You can see it on that app?" I don't know why I'm so appalled. "Wait—"

"You have a new patch on. Don't worry about it."

The patches last ten days at a time and communicate my brainwaves to the app. Normally, I don't care. It's a peace of mind thing, and mainly for everybody else. I can feel what's happening in my brain, and if I can't, then it's too late.

"Okay…what does the app show, then?"

"The wave has been weird since I got to California. Don't you ever look at it?"

"Not that much, no."

"The blue wave's been fuzzy since the first dream. It still looks like a wave, but the top of it…" I feel him shake his head. "The top of it looks wrong. When the second dream happened, it got worse. Got so bent out of shape that it almost touched the red line. It's more normal if you sit with your dad. The second he puts you down—"

"I take it back. The thing before wasn't embarrassing, but this is."

"I don't care who you have to sit with, as long as you're alive."

"What about you? Do you make a difference?"

"Yes. When I hold your hand, it stays in its normal rhythm."

"Well." I don't know what to say about that. "Good."

We go back into the family room. It's clear everyone ran away to shower and change, because it's all clean soap in the air.

"How was it?" My dad asks, a surprising lack of awkwardness in his voice, given that everyone knows about the shower.

"Good," Hercules answers.

"Hello? I'm still here."

Hercules uses that moment to put me back in my dad's arms. I hadn't noticed the pressure at my temples, but as soon as my head's on his shoulder, it goes away. Hercules settles in next to my dad and reaches across for my hand.

"Hi, sweetheart." My mom leans down to kiss my temple.

"Mom. It was a shower. I'm okay."

"Of course you are."

"You don't all have to sit in here with me. I'm sure there's better things to—"

"Do we have a consensus, then?" Zeus comes in, the air in the room shifting.

"No," Poseidon answers. A door shuts.

"A consensus about what?" I ask, since I clearly wasn't paying attention before.

"When to leave," my dad answers.

"To go *where?*"

"The mountain."

It's where I spent the first six years of my life. It's where I was born. There's no reason my entire soul should recoil from this idea.

"Why would we do that?" I try to sound like a rational adult and not an irritated kid. I totally fail. "I don't want to leave."

"It's the best place to attempt a readjustment for your painkillers." Dad's tone is too even.

"We have dirt here, too. Have Demmy come here and grow as much as she wants."

"It's not the same. And there's more space on the mountain without light leaks."

"Dad—"

"We're going." He doesn't snap, but there's a finality about the words that shocks me into silence. His game of agreeing with me is over now. "It's beyond us here."

It comes back to me that he's the one I asked to kill me.

*You said his name.*

I hope to God I didn't call him Daddy when I told him I wanted to die.

That's the thing he can't live with. He'll do anything to stop that from happening again.

"Okay."

"I'm sorry," my dad says.

"It's okay."

But from the way Hercules's hold on my hand feels distant and wrong, I'm sure it's not.

# CHAPTER
# FOURTEEN

*Hercules*

T HE DISCUSSION ABOUT GOING TO THE
mountain continues.

I stand it for as long as I can, feeling sicker
and sicker, until finally I have to do something about it
or throw up on the floor.

I'm not going to be the person who causes a fucking scene when Daisy might die.

"Persephone." Her name feels awkward in my
mouth. Maybe it would be better if I called her Aunt
Persephone, like Zeus and Poseidon's kids do, but I've
never been able to bring myself to do it.

"Right here." She sounds like a sunny day, like a

flower opening to morning light, and she's on the right side of the room. I thought she was on the left, with Poseidon.

"Take my spot for half an hour."

"Hercules," Daisy says.

"I'll be right back." I squeeze her fingers and get to my feet before she can ask me to stay. I have to move. I can't sit here while they casually discuss taking her to that mountain to die.

That's what it is. That's what it means. I don't know what made them so certain that it would save them, but it doesn't feel like that to me. Demeter is poison. In small doses, she can help with pain. More, and the painlessness ends in death. With Daisy at the gates. And if they're taking her to the mountain, she needs more.

It's a death trap. It's a fucking *death* trap.

Persephone slides into my spot and murmurs to Daisy. Everyone in the house tried holding her hand while she was asleep, once we figured out that she has to sit as close as possible to Hades, preferably in his arms, to get her brain waves under control. Next to mine, Persephone and Zeus have the greatest effect.

They should be fine without me, then. The two of them together should be enough to keep her stable until—

Until she dies, or gets better. I guess those are the only two choices. Those are the choices for everybody in the world, except for me, and I'm so pissed about it. Anger burns through me like boiling oil, so hot that when I toss gym clothes onto the bed in the guest bedroom I end up following them with my fist into the mattress.

Five times.

Ten.

Finally, I get a fucking grip and put the clothes on, never mind that my hands are shaking. I go back down and take a hall that goes the opposite way from the family room to the gym. It's high afternoon, sun streaming through the windows, and it makes me want to be sick again.

The sun is a fucking crime when Daisy can't even be in the same room as a nightlight. It shouldn't be coming up at all when things are so uncertain with her.

I stare around the gym like I've never been in one before, then go to the treadmill like a robot.

I've been walking for three minutes when Ares appears at the doorway. He takes one look at me in the mirror and blows out a breath. "Fuck, man."

"Why are you here?"

"You're pretty stressed. Been sitting in a room in the dark. Thought you'd want to talk it out."

"What is there to talk about?"

"I don't know. The big plans, maybe." He strolls across the floor, taking up a spot next to the treadmill.

Apollo rushes in. "You dick. You said you'd wait for me."

"Are you assholes coordinating? There's nothing to talk about." How many times do I have to say it?

"Like I said," Ares goes on like he wasn't just called a dick *and* an asshole. "There are plans being made. You have to have feelings about them."

"It doesn't matter to me where they go." I punch the button to stop the treadmill, then go over to a shelf with a bunch of weighted bands in it like I came in here with a plan. I didn't, but I find a band that will work and wrap it around a bar in the wall. A weight bench is close enough to nudge with my foot, and I sit on it like the prick that I am.

Ares and Apollo circle. They're both relaxed in the mirror. Apollo's eating ice cream out of a red bowl. Pollux was right—he *is* the pretty one. It's the only word that comes to mind at the sight of his face. Any person on earth would know that, especially when he's standing next to his brother. Ares is a handsome guy, but his features are stronger. Not quite so fine. I wouldn't call him rough. Pretty, though? No. Not like Apollo.

Ares catches my eye in the mirror and narrows his. "*They*?"

"Yes. It doesn't matter where they go."

"Who's they?" Apollo asks around his spoon. "Because as far as we knew, *they* meant—" He waves the spoon in a wide circle. "All of us. Are you not including yourself?" I don't see any point in lying. I wrap the band around my fist, fix my posture, and pull it back.

"No."

They exchange a look.

"Are you fucking kidding me? There's a mirror. I can see you clowns."

"Clowns!" Ares puts a hand to his chest. It's a very Zeus move, and I scowl at him, an expression he does not return. "We're concerned."

"There are other people to be concerned about."

"Of course we're concerned about Daisy. And about Dad."

"You mean—" I wish they would stop saying that to me. They can't peer pressure me into it. He's not my dad, and he doesn't want to be, and that's the end of it. "*Her* dad."

"No, we mean *our* dad." Apollo's light as a breeze. He eats ice cream and raises his eyebrows, looking at me pointedly in the mirror. "You've met before. His name is Zeus."

"He's fine. If you don't believe me, go talk to him."

"We didn't think he'd be interested in a chat." Apollo's spoon *clinks* on the bowl.

"You're his *sons*," I shoot back. "Why wouldn't he talk to you?"

"Because he thinks his brother's going to die." Ares taps his fingers on his opposite arm like it's a thorny logic problem to solve. "And Daisy. That's his niece."

"That's *your* girlfriend." Apollo thinks he has a winning argument.

"She's not my girlfriend." It's an automatic answer, and it feels like a lie. But not because she's nothing to me. I wanted her to be nothing, because that would've

made living next door a hell of a lot easier. Because…
she's so much more to me that *girlfriend* feels like a
cheap joke.

"Do you shower with girls who aren't your girlfriend often?" Ares asks.

"Shut the fuck up, Ares."

"I think the more pertinent question is, do you *bite*
girls who aren't your girlfriend often?" Apollo's teeth
meet his spoon. "If you do, you might want to rethink
it. I would, if Hades almost killed me, and—"

"I could kill you. Did you know that?"

He holds up his spoon-hand like he's surrendering.
"A friendly question between brothers."

"We're not brothers."

"Oh my God." Ares tips his head back to stare at the
ceiling. "What's wrong with you, man?"

"A bunch of shit we don't need to get into."

"Zeus told you about our mom. You could at least
stop being such a monumental prick and share some
facts about your life with us."

I've completely lost count of the reps I've done, so I
switch to the other arm and start over. My left shoulder
isn't fucked, but if I don't do all the exercises equally, it
*will* be. How's that for a cheap joke?

"What is this?" I ask him in the mirror. "You told
me about your mom. I didn't say a damn thing to you.
And if Zeus ran his mouth to me, then he probably ran
it to you, too."

Ares doesn't look at Apollo. I can tell it takes genuine effort on his part.

"We know she worked for Zeus," Apollo says. "We know she left, and was killed."

"Does that make you think we have something in common?"

Apollo *does* glance at Ares now, his eyebrows raised. "…yes. Having a similar situation happen to you means that you have something in common. Obviously, that's not all."

"What else do you think there is?"

"We—" Apollo motions with the spoon again, encompassing all three of us, slowly, like I might not get it otherwise. "Are all part of the same family. In fact, the three of us—" He motions again, and I really am going to kill him as soon as I'm done doing these fucking physical therapy exercises. "Are part of the same *nuclear* family, which is when—"

"I know what a family is, jackass."

"Then why are you pretending not to be part of it?"

"Because I'm *not* part of it. I can't fathom how that's so hard for you to understand."

"Do you think there's some secret criteria?" Ares asks. "Because legally, you're in the family. You know that, right?"

"Legally?"

"Do you…not remember the paperwork?" Ares arches an eyebrow, and I have a cold, sinking feeling. I can't help remembering things from my life. It would be easier if I could forget, but I can't.

I break eye contact and switch arms. Back to the sore, fucked-up, re-broken one. I know it wasn't actually broken from the dreams, but it sure as hell feels like it.

"Zeus collected me from jail. There's always a lot of paperwork for that shit."

"He collected us from his shelter," Ares says. "Did he tell you that?"

"No."

"We went there from the hospital." Apollo addresses this to his bowl of ice cream. After that, I keep my eyes firmly on the weighted band. "Some pricks from social services wanted to take us, but we ran."

"That's a good call."

"Oh, so you know about those motherfuckers, too," Ares says in a jovial tone. "Because you *also* ran away from them a time or two. Or ten."

"More than ten. You're lucky if it was just the once."

"It wasn't once. The time at the shelter was the last time, because Zeus took us home."

"That must've been sweet."

"It wasn't." How much ice cream does Apollo *have*? Is he eating tiny bites? I can't fucking tell. "Ares and I got in a fight, and we both thought Hades was going to kill us because he looks like a murderer."

Ares sighs. "He doesn't look like a murderer. He looks like his eyes are the wrong color, which they are."

"They're not the wrong color," I snap, and both of them stare at me, wide-eyed.

"Dude," Apollo says. "You don't have to go to bat for your father-in-law. This is all in good fun."

"I'm not going to bat for *him*. And he's not my father-in-law."

"Shit. Right. Your girlfriend."

I close my eyes and concentrate on not strangling him with the band.

"He took us to the farmhouse where they grew up." Ares, coming in so fucking clutch with the change of topic. "Has he told you about that?"

"I didn't want to know."

And I couldn't ask. I was so angry for the first six months, and it never went away, not even when the charges were dropped and my life was a *life*. Being angry had kept me alive for five years on the street. I couldn't put it down because I had a bed and a bedroom and nice clothes.

The only thing that ever shut it off was Ollie dying right in front of me. It became a dead thing along with him.

"You could talk to him about it," Ares says, like it's simple.

"No, I can't."

"Why not?"

"Because he offered to tell me about it when I got here, and I couldn't ask. And now it's too fucking late."

"The paperwork says it's never too late," Apollo says.

"What fucking paperwork?"

"The paperwork that says you're in the family. Zeus adopted you, the same as us."

"I know that." I knew that. Didn't I? I fucking knew that. I knew it in some part of my mind. I had to have known that. But I didn't believe it. "I've never seen whatever papers you're talking about."

"They're in his office." Ares shifts his weight from foot to foot. "In the top drawer of his desk. The one on the left. In case you ever wanted to look."

"Is there a point to all this, or are you here to drive me out of my mind?"

"Why aren't you going to the mountain?" Apollo asks, blunt.

"Because."

They both wait. I do ten more reps. Switch arms. Switch back. New exercise. They all blur together by now. They're all fucking pointless, because none of them is going to save Daisy.

"Because...why?" Ares meets my eyes in the mirror. "We thought it was the family thing. You're allowed to go there. You've...you've been there, haven't you?"

"A couple times. Yeah."

"So if your girlfriend is, like—" Apollo starts.

"Those were before." I instantly regret saying this. I don't want to talk about this with Ares and Apollo. I don't want to talk about it with anyone, but least of all these people who might, in a legal sense, have a point about being my brothers.

It's not a good idea to be brothers with anybody. That's what we called each other in the Army. That's what I called Ollie, and it did him no good in the end. It won't do Ares and Apollo any good, either.

And Zeus—I don't know about him. It would probably be best if he got himself out of the habit of thinking he had three sons, or pretending to have three sons, or whatever the fuck he's doing until he starts regretting me.

"Before what?" Ares prompts.

"They were *before*. It's different now. End of discussion."

"Yeah, right. Before what?" He's moved in, a glint in his dark eyes. Apollo is pretty, but Ares goes out of his way to look softer than he is. Gentler. Less dangerous. He's stopped doing it. "Say it, Herc. It's us."

"I don't care if you're—"

"Come on. Say it." Apollo purses his lips, staring at me in the mirror. "If you don't, we'll follow you around until you either kill us or say it."

"Try me."

"Just *say* it," Ares insists. He's the oldest, which should make him less of a jackass, but that hasn't happened yet. "Tell us why you won't stay with Daisy. *She's* going to want you there, so it's pretty fucking weird that you won't get in the car with the rest of us, get into a helicopter, and—"

All I'm going to do is take the band off the bar, but my hand has other ideas. I'm off the bench before I can stop it. My hand wraps around the bar, and it doesn't matter that it's bolted to the studs. The metal underneath my palm feels exactly like a jump bar, exactly like the one I used to launch myself out into open air hundreds of fucking times, and I'm back in it.

Wind in my face. Ollie next to me, his hair visible under his helmet. The parachute we didn't know was faulty until it was too late.

The fall.

The fall.

The fall.

The landing.

Pain wrenches through my shoulder at the same moment the bar rips out of the wall. The mirror looks like the view from between those stone gates, and there's nothing but empty air and earth coming up. Earth slams into the mirror, but it's not earth, it's Ollie, his eyes already dead, chest not rising, and I can't reach through glass to get to him. Even when I *could* reach him, it wasn't enough, I couldn't save him.

The glass shatters.

There's shouting. I can't tell who's saying anything, only that there are hands on my shoulders. One of them digs into broken bone and I swat at them, completely fucking ineffectual.

"—glass," Ares says. He's got his hand lower down on my arm now. "You'll cut yourself. Stand still."

He brushes at my clothes. Apollo has my other elbow, and he's not letting go, like he thinks I'll make a break for it. Where the fuck would I go? I can't breathe. I've never felt anything like this in my life, unless I have, and I called it adrenaline or emotion or weakness. My teeth feel like they could crack in my jaw. I want to scream, or cry, make an unholy sound. I can't do that in front of these people. I won't.

I can't get it to stop.

"Come over here." Ares doesn't have to pull very hard to get me to move, but there's only so far I can walk. My legs feel all fucked up, too. Ares flickers into view. First, his eyes, which remind me of Ollie's, and then his hair, which doesn't. It's not quite as curly. "Let me have that."

I don't know what he's asking for until he takes it out of my hand.

It's the bar from the wall, with pieces of the studs in it.

Ares tosses it to the side of the room, where it lands on a rubbery mat. Then his eyes are back in front of my face. His hands at my cheeks. I'd normally tell him to fuck off, not to touch me, except, actually, I can't remember the last time he was this close.

"Nothing's going on." His voice is light and even, like a huge-ass glass mirror didn't shoot pieces of debris at us. "Do you know where you are?"

Falling through thin air. "Yes."

"What was in that mirror?" Ares's eyes briefly leave mine. He looks over my shoulder, then tilts his head toward the door. Someone else moves, close by. I don't know who it is until he goes past. Apollo. Where the fuck does he think he's going? I don't know. I don't care.

"Ollie died on a jump." I hear myself say it more than I feel myself say it. My lips aren't connected to my brain. Nothing's connected. I'm still in midair.

"Ollie," he says softly, and then his eyes get wider— recognition. I know I talked about this before. I came *here* from the hospital. How long was I in that sea of painkillers? A week, maybe two. There was at least one surgery after that. "I thought you meant he got hit when you were on the ground."

"He fell. We fell. His parachute didn't work."

"You don't want to go in the helicopter."

"I'm not some—I'm not some pussy. I'll go in a fucking helicopter for her. You don't understand."

"I'm trying to understand, buddy. Keep talking. You need some more air in your lungs. You look like a ghost. Do you know you're not in a helicopter now?"

Not really. "Yeah."

"You're not. You're on the ground, but you're not at home."

"No shit."

"This is Hades's house. Home is next door."

The next thing that comes out of my mouth is a laugh. It's horrible and wrong, and I can't even get the air to sustain it. "Is that where it is? Could I go back to before all this bullshit? Would that be okay?"

"Before what? Before Ollie? Before your mom?"

"You don't understand." Fuck—*I* don't understand.

None of this makes any sense. I keep seeing night air and clouds, hear helicopter rotors beating and beating and beating, and I shouldn't be able to. This whole room is full of sun.

"What's going on?"

Fucking great. It's Zeus, and I can't even punch him. I can't even look at him until his face is near Ares's.

"He freaked out and pulled the bar out of the wall." Ares says it under his breath, as if I'm not going to be able to hear him from six inches away.

"Okay." Zeus smiles when he says it, like a pile of shattered glass and ripped-apart studs are the very least of what he's encountered in his life. "Herc, is this about going to the mountain? We can make different plans if you can't go."

It stops my entire brain.

Zero thoughts pass through. There's only the clouds and the rotors and the rush of wind.

"What?"

"He thinks he's in a helicopter," Ares mentions.

"No, I fucking *don't*. I'm asking what the—what the hell you're talking about."

"We don't have to go to the mountain," Zeus repeats, slow enough for me to understand through what's obviously a complete mental collapse. "If you can't go, we'll figure it out."

"*She* has to go. Daisy has to go. That's what all of you decided."

"Daisy can't go without you. And she needs you."

"No, she doesn't. She needs her—her—her—" I have fucking lost it. "Her dad. Not me."

"She needs both of you." Zeus has taken Ares's place, and it was so seamless that I didn't see either of them move. One of his hands is on my shoulder. My left shoulder. The one that doesn't hurt. "Are you thinking of Ollie?"

I'm always thinking of Ollie. Not a day goes by that I don't think of him, or my mom.

"She's the third one."

A hint of a frown. "Daisy?"

"Yeah. She's the third."

"The third…what?"

"The third person I couldn't make the trade for. But you don't fucking get it, do you?"

He pauses, and I know he's forcing himself not to say *nobody wants your trade*. "No, I suppose not. Can you explain it to me?"

A hot surge of anger is all that makes the words possible. "My mom only had me. Ollie only had me. There was nobody to hate me afterward. You can still save yourselves. You figured it out in time."

"Figured what out?"

"That I'm fucking useless. And you know what? I can't do it." That awful, soulless laugh lurches out of me. "I can't do it again. I can't be the one who's left. I'd rather die, and I fucking *can't*."

I refuse to think about why he's blurry, and why my face feels hot, and why I'm choking on nothing.

"I get it." Zeus squeezes my shoulder. "I understand. I have to ask you a question, though, if you're okay."

This is the kindest lie he could've offered me. "I'm *fine.*"

"You sure?"

"Yes, asshole. I'm f-fine."

"Okay. What do you think about getting changed and coming back to the family room? Daisy's asking for you."

# CHAPTER
# FIFTEEN

*Daisy*

THE MOOD IN THE FAMILY ROOM IS TENSE when Hercules comes back with Zeus.

My mom pats my hand and stands up without a single second of hesitation, and then he's back at my side, his fingers intertwined with mine.

That feels better.

Everything else is getting worse.

I can feel the nightmare coming, but it's in this bizarre holding pattern where it's at the edge of my consciousness. Sitting there. Not getting any closer. Not backing off. I didn't know it could stabilize like that. I don't know if that's a good sign or a bad sign.

Hercules leans over and rests on my legs, his hand still in mine.

I can reach his hair with my free hand. I've been playing with various curls for a few minutes before I realize he's asleep.

"We have to talk about an alternate strategy." Zeus sounds like he's at a party that's happening in a library.

"Why are you whispering?" Poseidon asks.

"I'm not whispering, I've lowered my voice, because Hercules is sleeping." Zeus seems to understand it without anyone saying anything. I don't know how, since there's literally no light in here. Maybe he can feel it.

Wouldn't be that weird, all things considered.

"How the fuck do you know that?"

"Is that really the most important thing, Poseidon? Jesus Christ."

"Fine. What do we need an alternate strategy for, prick?"

"For the mountain. We might not be able to go."

My dad doesn't move. It's the exact opposite of a startle, which is how I know he's genuinely surprised. "Why?"

"Hercules has a problem with it."

"With the mountain? He's been there. We've all been there, even me." Poseidon might be more shocked than my dad. My dad and Zeus sometimes joke about how he wouldn't visit the mountain for years at a time. I thought they were exaggerating, but…maybe not.

"He has a problem with the helicopter flight."

There's a beat of silence. "*What?*"

"Poseidon, would you shut the fuck up? Or at least talk a little more quietly so we can have this conversation?" Zeus's party voice frays a little at the edges, but he holds on.

"What?" Poseidon whispers.

"It's about Ollie."

My dad and Poseidon exhale at the same time, and my dad repositions, letting the arm of the couch take more of his weight. "How much of a problem are we talking about?"

"Significant," Zeus answers.

"How significant?" whispers Poseidon.

"First." I can't see Zeus hold up one finger, but I know he's doing it. "You've made your point. And second, Hades, there's a fuckload of broken glass on the floor of your weight room, and one of the bars has been quite literally torn out of the studs. Ares thought he was having a panic attack."

"He was—" Poseidon's too loud, and Zeus cuts him off with what sounds like a hand over his mouth. After a few beats, Poseidon continues in a voice just above a whisper. "He was in the Special Forces. The man doesn't have panic attacks."

"Please." My dad might be the quietest of all of them, but he's still the most cutting. And this isn't even him at his *most* cutting. "I know you've had men on your crew face similar issues."

"But he's Hercules." Poseidon's not making a joke. I can hear him frowning. "He was always a tough bastard."

"Apparently, he has some concern that Daisy is the third person he won't be able to save," Zeus says. "He's never seemed particularly superstitious to me, but it has meaning for him. And regardless of whether his concern is justified—"

"Of fucking course it's justified," Poseidon interrupts.

"*Regardless,* there's no way we can put him on the train and put her on a helicopter. They both have to go together. He's under the impression that somebody else can take his place with her."

"That's not the case." My dad's worried, which makes *me* worried. More worried, I mean. I'm already baseline worried, given...the situation.

"He said he didn't have as big of an effect. That's what he said." It's harder to keep my voice quiet than I thought it'd be. "Was he wrong?"

"What did he say, exactly?" Zeus asks.

"He said all he did was keep the wave in rhythm. Not below the line."

Zeus sighs. "Then yes. He was wrong."

"How?"

"The rhythm is as important as the height. It's hard to see that when there's seizure activity, because it's at the top of the graph, but it's just as important."

Hercules breathes, his body moving gently up and

down. He's heavy enough that I know he's actually sleeping. Not faking it.

He's exhausted.

I'm exhausting.

A witch who puts visions in his head.

This whole thing is too much.

"What are our other options?" My mom is calm, too, and honestly…I'm not sure how she does it. Even at his calmest, my dad feels like an inhuman strength that's barely being kept in check. Then again, she told Zeus and Poseidon to *get the fuck in the house*, and that was enough.

Brute strength isn't the only power.

My mind catches on what Zeus said and repeats it back to me, over and over, as the conversation stirs softly around us.

*He has some concern that Daisy is the third person he won't be able to save.*

People say *things come in threes* all the time. That doesn't make it true. The idea that the vastness of the universe results in such a regular pattern can only be an idea. It can't be reality, because life is too big and chaotic for that.

But…does it matter? If our human experience tells us that the rule of three is a pattern that can be counted on—if we *all*, in some shape or form, believe that it's true—then maybe it does.

Then maybe he's right.

At the end of the day, when we get all the way

around to the beginning of that logic circle, what matters is Hercules.

If *he* thinks that me being his third person is significant, then it is. If this is the thing he can't do, if this is his breaking point, then none of the rest means anything at all.

I run my fingers through his hair, tracing the pattern of one of his curls, as gently as I can. I don't want him to wake up if he's tired.

*You don't think you're good enough,* I think at him. My parents' voices are like a stream running through the room. Chilled water and sparks of sunlight. Poseidon's is bigger, like the ocean, and Zeus sounds like a party. A small, quiet party. Your family, gathered around the table, singing the birthday song in the backyard.

"—friends with connections. Hades, are you willing to—"

"—before. We shouldn't put them in a position where they feel responsible," my mom says.

"Oh, *fuck* not being responsible. We live in a fucking society." Poseidon, voice rising until Zeus shushes him, the noise like the foam of a whitecap.

"Demeter said she would come." A glass of champagne. Clapping while they cut the cake. A broad smile. Air moves, like he's shutting the door behind him.

This brings the room to a halt, my dad's arms tight around me. "When?"

"Just now. She and Gio can be here tomorrow morning."

"Why not tonight?" my dad asks.

I'm still trying to figure out why Hercules could possibly believe he's not enough for this, not enough for me, why he could possibly think he's not important, so I miss the first part of Zeus's explanation.

"—workers," he's saying, when I remember to pay attention. "They'll be here at dawn."

"To do what?" I ask. "What is she going to do?"

"You need new painkillers, otherwise we can't solve the rest," Zeus answers. "She'll have to touch you to know how to grow the hybrids. And then—"

"I don't think the soil on the mountain is as important as you think," my mom says. "Growth shouldn't be a problem, as long as the processing is the same."

"There's no reason to think—" I should let Zeus finish his sentence.

I should.

"What about Hercules?" I'm the thing we're trying to fix. I know that. But it seems...shortsighted to focus all our efforts on saving me if he needs help, too.

"What about him?" My dad's tone is unexpectedly gentle, and it makes me want to cry. It makes me feel young and fragile and exhausted. I *am* those things, I guess, but I don't want to be.

"What are we going to do for him?"

I expect another awkward silence, but Zeus is right there with a response. "Whatever he asks for."

"You know he won't ask for anything. You know that."

"Whatever he needs, then."

"What if it's *me*? What if I'm the thing he can't afford to lose?"

"Daze," Zeus says, because my dad is holding his breath, and I'm pretty sure he can't say anything at all. "None of us can afford to lose you."

"But what if I'm not cut out to be in the world? You would be okay. You would be—you could survive it. What if he can't?"

Footsteps approach, and I think my dad might've died, because he's still not breathing. Zeus gets down close, one of his hands going to my dad's knee and the other hand going to my face.

"Don't say it." My breath is shallow, every one of them hard to take, and I barely have the energy to stay awake. I'm already dizzy. "I don't want to hear it right now."

"I won't."

"It's not like I want to die."

"I know that."

"I *don't*. No matter what I said when I was—I *don't*. That's not what this is about, so don't make it about that."

If he does, I'll…well, I'll probably pass out, and at least that would be the end of the discussion. But if I *don't* pass out, I'll have to sit here with this horrible crush in my chest and tears stinging my eyes and a giant hollow pit filled with desperation.

It's not great.

"I wouldn't." Zeus doesn't move his hand. He lets it rest on my cheek. "I get it."

"Do you?"

"Not all pain is physical."

My dad's chest hitches, one time, and then he breathes like nothing happened. A rock-steady rhythm. I pretend not to notice Zeus patting his knee, or the undercurrent of an earthquake low in the air. I'm almost certain that Zeus is covering it like a breeze, trying to counterbalance it with…not joy, really, more like…

More like peace.

But it's hard. It has to be hard, with the tug of the nightmare still crouched in the corner of my mind.

Maybe it won't be so difficult if I stop fighting it. Breathing it out feels like it'll never be enough, but it's all I have.

"I know you're worried about him." That's not… what I expected Zeus to say. I thought he might say that I didn't *need* to worry about Hercules, or reassure me about how he can survive whatever life throws at him. It's a massive relief when he doesn't. "I also know that you won't stop worrying about him, and I wouldn't ask you to. I want you to know that if anything happens to you, he won't be alone."

Jesus. How does he *do* that? He's not promising that Hercules will be okay, because we all know he wouldn't be. He's not even promising that he, or anyone else, will have what Hercules needs in the event of my brain-betrayal demise. He's giving me a promise he can keep.

"Okay." I let my next breath out as slow as I can. "I'm not planning on dying, though. I don't want that."

"I know," Zeus answers.

"Daddy," I say.

"I know. Of course I know." I'm not at all surprised that my dad's stress doesn't show in his voice. "I'm not holding it against you, Daisy. That would be hypocritical."

That's enough to interrupt the emotional rockslide in my tired mind. I lean harder into his shoulder, but not because I want to, necessarily—my entire body feels heavier and less manageable. Or my mind is less able to manage it. I'd be terrified of that if it hadn't gone on so long already.

"What do you mean?"

Him saying he's a hypocrite could only mean one thing, and it doesn't fit. My dad is the strongest man I've ever known. He'd never ask for anything like I asked for, no matter how out of it he was.

"I mean that Zeus doesn't hold it against me, so I'd be a hypocrite to hold it against you."

I don't know what to say. I don't actually want company when it comes to this thing I've done, this thing I've asked for, this thing that's *still* making everyone's life harder.

It's nice not to be the only one.

There's not much use in wishing I was, though.

"If it helps." Zeus runs his thumb over my cheekbone, and the strangest memory surfaces of being very, very young and waking up in Zeus's arms instead of my dad's. I couldn't begin to say what my parents were doing, or if I'm making it up, but I remember it so clearly. "You remembered your manners when you asked. And you didn't call your father a motherfucker and tell him you hated him in the same breath."

"Wow, Dad."

My dad snorts. "I can't be blamed."

"We would never blame you." Zeus's voice is so easy. I could almost believe it didn't hurt him at all. "You're a sweetheart."

Somewhere close by, my mom laughs. I can tell she's crying, but she's keeping it quiet.

"Everybody knows that." Poseidon sounds exactly like he's lying in a hammock on his ship. My brain probably *is* shutting down, because I know for a fact there's not a hammock in here. "Mention Hades's name anywhere on the globe, and all the guys say he's a sweetheart."

My mom giggles, and I hear the moment she gets caught up in her laughter and loses control of it. "I—" A strained gasp. "Excuse me for a minute."

She rushes for the door. It opens and closes, and then there are the softest footsteps in the history of the world, running fast. Her voice is distant when she bursts out laughing. In the dark, it sounds like an entire garden. Brigit's golden voice and Ashley's rolling brook join her, and you know what? This will be what I miss if I die. Not only being alive. Not only Hercules. Being able to listen to them. I know it's not the most feasible plan to live in complete darkness for the rest of my life, but I'd do it if I still had this. The party I described in my mind to Hercules.

"Unbelievable," my dad says. "My own wife. I blame you, Poseidon."

"Sorry," Poseidon whispers, but he's not. He's smiling. It's in the shape of the word.

Zeus lets out a soft, cocktail party laugh. He pats my dad's knee one more time, pats my cheek, and gets to his feet.

"Now." Clothes meet furniture. He's probably sitting in his favorite chair. "What should we do about Demeter?"

Poseidon groans. "Are we ever going to stop having this conversation?"

"Since she's our sister, probably not, you unfeeling prick. I meant—where do you think she'd like to stay?"

"She'll stay here." My dad's firm about this, and fast.

"Um." Poseidon rustles around. Can't tell what he's doing, but he doesn't sound like he's in a hammock anymore. "Is this—are you being funny?"

"Does it sound like a joke to you, Poseidon?" These words are diamonds, sharp and precise.

"It all sounds the same coming from you. That's why I'm asking."

"Do you think I would *joke* at a time like this?"

"It wouldn't be the worst idea."

My dad moves, shifting like he's going to stand up, and I hear Poseidon jump to his feet.

"Sweet Mother of God, Hades. Would it kill you to lighten up for once in your life?"

"How did you know he was coming for you? He didn't, like, get up. There's an entire other person on top of him." I *wish* I could dissolve into laughter, but that would wake up Hercules and take the rest of the energy I have. Maybe for the day, but maybe for my life.

"Instinct," answers Poseidon. "Live with a high-strung motherfucker like him for long enough, and you get a sense of when he's—"

"Teasing you?" I ask, innocent.

"Trying to murder me," Poseidon shoots back.

"He's a sweetheart. He would never."

My dad laughs again, but he swallows the sound, and then he's absolutely cracking up, his shoulders shaking, breathless.

"Demeter can—" Dad seriously sounds like he can't get enough air, he's so delighted with himself. "Demeter can stay at your house, Poseidon. You two have a friendship now. You could let her sleep—"

"Hades, shut the fuck—Jesus. Shut the fuck up." Poseidon's laughing too. It's muffled behind his hands, or his arm.

Zeus is the last one to break. He has the prettiest laugh out of all of them. He's been the one shushing everyone else all this time, but he's also the first to laugh the loudest.

"I hate all of you," Hercules mumbles into my legs. "So fucking annoying."

That makes them laugh even harder.

It's a long, long time before they can stop. My mom comes into the room three times, still laughing, and leaves again before anybody can stop to tell her it's fine.

Finally, Zeus clears his throat.

"Okay." His voice is wobbly and strained. Anything could set him off, and part of me wants to. I'd rather listen to them laugh than listen to them cry and worry. "Anything we need to do before Demeter gets here? I'd imagine we'll be in this room until she can test some options and find one that works."

"Yes," I say, before anyone can get ahead of me and laugh for another hour.

"What is it, Daze?"

"I want to sleep in my bed tonight."

I don't say *one last time.*

# CHAPTER
# SIXTEEN

*Hercules*

DAISY IS SO WORN DOWN ALREADY THAT IT'S only a matter of waiting until she feels like it's *bedtime*. She makes it until shortly after ten. Not that the light in the house is any different. It's always dark, now, and it will be unless Demeter comes through with miracle painkillers. From what I understand, she's done it once before, not twice, so there's not so much third-in-a-list-of-threes bullshit hanging over her upcoming visit.

Hades carries his daughter upstairs for the night, staying in contact for as long as he can, and then we start a production that has a real last-time energy.

I hate it.

This isn't the last time Daisy's going to sleep in her own bed. It's fucking not. Even if it feels like that.

She arranges her head on the pillow, and both her parents hover around and kiss her goodnight. Persephone's the only one who manages to pull off acting casual, and then she has to drag Hades out by the arm. Impressive, honestly. She must have some secret power over him.

Then we're alone in the dark.

I get into the bed next to Daisy and pull her into my arms. She lets out a contented little sigh.

"Baby." She could be asleep already, with how tired she's been.

"Yes?"

"What's the deal with the bed?"

"It's…" A long pause. "A semi-firm mattress, and I'd say I've had it since I was sixteen, but I'm not sure if—"

"Why did you want to sleep in here?"

"Give my dad a break."

Her hair is so soft. There's not a single knot in it. I run my fingers through it again and again with no resistance.

"I don't think he wants a break."

Hades isn't taking one, anyway. He's sitting in the hallway outside the door. Zeus is monitoring the app to make sure the distance doesn't kill Daisy. The plan is for him to move away from the bedroom in fifteen-minute increments so we don't set anything off.

"It could take a while to grow the right flowers for the painkillers."

"What flowers?"

"They're *made* from flowers. Demmy made them for Dad first, with—with—" A huge yawn interrupts her, and a pure, cold terror clutches at my chest. There's no nightmare in the room now. None of the dread, or the pressure, or the sense of something hovering in the dark. I can't even feel it in the distance. "A certain kind of moonflower. And poppies she bred."

"She did that for him, and he keeps her on a mountain?"

Daisy laughs. "He doesn't *keep* her there. She and Gio want to stay."

"He was keeping her there before, though."

"That was different. *She* was different. And it was a group decision. But *anyway*, nothing bad's going to happen tonight."

"How do you know that?"

She shrugs. "Can't feel it waiting."

I can't either, but I don't like it. This feels like the silence before an ambush, only there's nothing I can shoot, or tackle, or bomb to hell. My shoulder aches the way it did when I was recovering from surgery. Even if this nightmare *was* a physical being, I don't know if I'd be strong enough to wring its neck.

Can't say I love that feeling.

"What are you worried about?" Daisy asks.

There's a quiet shuffling in the hall. Hades, moving

down a few more feet. Zeus's voice is a brighter hum, and from farther off, Persephone's is like a night bloom.

Oh. I get it now. Midnight blooms.

"You."

Daisy hooks her hand into the neckline of my T-shirt. "You've done so much for me. Do you know that?"

"It's not enough."

"Hercules." I want the feeling of her fingers on my skin imprinted there for the rest of my life. "Brains are complicated. Nobody expected you to be able to help mine, at *all*. I would never expect that from you. I wouldn't be disappointed if—"

"Don't say that."

"Don't say what?"

"Don't say that it's fine if I can't save you. It's not fine. You should be able to count on me." My throat feels bruised, and my ribs, and that deep ache is spreading all over my shoulder, getting sharper every second. "My mom should've been able to count on me. Ollie should've been able to count on me. I'm so fucking sick of letting people I love down."

She's still, but she's not asleep. "I don't think any of those people would agree with you."

"They should."

"Well, *I* don't. You haven't let me down. And you can't."

"Yes, I fucking can."

"Are you refusing to kiss me?"

I bark a laugh. "Jesus. No."

"Then do it," she insists.

I lean in for a soft kiss, one that's appropriate for a woman who might literally fucking die soon, and Daisy hooks her arm around my neck and yanks me in for a rough one. She bites me like she did the first time. It's hot and desperate, sharp teeth and sweetness, and when she's kissing me, I could forget that her painkillers failed, I could forget that we're out of tricks to stop her seizures, I could forget that there might not *be* an answer that arrives in time.

I taste her like there's no tomorrow.

I'd fuck her, too, but we've come to a silent agreement that fucking might be counterproductive right now. Without an active nightmare threat, we can't risk spending her energy on a rough fuck, or even a gentle one.

Her hand is tangled in my hair when she pulls back, gasping.

I like the sound of it until I realize she's not gasping because she wants to fuck, she's gasping because she can't catch her breath. She doesn't have enough energy to catch her breath.

I pull her against me on instinct. "Relax, baby. All the way. Don't hold yourself up at all."

Daisy half-asses it.

"I mean *all* your weight, on me, right now. Your shoulders are still tense." She only *begins* to relax when I rub her back, her head getting heavier first, then the rest of her. "You have to stop pushing yourself up. I'm not going to kiss you again."

"Mean," she exhales.

Voices rise a little in the hall.

"That app's probably going crazy. If you don't want a family reunion in here for the night, you have to keep breathing."

"Want," Daisy manages. "Sex."

"God. You're such a slut for me."

"Yeah," she agrees on a high, strained breath, like a laugh.

"Try again tomorrow."

"In." I want to replace my lungs with hers. I don't know what's gone wrong. If she's so damn tired that she can't breathe, or if her body's taking emergency measures to save her, or if it's her brain—I don't know. But she can have my lungs. She can have my life. I don't care. "The—family—room?"

I let out a resigned sigh. "If you want me to fuck you in front of your dad, then…I guess I don't have a choice."

"Ew," she breathes.

"I'm sure he'd close his eyes."

"*Ew.*"

"Baby." I hold her head close to my chest and wait for another wave of tension to leave her. "I'd fuck you anywhere."

"Gross," she whispers.

"Commitment," I whisper back.

"That what you are? Committed?"

That sentence took it out of her. She settles onto me with a sigh, and it takes everything I have not to shiver underneath her. Not to let all my muscles shake. Because a small, cowardly part of me wants to get out, get out, get *out* before I have to watch her die, and the much larger part knows that I won't leave her until the bitter end, even if it makes me wish for a death I can't have.

"Yes. You're stuck with me. I took an oath. Plus, your uncles and your dad sent me to protect you. I'll do whatever I have to do. I'll do everything I can. Don't worry, baby. Just rest."

Daisy makes a soft sound. *I.* That's what I think she says, and I brace for the rest. Please, don't let it be *I love you.* Please, don't let her love me when I can't save her. Please, let her love me anyway, even if it's only for one night.

She doesn't finish the sentence.

There's nothing to look at in the dark, so I'm fully free to concentrate on her breathing. On the feel of her in my arms. On her exact weight.

Jesus. I don't *need* to memorize these things. She'll be okay tomorrow, and the next day, and the next.

But then—there's never a guarantee, is there? One minute, your mom is alive. The next, her neck is broken and she's never coming back. One minute, you're still falling, still suspended. The next, you're crushed on the ground. One minute, the woman you love—

Fuck me.

I memorize her in the dark. Her breathing goes back to normal as she falls more deeply asleep. The voices in the hall move farther and farther away.

All quiet now.

I catch myself dozing off, in that weird space between sleeping and dreaming. Not a nightmare—actually dreaming. It happens twice. Maybe three times.

The ache in my shoulder gets stronger. A similar ache starts up in my ankles and moves up through my calves and my knees and my thighs.

It's not the first time I've been pinned in an uncomfortable position. This hasn't lasted nearly as long as some of the bullshit ways I had to crouch in the Special Forces to stay alive.

It should be nothing.

It's not nothing.

I do as much as I can lying down. I stretch my legs and my arms and my neck. It works for about five fucking seconds.

My heart starts to race.

If it keeps going in that direction, I might have a heart attack and die, and then I'd be letting Daisy down in the most fucked-up way possible. The one thing I've never attempted to survive is major organ failure. And if I can't die *for* her, then screw it. I'm not letting it take me by surprise.

Like any mission, I plan it out. I need to get out of the bed and stretch. I'll walk down the hall to the bathroom. My phone is on the charger there. I'll check to see how much of the night we have to get through. I'll come back.

Two minutes at maximum.

Before I make a single move, I scan the space as objectively as I can, given that we're dealing with killer nightmares *on top of* an unknown hostile party who could make an attack at any moment.

Nothing seems out of place.

Waiting too long is as dangerous as moving without a plan, so I count to three and go.

I ease myself off the bed, touching Daisy until the last possible second, and head out of her bedroom, into the silent hallway.

It's steps to the bathroom. I shut myself in and feel for the switch that turns on the emergency lights. They're a faint red glow, and even that seems bright after so many hours in the dark. That's enough to get my phone. The screen's brightness is already down, thank fuck.

It's a minute before three in the morning.

My stomach drops at that 2:59. Three in the morning has no meaning. It's not a special time. It has nothing to do with life or death.

All it means—*all* it means—is that we're not far from dawn. Daisy's almost made it through the night.

I splash water on my face, dry my hands, and step back into the hall.

A scream obliterates the silence.

It's the most harrowing sound I've ever heard—at home, on the battlefield, *ever*. It overrides all the instincts the Army drilled into me and all the ones from living on the streets, too. I can't move. I can't think. I can't tell which direction it's coming from until the person screaming takes a huge, wretched breath and screams again.

And then I understand *who* it is, and I'm nothing but terror and adrenaline.

It's Hades.

There must be a curtain open in the main bedroom, because I can see his outline through the door. Persephone's, scrambling out of the bed.

"Hades." She's too loud. I've heard fear in a lot of people's voices in my life, but never like this. "Hades. *Hades.*"

Footsteps *thud* on the stairs as Conor starts barking.

Hades's scream cuts off into an even worse silence, and then he *runs*.

I can't see his face. He's all shadow, and I slam my back against the wall in time to get out of his way. Conor's with him, barking and barking and barking.

He collides with someone at the end of the hall.

"Hades," Zeus says. "Hades—Hades, stop—"

Somebody throws up.

"Fuck," says Poseidon. "Both of them? Or just him?"

Conor's barking gets muffled, like he's biting at someone's pants, and light glows.

It's one of those balls, in Poseidon's hand. Zeus has Hades's shirt in his hands, a syringe held in his teeth, and Hades pulls himself away from Zeus and stumbles into Daisy's room.

The pressure is like a pair of hands clapping at my ears. Jesus, fuck, that *hurts*, it all hurts, but I move anyway. Push past Poseidon, who has his arms around Conor.

Hades is at the side of Daisy's bed, his hand over hers. She's still sleeping, her eyes closed.

"*Don't*," he shouts, like he doesn't have control of his voice. Fucking terrifying. He always has control of his voice. "Don't. Don't. Not. Happening. Yet. Wait."

"I can't wait," Zeus answers.

"*Wait*," Hades insists.

Daisy opens her eyes.

Black. Behind her. A pressurized cloud. Hovering in the space between the light and the dark, ready to fucking pounce.

I'm halfway there by the time she screams. I don't have a plan. I throw myself around Zeus, crawl onto the bed, and put my hand on her chest.

It pulls me in by the neck. I fall through night air, the floor of my mother's apartment, and land hard on my shoulder on an unforgiving stone floor.

Daisy's here.

Black dress. Bare feet. She faces away from me, toward the gates. The pull is even stronger here. This must be what it's like to notice gravity, only worse.

Like noticing it at the same time you notice there's no parachute.

She turns her head and looks at me, face solemn. "They already went through."

It's eerily quiet in the stone room. As quiet as it was before Hades screamed. "Who?"

"Conor and my kitten."

I can't see a fucking thing through those gates. Nothing but shimmering black. "What's on the other side?"

"Death," Daisy answers. "I'm afraid to go through."

"Because you think it won't let you out?"

"Because I think I might want to stay. It doesn't hurt here. But...I need to get my dad's dog. I need to get my kitten."

I can't blame her.

I can't let her do that, either.

I'd never forgive myself.

And finally, *finally*, after a lifetime of wishing I could just fucking die, a realization clicks into place.

"I can go with you. It can't touch me."

Her eyes light up. "You would do that?"

"Tell me not to go with you."

She cracks a smile, and the stone room vibrates. "No."

I take her hand in mine, lift it to my lips, and kiss her knuckles. "Then let's go."

The gates pull at us, *wanting* us, and it's a relief to

stop fighting. Daisy walks at my side until there's no more stone floor, until we're there, until it's time.

"Do you think we'll die?" She peers up at the gates like they're an exhibit in a museum. A piece of art.

"No. I won't let you die. No matter what."

She takes a breath, and we step over the threshold.

It's not an apartment, or the ground in hostile territory. It's not even a stone room.

There's...

A field.

A wide, grassy field, with trees in the distance and the sun peeking over the horizon. It's absolutely gorgeous. I take a step farther in without thinking. My shoulder doesn't hurt. *Nothing* hurts. Not my heart. Not my soul. Nothing.

Because...

My heart isn't beating.

I was wrong. I was *wrong*. A wild certainty moves through me like a breeze. I can't die out there, but in here?

In *here*?

I can.

I can make the trade for her, but only here.

"Conor," Daisy calls.

Her voice *shocks* me. It's her voice, but darker, more expansive, ringing with power. Conor comes bounding over a low rise in the field like he's compelled. I track him over the grass, following him, and so I don't see her until he sits at her feet.

I stop breathing.

Daisy bends to pet Conor's head, gracious, grace-ful, and...not herself.

She's at least as tall as Hades. Taller. Her arms are covered in what look like tattoos, but I don't think they are. They're too...alive. Like veins of power all over her skin. Green and silver, in beautiful twisting patterns that end at her knuckles.

And...

She has wings.

Huge, black wings that flicker in and out of view every time I blink.

"Daisy?"

She lifts her head, straightening, and my heart flails.

Daisy's stunning.

A sharp, harsh beauty my body knows isn't entirely human. It's more. The color is back in her face. Pink cheeks. Red lips.

And black, *black* eyes. There's no white.

When they meet mine, I feel her.

I've always felt her, but now I feel what she's doing. It's like a river inside my mind. A soft, searching touch.

This is how she finds the nightmares.

New meaning crashes in, strong enough to shatter my bones. This is what her mind does. It looks for pain and amplifies it into screaming nightmares.

Except Daisy doesn't want that. She's never wanted to hurt other people. She wanted to save her family from pain so much that she moved to the opposite side of the country.

All this power is a weapon, and she turns it on herself. She keeps it in her mind. Hurts herself instead.

A necklace glints at her neck. It's a black diamond, held in a twist of—platinum? A delicate chain with flower petals in the links.

"Can I keep that for you?"

Daisy smiles, and her teeth—they're *actually* sharp. They look deadly. A beautiful nightmare. "Keep what?"

"Your necklace. It's gorgeous. Tell me I can't have it."

Her smile widens. "No."

I approach her like she's not the most powerful person I've ever known. I go to her like she's the woman I've spanked and fucked and held while she cried. She *is*. Like the diamond necklace, eternal and fragile. She's both. She's mine.

Daisy bends her head. I expect the necklace to fight. To cut me, maybe. But the clasp comes undone beneath my fingers, easy as anything, and I put it in my pocket.

"Where is your kitten?"

The smallest frown curves her lips. "I don't know."

Conor hasn't moved from her feet. He's in thrall to her, and her hand drops to stroke his head. It's a gesture that's entirely Hades. Daisy's never been tall enough to pet Conor like that.

I look over the field in the rising light. "Kitten," I

call, softer than Daisy, because my voice is still the same. "Baby."

It mewls, and I find it at my feet. Its pink nose nudges my pants, and it circles one of my ankles, its tiny body warm and purring.

I lean down and take it in my palms. It curls into a ball, purring louder.

"You're very strong," Daisy says, her voice reverberating through everything. "She's never come to me."

"I didn't need to be strong." I stroke the kitten's head with one finger. "I wasn't afraid."

"Afraid of what?"

Of seeing her as she is. I've never been afraid. I'm not afraid now. Just in awe.

I hold my free hand out to Daisy. "Tell me you won't come with me."

"No."

She takes my hand, and I stifle a gasp at the feeling.

Like a laugh in the dark. Like razor-sharp nails. Like a nightmare.

A beautiful, righteous one.

I lead her toward the gates. It's the same shimmering dark. The closer we get, the more it tries to push us away. Push *me* away. Daisy doesn't seem to feel it.

"What's on the other side?" she asks.

"Life."

She laughs like I've told her a wonderful joke.

We stop at the threshold, and I kiss her knuckles. "How do you feel?"

"So good." Daisy rolls her shoulders, her wings moving with them. "Like I could *run*."

"Would you run with me?"

She wrinkles her nose, grinning, and it's the most human she's looked since we got here. "Not too far, I hope."

"No. Not too far."

My teeth hurt already. The *push* from the gates is almost unbearable. It wants us in here, but it can only have me.

I smile at her like it's a game. The kitten mewls. Conor huffs and gets to his feet.

"Ready? Set?"

"Go!" she shouts, and races through.

The stone room seems longer than before. I run at a dead sprint, and Daisy's right there, right with me, her hand in mine. She laughs out loud, and her voice is half and half.

I need her power to make it to the other side.

To that door on the other side.

Conor runs like he's a puppy, sprinting and sprinting, and claws dig into my shoulders. The pull of the gates is alive. It rips at my shirt, but I don't stop. I don't stop for anything.

"Oh!" Daisy gasps, and her hand gets smaller in mine. "Hercules—"

"Not much farther. Come on."

I move my hand to her elbow and bring her with

me. The stone underneath us starts to crack, dark pushing through it like weeds. *Not a seizure. Not now.*

Twenty feet to go.

"Hercules."

Ten.

"There's nothing there!"

"There is. There is. You can't see it yet."

Five.

I can see it. The outline of a door.

We're two steps away when the handle materializes. A black doorknob, made from the same stone as the floor. I wrench it open while the gates try to take my hair out. While that power wraps around my ankles tight enough to crush them. Too fucking bad. I've survived worse than this, and I'll get her through if it's the last thing I do. The pull takes my right wrist and *yanks*, my shoulder collapsing, and I hold the door open with my left hand and shove Daisy through. Conor bolts across after her.

This is the only thing I've ever needed to be strong for. This is why I had to make it. To keep living when I wanted to die.

This.

I don't want her to go, but I want her to *live*. I can't argue with that. Peace settles in my chest, even as the gates ramp up.

It feels like a tornado. Like hands made from shrapnel grabbing at my arms and legs. Daisy stares up at me, herself again, lips parted in shock.

"Hercules, *no.*"

I tip the kitten into her arms. It's so easy. It takes almost nothing. None of my strength. None of my pain. It's the easiest trade I've ever made.

"I love you," I tell her.

*I got you out. Don't worry about me. This is what I've always wanted, and I did it for you. Live. Live. Live.*

And then it's like falling out of the sky. I couldn't change gravity, and I can't stop the pull. It whips me off my feet, stone ceiling rushing overhead. I hit the threshold and it's like glass shattering.

I tumble out into the wide, green field and roll until I come to a stop.

The grass is dotted with thousands of tiny daisies, and the sun is above the trees. The air is sweet and fresh.

On the other side of the door, Daisy's alive.

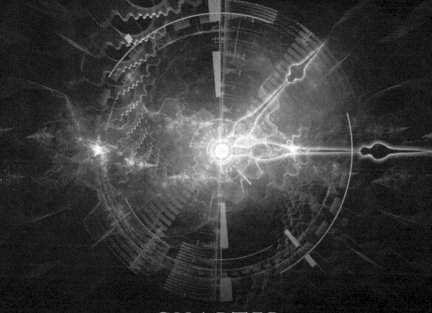

# CHAPTER SEVENTEEN

*Daisy*

THE DOOR SLAMS IN MY FACE, AND I'M AWAKE.
I'm awake?
I'm awake.

Breathing hard, like I've been running, and not an ounce of pain anywhere in my body. I can't remember the last time I didn't have at least the suggestion of a headache. I can't remember the last time I felt this good.

Am I still dreaming?

There's light.

Light in the room, and that should be—I should be screaming. It should hurt. I cover my eyes with my hands, but light leaks in past them.

It doesn't hurt, but it will. It feels like being…new? Like maybe this is what it was like to be a baby. Before everything was so fucked up.

Before Hercules loved me.

*I love you*, he said, and the kitten was so warm and small in my arms, and shadows pulled at his clothes and his legs and his hair and the door slammed and—

I suck in a huge, unholy gasp and lunge for him.

Hercules sprawls on the pillow, one arm out like he had it around me, perfectly still. Like someone made a statue and let it rest on my bed. His eyes are open. He stares at nothing.

"No." I climb over him and lose my balance. My knees hit his ribs, but he doesn't move. "Hercules. *Hercules.*"

He can't be frozen like this. He can't be unmoving like this.

He can't be dead.

Not like this.

Not when he loves me.

Not when I love *him*. Not when I want him with me forever, absolutely forever, until all the days in the universe are over.

"Hercules." His name comes out in a broken scream. What am I supposed to do? I'm the one whose brain shuts down at the worst possible moment. I'm not the one who saves anyone else. I make life scary and hard, and I don't know what to do. I push at his chest. Punch at it.

Grief rolls over me like a rockslide. It hurts in such a pure way. I don't think I've ever felt pain like this before—pain that couldn't be compared with what I already felt. This is new, like every muscle is bruised, but underneath, my body is fine. It keeps breathing even though it shouldn't.

I keep breathing, but he's *not*. That's wrong. That's nightmare-wrong. That's seizure-wrong. That's earth-rending wrong. I can't be breathing if he's not.

"Daisy." Someone puts a hand on my wrist. I think it's Zeus. I throw him off. "Daisy. We need—"

"Shut *up*," I scream at him. There's noise in the room behind me. I have no idea what it means, or who's in here with me, or what happened before. I remember a field and the sun in Hercules's hair and his huge hands cradling a tiny kitten. "Help me. *Help* me."

The voices blur together. Poseidon shouts. I don't know what he's shouting. I can't understand anything. CPR should crack ribs. I read that somewhere, but I don't know where to push. I pick a spot on his chest and drive both hands into it, throwing all my body weight behind it.

I know right away that his ribs won't crack.

It's physics. I'm not big enough to do it, and he's too strong. He's always been this strong. This is how he survived.

To die.

For me.

No. No. No.

"That's not what I wanted." I don't know I'm sobbing until I hear my own voice. "That's not what I wanted. I never would have let you in there if I thought that's what you'd do. *Why* would you do that? You don't have to die for people! You have to live for people! *Wake up.* Breathe. Stop doing this. *Wake up.*"

"Daisy." It's my dad this time, and I don't push him away because that would mean taking my focus off Hercules a second time. He's sitting on the bed with me. I don't know when he got here. "What happened?"

"He went through." Can he even understand me? The words feel misshapen in my mouth. Words are so unimportant right now. Explanations are so unimportant. "He went through the gates and shut me out."

Poseidon yells again, the sentence running together except at the very end. "—your ass in there."

"How am I supposed to do that?" my dad snaps.

"You were in there too, weren't you?"

"I don't know where I was."

"Hades, you *screamed.*"

Zeus breaks into sobs behind me, and another, softer voice smooths his over. Why can't I hear them clearly? There's something else that feels louder than they sound.

I choke back my own sobs and force a breath into my lungs.

The nightmare's gone.

There's no nightmare.

I'm not in any pain. Not the way I have been since

before I left for California. My eyes are starting to burn, the very, very beginning of pain, but that—that makes sense. I've been in the dark for a long time. It's not catastrophic. It's not a warning.

Conor's not barking. I'm okay.

But I can still feel…

I can still feel the gates. They're nearby, but they're not in my own head anymore.

Maybe I've lost it. Maybe there's no such thing as reality for me now.

Or maybe Hercules has the gates.

"He came with me to get Conor and the kitten out. He came with me, and he brought me back out again. There was a door, and he—he pushed me through it, and it shut, and—"

I squeeze my eyes shut, my hands over his heart, and try to go back in.

Nothing happens.

I don't know *how* to go back in. I've never done it on purpose. It happens to me while I'm sleeping, and there's no way I can fall asleep, unless—

"Knock me out." I look over my shoulder and meet Zeus's eyes. He swipes furiously at the tears on his cheeks. "Knock me *out*."

"You won't dream," he says.

"*Fuck*," I scream at Hercules. At everyone. How am I supposed to do this if I can't get back into my own dreams? How can this be a good thing if it comes at the price of Hercules's life?

It can't. It can't.

I push harder at his chest. I push hard enough to break ribs. No air moves in and out. No breath. None. None. I keep trying. Keep trying.

I can't try to break his ribs and stop myself from sobbing, but when the first one tears out of me it makes me *furious*. How can I be sobbing while he's dead? How can I be strong enough to cry all over him while he's dead?

How could he die?

He didn't think he could die, but then—

He never went through those gates. How would he have known?

"Damn it, he knew. He knew. That's why he said he loved me."

"Daisy—" My dad puts his hand on my arm. Soft. Like he might stop me, if he has to.

I whip around and meet his eyes. "*Daddy*. Help me. Help me. Save him. Please."

I've never felt this helpless in my entire life, and I've spent the whole thing at the mercy of indoor lighting.

My dad can be less than all-powerful later. Not now. Right now, he has to go back to being the man I always thought he was, and *fix this*. He's the only one who can do this. The proof is in his eyes. He's the only one who's ever understood what that's like, and he has to be the one who can help me. We're the same. We're the *same*.

Poseidon's talking again, so fast he's tripping over

himself. My dad turns his head to listen, but doesn't look away from me.

Zeus answers.

Their voices are getting clearer, and that means the gates are slipping away.

"You have to do it now," I sob at him. "You have to save him right now. Daddy. Please."

"It might—"

"Don't tell me it's too late. It's not too late. I can feel it. I can feel the gates. He's in there, and you can go through and get him out, but I can't—I can't. He took my necklace, and I think that means—I think—you have to save him. You have to do it *now*. Just help me. Please, help me."

Poseidon, again. I get more words than last time. "—*you* saw—battle on Haven Island, around you—chance, it has to be—fucking prick and do—*hurry*."

If he waits long enough for me to hear a full sentence, this is over.

Every one of my heartbeats is another second closer to *too late*.

Every single one means I'm alive, and Hercules is closer to being permanently dead.

"I can't do this without him. Daddy. I can't. You have to bring him back to me. You have to tell him he can't stay there. I do *not accept his trade*."

He takes a deep breath. Lets it out.

"It might not work."

The sound that comes out of me isn't a word. It's a

furious, frustrated scream through my teeth, because we're running out of *time*. How can they not see this? How can they not at least try? If it doesn't work, then we'll know in ten seconds. If it doesn't work—

"Okay," Dad says.

My voice is going. Tearing itself apart. My heartbeat is so heavy in my chest that it could burst through and kill me, and wouldn't that be ironic.

"Okay," he says again.

Calm covers up the terror and grief, but so light, like sunshine on water. It ripples like waves. It's not steady, like Zeus must not be steady, but this is all he can give. It makes my sobbing less violent, at least. I'm less likely to throw up all over Hercules.

My dad moves closer and takes my wrists. He moves my hands gently, gently into a slightly different spot on Hercules's chest. Below the calm, I get another jolt of fear—there should be a heartbeat under my palms, but there's not.

I need him to have a heartbeat.

I need him to be here.

My dad puts his hands over mine, and I could die of relief. It's premature, and I know that, but if he's trying, there's hope.

He closes his eyes.

For another pounding, thundering heartbeat, nothing happens.

Then a crease appears in his forehead. It's the only outward sign that this is costing him anything at all.

I don't know how that could be possible, because I *feel* it. The intense, unrelenting pressure of his mind. His power? Whatever it is, I don't know how he survives it minute after minute. It's the weight of the world, crushing, crushing, crushing.

And that—that can't be the solution. I don't need to destroy that stone room, or the gates, I need him to *get there.* I need him to bring Hercules back to life, and that won't happen by crushing his heart.

"Persephone." My dad doesn't open his eyes.

Mom's at his side in an instant, leaning in close, her head on his arm. Her silver eyes meet mine as she reaches for his hands. She doesn't smile at me. Doesn't say a word. But her eyes, which have been soft and warm and gentle all my life, are steely.

The moment she touches my dad's hands, I feel her, too. This time, I can't hold in the gasp. It's like gold thread through my veins. Roots tunneling into the earth. The wild thrash of flowers opening. It's equal and opposite to my dad. Every bit as intense, and it's all flowing directly through me and into Hercules.

"Follow it," my mom murmurs.

"I can't," I say.

But she's not talking to me. My dad lifts his head and rests it on hers.

I hold my breath.

If this means it's my fault that he dies, too, then—

I don't know what I'll do. Scream for the rest of my life. Cry until I'm dead.

Understand exactly how Hercules felt.

But my dad keeps breathing, even as his brothers arrive to hold him upright, to keep him from crushing my mom.

"Please." Everybody in this room is already doing as much as they can. I'm not talking to them. "Please, come back."

# CHAPTER
# EIGHTEEN

*Hercules*

DAISY WAS RIGHT—NOTHING HURTS HERE. For the first few seconds after I stop rolling, I don't move. Everything about this place is peaceful, and not in an ambush kind of way—actually peaceful. My nerves have been trained by years on the street and in battle to constantly scan for threats. I do it once out of habit and know that I'll never have to do it again.

I'd been focused on Daisy before. Daisy and her dark, nightmare beauty. Daisy and the incredible strength of will it takes to turn that inward instead of letting it out. She lasted a long time, doing that, and in the end when her strength failed, the effects were mostly on me. That's okay. I'm strong enough to handle it. Better me than anyone else.

Better me here than her.

Her family needs her. And for once, I didn't fail them.

I lie on my back on soft grass. Not a single piece is withered or sharp, and the ground cradles me like I was born from it. I'm so comfortable that I think the dirt is making it happen, or the grass, but eventually I decide that while the grass is incredibly soft and the dirt beneath is as springy as the most expensive mattress, it's my body that's different.

My shoulder has bothered me since I crushed it trying to save Ollie, but the pain is gone. All the small hitches and tugs from the scar tissue have vanished. There's no referred pain in my back, no soreness in my scapula from forcing my posture into a position that would take off the pressure. No nagging pains in my ankles or knees. No surprise phantom pains in the scars on my hands, which were made when I tried to drag Ollie somewhere, anywhere, he could be saved.

There is no threat to respond to. There is no call to answer. I'm as free as I ever have been, lying in a field of daisies, looking up at a blue-gold sky. At the morning, coming to life.

I run my palm over the tiny flowers. They're silky under my skin, fresh and new and safe.

The one disconcerting thing is the lack of a heartbeat.

I felt it fade when we were both here, but there were more pressing things to worry about.

Is it there, but quiet?

No. I hold my breath and listen and find I also don't need to breathe. It feels good to do it, though. It feels good to inhale sweet early summer and morning flowers in bloom and a scent that I want to call sunshine.

I let out a laugh at that. What does sunshine smell like? This, I guess. Like holding hands with Daisy.

I put a hand over my heart, then at my neck. Still no heartbeat.

"I did it," I announce to the flawless sky. "I did it."

"Did what?"

I'm not startled, exactly. I don't think anything here would hurt me, but I didn't know it wasn't empty. Anticipation feels like fresh air. Excitement feels like more sunshine.

I push myself to sitting, and—

"Mom! *Mom.*" No idea what I do to get to my feet, only that I'm looking up at her, and then I'm looking down into her face. I'm *touching* her face. I'm touching her, my hands on her cheeks, and she grins up at me, her eyes shining. They're my eyes, the color of honey, and she gave me my curly hair, and I never thought—I never— "Mom."

"Hercules." One of her hands rises to cover mine, and it feels so *small.*

"You shrank."

She laughs, and here, in this place, there's nothing but delight in it. No hidden stress. No pain. No fear. "You grew."

"I missed you."

Her smile softens. "I've been here. I hope you didn't worry."

"Mom." I twist one of her curls around my finger and an old, old memory floats in. How little was I? Young enough to sit in her lap. I'd been resting there, my head on her shoulder, playing with her curls. The background is a blur. It doesn't matter where we were, only that we were together. "Of course I worried. You're in an empty field."

She wrinkles her nose. "Empty?"

"There's nothing here but grass and daisies. And a few trees, I guess. How can you live in the trees?"

"Is that all you see?"

I lift my eyes from her face, but I keep my hands where they are. I don't want her to disappear.

"Yep. Grass. Flowers. Trees. Sky. It's a beautiful morning, but it's not a life. I guess it doesn't have to be one, if—"

"You can't see it," she says softly. "Here."

My mom puts her hand over my eyes. If I still had a heartbeat, it would pound at the idea of being lost in the dark—what if I can't find her?—but my heart isn't beating, and all I feel is the mildest chill in my lungs.

"What are you—"

"Look now." She uncovers my eyes.

"It's still the sa—"

I never finish saying it's the same, because it's not true.

The field is still there. The grass, the daisies, the trees, the sunrise.

But the hazy, unbroken line of trees has opened to reveal a lush valley. A sparkling river. Houses tucked nearby. Behind them, light glints off a small lake and onto a blonde woman sitting on the shore, whistling at a fluffy white bird. A dark-haired man sits behind her, his head bowed to kiss her shoulder, and even from this far away, I can tell they're in love. I can hear her laughing at him. A name like *James*. This is what I imagine a painting of paradise would look like.

It all blurs into a fuzzed-out palette of greens and blues, the tree trunks reduced to dark streaks on the periphery. I might not need to breathe or have a heart that beats, but I can still cry.

My mom puts her arm around my waist and leans her head against me. I wrap my arm around her shoulders and look and look and look. *Should* I have sent Daisy back? This place is wonderful, and she would love it. Nothing would hurt her here, either.

No, no—losing her would make the world bleak and awful. She has a family that needs her. It's always been better for me to be the one. Instead of my mom. Instead of Ollie. Instead of her.

Fuck. I love her so much. That part hasn't stopped

at all. It's maybe even bigger, this feeling like a butter-fly-flutter pulsing against my chest.

"Which one's yours?"

My mom ignores the awkward way I wipe at my eyes and points. "That one."

Nestled at the edge of the trees, overlooking both the valley and the field, is a cottage. It's like the one we talked about. The one she dreamed of. It's close enough to the—village? Town?—that she's not alone, and close to the running water of the river, but it has space around it.

"You always wanted a yard." The words don't do justice to the wild joy I feel for her, so strong it's al-most painful. Another thump in my chest, this time with pressure.

"I have a *huge* yard." She sounds slightly awed, like she's discovering it for the first time, but of course she's been here all along.

"Tell me how it's been." Impatience comes on sud-denly, though I know, I *know*, there's no rush. In a place without heartbeats, how could there be? "Tell me you've been okay. You've been happy. Please say you've been happy."

"I missed you." My mom squeezes me. "So much, Hercules. But I've been fine. I've been comfortable."

"Not happy?"

"Happy, too. It's different, when you've left your son."

"That wasn't your choice. You didn't mean to do it."

"I should've found another way to survive. I knew the risks I was taking. I'm sorry I only understood that when it was too late."

"Don't ever—" I don't need air, but I want more of it. A tight grief wraps around my ribcage. "Don't ever apologize to me. I should've been there for you. I should have stopped him. I should've taken your place."

"Oh, Hercules." My mom turns to face me and wraps both arms around my neck, pulling me into a hug that reminds me of every hug she gave me before she died. It doesn't matter that I'm much taller now. "That's not how it works."

"Yes, it does. I thought it didn't for a long time, but it does. I traded for Daisy."

"Daisy." Her name sounds even sweeter when my mother tests it out. "You love her."

"Yeah." My voice breaks, which I'm not proud of, but who cares? It's me and my mom in a field by the cottage. There's nobody else to hear. "I didn't think much past the part where I'd give my life for her. I didn't think that *if* I could ever die, I'd…you know. I'd keep going afterward."

"Came as a shock to me, too."

"Mom, this whole thing is so fucking weird."

"Jesus, I *know*."

I laugh into her hair, a huge belly laugh, and she laughs, too. When else was I supposed to deeply consider that Daisy's nightmares might be real and connected to a physical place? Or is this a spiritual one? What kind of wonder-of-the-universe bullshit is this?

When we've both recovered from the laughing, I spend a minute breathing. A drop of water lands on me, but when I look up, the sky is as brilliantly clear as before. A dragonfly sails past, drawing my attention back down. Now that I can see this place clearly, I can also hear it. Birds sing in the forest. I bet if we started walking in that direction, the trees would be closer than they appear.

I get a little distance so I can look at my mom. *Really* look at her.

"You finally got nice shampoo."

Another laugh. "I did."

"And the dress?" She's wearing a pale green dress with a white…overdress? It's not an apron. It's like nothing she ever wore when she was alive.

"I felt like wearing it." Mom raises her eyebrows. "It has pockets."

She sticks her hands into them and wriggles her fingers to prove it.

"What do you carry around with you?"

A smaller, more private smile lights her face. "Any guesses?"

"Not really." I can't imagine what you'd have to carry in your pocket in the afterlife. Or in the nightmare-afterlife. Or whatever this place is.

She holds out her hand. A shiny quarter glints in her palm.

I cover it with mine so I can feel it there. Trace the outline with a fingertip. Turn it over so I can see the year stamped on the opposite side.

"You kept it?"

Mom's expression turns solemn. "Oh, yes. It was the start of our savings for the cottage. Don't you?"

"I thought you would've spent it."

"I kept it in my pocket until I left you. And I keep it now. What do you keep in your pocket?"

I hadn't bothered to look down at my clothes. When I do, they're...mostly the same, but far more comfortable. Loose pants. A shirt made from the same cloth.

"Oh, for Christ's sake. I can't wear white. I'll fuck it up."

My mom touches my chest, and the pants turn to my favorite jeans. The shirt turns a dark green. I'm still barefoot, which is good, because who needs shoes in a place like this? Nobody.

"You looked nice in white, though."

"Thanks." I take out the necklace and show her. "This is what I keep in my pocket."

She studies it seriously, and I feel like a little kid, bringing her home a worksheet with a sticker on it. My mom's eyes linger on the black diamond wrapped in the silvery chain. All the minuscule leaves and petals strung through the links.

"You're holding it for her?"

"I think that's why this worked. I don't know. It's

also pretty fucking weird, but...I think she'll be safe now. I hope she will."

"I'm sure she will." No doubt in her voice, and it feels so good to trust her again. I haven't felt like this since I was small. I can't remember a feeling like this, except when I was with Daisy, and that was...that was right. I was worried about my own bullshit, but at the end of the day, it was right.

The sense that I need to hurry the fuck up flickers to life again. "Can I ask you a question?"

"Anything." Her eyes are still on the necklace. She touches the black diamond with care, like it's not a diamond and basically indestructible.

"Why didn't you tell Zeus about me? We could have been okay."

My mom's eyes snap to mine, her hand curling over the necklace. A smile starts, then falters, on her face.

"I would have thought...oh, Hercules, I would've thought it was obvious."

"*What's* obvious?" Oh my fucking God. "You did *not* sleep with him. Tell me you didn't sleep with him."

"What? No!" My mom takes a big breath and bursts out laughing. She laughs until tears sparkle on her cheeks in the soft morning sun. I cross my arms over my chest and watch, wanting to laugh with her, stuck between being embarrassed for no reason and wanting to know what's so funny about the idea that she might've slept with a man who owned an entire whorehouse. "I'm—I'm sorry, Hercules, that's not what

I meant. No. I didn't sleep with him. I didn't want—I didn't want him to think I'd taken anything."

"Like…what? His sperm when he wasn't looking?"

She covers her mouth with her hand, obviously struggling not to laugh, and takes a deep breath. It takes her two tries to let it out.

"The night you were…well, I'm fairly certain it was the night you were conceived. I was—"

I hold up a hand. "Mom. I'm begging you."

"I was *starting to fall asleep,* and there was—" She pushes her fingers through her curls and shakes them out, and it's so familiar that my heart feels like it could beat. "I don't know how to describe it. Like a bolt of lightning came through my room. A very—a very pure energy, and strong. And I always thought…" Her eyes turn thoughtful. "I always thought he had a kind of… aura about him. I thought maybe it was the force of his personality, or—who knows. It could have been anything. But that's what it felt like. It felt like he'd lost control of it, somehow. It went—" Her hand brushes over her belly. "Right there, and it didn't go away."

"Wow."

"Of course I should have told him. I could have," she admits. "He was fair to us. But when it happened, he was too…" Mom pauses, seeming to search for the right word. "Not angry. It wasn't that he was angry. He was…hurt? Grieving. He seemed like he'd lost someone important, and I was afraid that I'd taken something else. So I left, and I didn't say anything."

"You could've told *me*."

"In the beginning, I figured it didn't matter. I was never going to go back. You were never going to cross paths with him. Then I decided I'd wait until you asked about the...the more obvious evidence."

"*What* obvious evidence?"

She blinks. "Sweetheart, you have golden eyes."

"They're brown," I shoot back. "They're like yours."

"Mine aren't gold."

"Neither are Zeus's." He has brown eyes, too. They're brown. They just—they have gold in them, too. The first day I was in his house, the first private conversation we had, I remember thinking *he's got golden eyes*. I cover mine with my hands. "You should've *told* me."

"Now I have. What else do you want to know?"

"God." I drop my hands and take in the sight of my mother, beautiful, happy, whole, in a grassy field, on a lovely morning. "Everything. But there's no rush, right?'

She brushes her knuckles over my cheek, then presses her palm flat over that spot.

My mom looks...

Sad?

"I'll stay with you in the cottage, Mom. We have time."

She opens her mouth. Hesitates. "You don't want to stay here, Hercules."

"Yes, I do. This is what I've always wanted. Since you. Since Ollie. I always wanted to do this for someone, and this time I did it."

"Oh." I didn't know you could get so much emotion into one word. "I'm so proud of you. I love you so much. I've missed you so much. But this isn't what you want. And someone is here for you."

A shout echoes from the valley. Down below, alongside the clear, glittering river, a person sprints toward the hill and our field.

I would know that run, and that hair, absolutely fucking anywhere.

"Ollie!" I shout, and he's far, but I can still see when he picks his head up and beams. There's the flash of his smile, just like I remember it, and he's not dead on the ground, the life knocked out of him, he's running as fast as he can. Like he was born to run by a river. It's a graceful, loping run, like he could hop into—I don't know. A chariot. Into flight. Any second, his feet could lift off.

Jesus, I'm so happy to see him. He's okay. I'm laughing before I understand it's me.

"If you mean him, then I *have* to stay. He's my best friend."

My mom turns my face back to hers, and then keeps turning, to the other direction. "Not him, sweetheart."

Hades walks through the grass in long, easy strides. My breath stops at the sight of him.

It's jarring enough seeing him in full sunlight. In the eighteen months I lived at Zeus's house, I saw Hades out in the sun twice. Maybe three times.

Even *more* jarring is how perfectly fucking normal

it looks on him. He's tall and blond. The light catches in his hair like a halo.

But what I can't believe is that he's the same.

Daisy *wasn't*. When we were here, she wasn't hiding anything about herself, and she was a goddess. The way she looked is burned into my mind. Those black wings. Her black eyes. Her beauty. A true, terrifying beauty.

Hades looks like himself. He's always been exactly who he was. He didn't hide it from anyone.

I don't know which thing is scarier.

A dog circles his feet, bounding through the grass, stopping to sniff at flowers and brush up against him, its tail wagging and wagging and wagging.

It's a big dog, but it's not Conor. Conor's all black, his coat shiny, his frame sleek despite how fucking enormous he is. *This* dog is mostly German Shepherd, and part some other breed. It's tan and black with hints of red and it's beside itself. I've never owned a dog, but you'd have to be a fool to miss the unadulterated joy radiating off that thing.

I give Ollie the universal *give-me-a-minute* gesture. He mouths *seriously?* but he's still smiling. His run slows to a jog, and I take a step toward him. Can't stop myself. My mom puts her hand on my back like she's going to stop me.

"I'm fine," I tell her. "I'm okay."

"You *are*," she agrees. "Everything will be okay. Don't run."

"I wasn't going to."

I wasn't. Running in the presence of Hades would not be widely considered a great decision.

There's that feeling again. *Hurry the fuck up.*

But why? I thought I had forever.

I was at peace with it. Now I don't know what I am. What *he* is, or why he's here. Every step Hades takes injects more confusion into my blood.

Do I even have a bloodstream anymore?

It feels like it, a little bit.

My mom said *not* to run, but…should I?

No. This is a field. It'd be pointless.

Hades stops a couple of steps away, the breeze ruffling his hair, and leans down to scratch the dog behind its ears. He strokes her head. "Stay," he murmurs. "Here."

The dog's tail wags even harder. She's too overjoyed to sit, but she pads around in the grass next to Hades's feet while he straightens up and slips his hands into his pockets.

There's something super fucking weird about his face. Maybe it's the relaxed expression, like he's visiting one of his vacation homes. The man is always a little tense, no matter what, but not right now.

He smiles at my mom like they've met before. "Alcmene."

She smiles back at him. "Hades."

"You *know* him?" What the fuck? How much has she been hiding from me? "Are you serious?"

"I know *of* him." My mom gives me a scolding look.

She'd have given me a lot more of these growing up if she'd lived. "He's known here."

"You've *been* here?" I'm starting to sound like an indignant prick, and maybe I am. I keep my arm around my mom's shoulders and narrow my eyes at Hades. "Don't you think it would've been helpful to mention that? At *all*? Even once?"

He looks out over the field, down at the daisies, and drops his hand to pet the dog. "I didn't remember."

"How could you *forget* this?"

Hades is unhurried, like we really do have all the time in the world.

"If I had to guess…" The dog pushes its nose into his palm, and he strokes her head again. "I might've come when I had particularly bad seizures. Of course, I have no memory of what happens while they're in progress."

"What the fuck," I whisper.

My mom pats my arm. "You have a beautiful dog," she tells him.

He looks down at the dog, his eyes shining. "For a little while."

"What's her name?" Mom asks.

"Rosie," he answers. At the sound of her name, the dog jumps up, her front paws on his thigh, and he uses both hands to ruffle her ears. "She's a good dog."

"I'd keep her for you," my mother offers, and I stare, because she's never had a dog in her life. She's never even talked about wanting one.

"Wait," I blurt out. Is she serious? My mom looks

up into my eyes with an expectant smile. "What do you mean, keep his dog? He's *here*."

"I'd like that." Hades ignores me and smiles at her again, and I finally figure out what's so wrong about his face.

His eyes are blue.

They're blue, not black, and I'd bet my life that nothing hurts him here, either. That thing he said about the seizures finally sinks in. If he was here before, how did he ever leave? How would he *choose* pain and suffering over this?

Hades glances at me like he can hear my thoughts. Because he hoped.

He hoped that things would be better one day. He didn't want to leave his family. He doesn't now.

"I can't stay." Hades gets down on one knee, puts his arms around the dog, and holds her. She pushes her nose into him. Ten or twenty dog kisses later, he releases her and stands. When he looks at me again, he's much more serious. "Hercules."

"I'm okay here. It's not a big deal. You can tell Zeus I'm fine, if he's worried."

"Daisy's waiting for you."

"She is?"

A solemn nod. "She was very upset when she realized what you'd done."

I wince without meaning to, because the first thing that flashes into my mind is winged, terrifying, endlessly powerful Daisy. "Is she pissed?"

The corner of Hades's mouth quirks. "She says she does not accept this, and I doubt I'd survive telling her the news that I couldn't convince you to come back."

Hope beats in my chest. Or is it my heart? I don't know. "I didn't think that would be an option. It seemed like a permanent trade."

"Listen." Hades looks rich and graceful and at ease. I can't imagine wanting to go back to the pain of his real life, ever, but he seems pretty sure about it. "I have no fucking idea how this works. My daughter asked me to get you back, so I'm going to."

"But—"

My mom clasps her arms around my neck and hugs me tight. "Don't keep her waiting."

"But I love you."

"I love you, too. Come see me later. *Much* later."

"But what will you—"

"I have a dog now," she says, like that's a serious answer.

I do *not* want to let go of her, but I force myself to look at Hades. "How does it work? Because I don't think I'm allowed to walk through that door."

"I didn't come through a door. Or the gates."

"How the fuck—"

He tips his head back, mild irritation showing through for the first time. "Again, I don't know how it worked. I'm fairly certain I can follow the path back out."

"What path?"

Hades tips his head forward, blue eyes narrow and skeptical. "Are you kidding?"

"No."

He gestures behind him, and the path is obvious.

In the field of daisies, blood-red poppies have sprung up everywhere he's walked. I just didn't see them until he showed me.

"Okay. We just walk back?"

Hades shakes his head. "I don't think we have to walk."

"Then—"

He holds out his hand like we're going to shake.

I ignore it and squeeze my mom tight. "I'm going to miss you."

"I know."

"I'm glad you're okay. But you don't have to have a dog if you don't want one. That's fucking weird."

"She's a sweet dog."

"You don't *know* that." Rosie licks my hand. Fine. Maybe she'll be okay company.

"I love you." My mom kisses my cheek. "Go and be happy."

"I love you too."

She lets go and pats impatiently at my shoulder. "Get going. I'm so excited!"

I put Daisy's necklace into her hand. "Keep this for me? I think you have a free pocket."

"Of course I will. Now go. *Go.*"

I don't know why we have to rush this part, but I

know we do. The tone of the pressure against my chest has changed. We have to get going, like she said.

I take one more look at this place where my mom lives—where she *lives,* she's okay—and turn to face Hades.

My hand is an inch from his when someone tackles me viciously from behind.

It fully takes me out, down to the ground, and Ollie lands on top of me, grinning like a fool.

"You *bastard,*" he shouts into my face. "You were going to leave without saying anything? I fucking *shouted* at you. You said *wait a minut*e. And then you were going to bounce?"

"I forgot, okay? Jesus. There's a lot going on." My face hurts from smiling so much. "Are you okay?"

He rolls his eyes. "*Yes.* For fuck's sake. It's great here. Thank God it wasn't you, Herc, you'd never have been able to appreciate it."

"Oh, and you can?"

"You have *no* idea how many people I've met. And how many of them are down to f—"

"My mom is *right* here." He grins even wider, and I take him by the shirt collar. "Say you're joking, Ollie, or I swear to fucking God I'll find a way to k—"

"A joke!" He laughs, and I'll never forget it. I'll get to remember it here, without any guns going off in the background, without worrying that I'll get him killed, nothing. "I was joking! Fuck. You're so serious. Have a little fun, would you?"

"Hercules," Hades says.

Ollie jumps up and pulls me to my feet. He reaches out and fist-bumps Hades, which is the most bizarre thing I've ever seen in my life. "Hey, man."

"Iolaus," Hades answers.

Ollie makes a gagging noise. "Nobody calls me that. It's Ollie."

Hades rolls his eyes. "Okay."

Ollie laughs like they've done this before, which… is impossible.

Or maybe it's not.

No idea.

Ollie slaps my chest, then throws his arm around my shoulders. "Get the hell out of here, Hercules."

Not much time left. "I'm sorry."

"Don't be. I'll take care of your Mom, like I've been doing."

"Ollie—" I warn.

With his free hand, he shoves my elbow forward. My hand knocks into Hades's, and he catches it. There's pressure like you wouldn't believe, a sensation like poppies pushing through the ground.

"Take care of yourself." Ollie's voice is so clear. Totally unchanged. The field is fading, getting smaller and darker with every second, and I have the most powerful urge to grab for it, to keep some of it, to keep *something*. But this place can't be kept, already losing form along with color, more of a suggestion now than a vision. "Take care of Daisy. Don't come back."

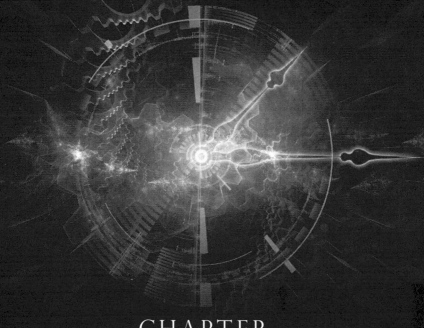

# CHAPTER
# NINETEEN

*Daisy*

THE GASP IS SO LOUD THAT I DON'T KNOW WHO
it's coming from.

It's both of them.

It's Hercules *and* my dad.

Hercules blinks, eyelashes fluttering, and I throw myself at him like I've lost it, which I have. He grunts when my full weight comes down on his abs and looks up at me, disbelieving, tears in his eyes.

"Daisy."

The shriek that comes out of me isn't dignified and it probably isn't appropriate and it's *way* too loud and I don't care. I don't care if anybody else is in here. I bury my hands in his hair and kiss him.

He doesn't taste dead. Not that—not that I've kissed anyone who's dead, but he's warm, he's *warm*, he's not cold and he's not still and he kisses me back with an amount of force that's definitely not appropriate for a crowded room.

His hands come to my face, and then he pushes me back a few inches to look at me. Stare, like he's not sure what I'm supposed to look like.

I slap his chest. "What were you *thinking*?"

Hercules's mouth drops open. His eyes get huge, like this is the most foolish thing anyone's ever said to him in his entire life. "I was *saving you*. You're not serious. I was thinking that I *love* you, and so I was saving you."

"I love *you*," I shout at him.

"I can hear you," he shouts back.

"Good, because I thought you were *dead*."

Then I burst into tears and collapse on top of him, his ribs intact, strong enough to hold me.

"Baby." His voice turns on a dime, and it's soft and warm and sunny. Hercules runs a hand over my hair, his other hand on my back. "Don't cry."

I push my face into his shirt. I'm going to pretend I didn't make a high, embarrassed noise.

"It's okay," he says, and kisses the top of my head. "I'm fine, baby. Don't cry, please."

"*You're* crying."

"No, I'm not."

"What is *happening* in here?" The voice sounds *so* much like my mom that for a second I don't know what's going on. My mom has been here. She knows what's happening. But then the shifting air carries over a light, almond-y scent. I whip around and *there she is.*

"Demmy!"

"Daisy!" My grandmother matches my tone, her forehead creased, hands on her hips. Her outfit is various shades of green, all flowing and artsy, and honestly, she could be my mom's sister. "Why are so many of you weeping openly? What could have happened this early in the morning? No one's dead."

Zeus is definitely weeping, and—so is my dad. Silently. He's also holding his breath, which can't be good for him, but he doesn't turn around. He doesn't move at all. He sits with his hand on his chest, his brothers' hands on his shoulders, my mom's hands on his face. Brigit and Ashley are arrayed behind them, each one with a hand on their respective husband.

Okay, so—a *lot* happened, and I've been too busy kissing Hercules to ask for details.

"Demeter." A softer voice. Much gentler. Eleanor, who is also like my grandmother, moves into the bedroom. "Shouldn't we ask questions once we send someone to help your husband?"

My dad gasps again. "*Mom.*"

He shakes off his brothers and turns, shoving his legs off the side of the bed and reaching for Eleanor.

She goes to him without hesitation. His arms go around her waist, and one of hers circles his shoulders, and she pats at his hair. I've never, ever seen his shoulders shake this hard.

I've never heard him call her *mom*.

"Sweet boy." Eleanor doesn't look surprised at all, and I wonder if he's called her that in private before, or if she knew how he felt about her. "Is it a headache?"

"No." Oh, God, he's *miserable*. "No."

"Tell me what happened."

Demeter glances around the room. "Daisy, why are you straddling that young man?"

I move to the side. "It's Hercules, Demmy. He's my boyfriend, and he tried to kill himself for me."

Demeter shoots a look at my mother as if to say, *are you aware of this Romeo character? If you're not, Persephone, you should be.* My mom just laughs.

Hercules sighs. "That's not what I did. Her nightmares were going to take her into the underworld forever, so I stayed instead."

"Young *man*," scolds Demeter. "What the hell would possess you? What a foolish idea."

"It was brave. And it was hard. And then Dad had to go in after him." This story makes almost no sense. I'm not sure how it was possible. I had to sit here, waiting, while some of the most important people in my life were dead. Or in the underworld. Or in a nightmare. I don't know. "Also, I love him."

"We all do foolish things for love," Demeter

allows. "Daisy, I thought you were in crisis. Have you recovered?"

"Oh, yeah. I thought I was going to die. But that wasn't the worst part." Hercules smiles at me from the pillow. He's blinked most of the tears from his eyes, but he looks tired. His cheeks are flushed like he wants to cry. "The worst part was when I thought I might live."

Demeter lets out a sigh. "There isn't a single member of this family who can explain things in a coherent manner."

"Hey," Zeus interrupts. "I've explained plenty."

"You're *weeping*," Demeter says. "You're in no state to tell me what I've walked into."

"Demeter." He sounds exasperated but fond, and he's still crying. "Tears don't prevent people from explaining things."

"Hold the fuck on." Poseidon has cried the least, I think, but he drags the sleeve of his shirt over his eyes anyway. "What's this about your husband?"

"He is a grown man." Demeter comes over to the bed, leans over to kiss my forehead, and puts her hand on my cheek. She studies my eyes while she does it, a frown tugging at the corner of her mouth. This goes on for several beats, and then she narrows her eyes at Hercules. "What did you say you did, young man?"

"Demeter," he says. "We've met before."

She makes a *hurry-up* gesture at him.

"I told you. I went into her nightmare. Daisy and I

went through the gates to get Conor and her kitten, and then I pushed her back out so I could stay in her place."

Demeter mumbles a sentence that sounds like *I will never understand men.*

"And what did you do there?"

"Stood around. Talked to my mom. Saw—"

"Did you have something of Daisy's?"

"Her necklace."

"*What* necklace?" I'm interrupting, but even as I'm asking, the details start to bubble up disconnected and dream-like, as though I'd been looking at things from high up. "Oh! I don't have that necklace *here*, but..."

"You did when you were on the other side of the gates. It was a black diamond with a silver chain, and the chain had leaves all over it."

"Did you keep it?" Demeter demands.

"Did I keep a dream-necklace? No. How would I have done that?"

"In the other place. Through the gates."

"I gave it to my mother for safekeeping."

Demeter breaks into a wide, pleased grin and reaches out to tousle Hercules's hair. "Good for *you*. You should be proud of yourself."

"Why?"

"It's complicated, sweetheart." She pats his cheek like he might not understand even if she told him everything. "Put it out of your mind."

"Um. I don't think—"

Demeter straightens. "The regular painkillers will

continue to work. I'll stay for a few days to make sure none of you are…" Her eyes travel over the room again. "Off the deep end."

Poseidon snorts.

"In the meantime." Demeter smooths her top. "We should go downstairs."

Zeus puts his arms around Brigit, who hugs him back. "Why?"

"There's a young man down there who tried to light your house on fire."

"Demeter." Poseidon gapes at her. "What the fuck?"

"He was unsuccessful, obviously. Gio's with him downstairs."

"Your husband brought him *inside*?"

"Yes? Where else would he have brought him? The mountain? Come on." She gestures to the door.

No one moves.

Demeter lets out an even louder sigh. "I didn't want to have to say it, but this is embarrassing for Hades. You don't have to stand around like emotional voyeurs."

"I'm not embarrassed," my dad mumbles into Eleanor's shirt. She smiles, her hand still moving through his hair.

"You should be," answers Demeter.

She comes to the side of the bed and helps us off. My mom comes to my other side, but it's Hercules who has wobbly knees now. Light from the bedroom windows is starting to filter into the hall.

Hercules and I are the last ones out, my mom waiting for us.

I'm at the door when my dad takes a deep breath.

"I saw Rosie." He's almost too quiet to hear, and breaks into rough, audible sobs.

"Oh, Hades," Eleanor says, and I reach back and pull the door shut behind me, my chest aching for him. He *would* be embarrassed about crying in a way that other people could hear, which he's never done, not once in my life.

Poseidon clatters down the stairs behind Demeter. "When you say *light Hades's house on fire—*"

"The young man was going to shoot a flaming arrow at the house."

"*What?*" shrieks Artemis from the bottom of the stairs. She's in pajamas, constant Apollo at her side, the rest of my cousins gathered in a clutch of bedhead and bewildered looks. "Can I shoot him with an arrow, then? Hi, Demmy."

Demeter dispenses gracious kisses to all the cousins. "Do you have your bow?"

"They took it away last time I shot someone with it, but they didn't hide it very well."

"Demeter, for Christ's sake," Zeus says. "No one is murdering the—young man? Are we talking about a teenager?"

"No, he is simply a fool." Demeter finishes ruffling Pollux's hair and goes through the living room, the rest of us following. "Gio?" she calls. "Where did you go?"

"In here," he calls back. There's a small library off the living room, and Demeter's husband is standing in it. His light hair looks shiny and gorgeous in the glow from a lamp on the corner table. It's having to compete with the sunrise.

A sallow-skinned man sits at his feet, his hands tied behind his back and a bruise darkening under his eye. He glowers at us as we get closer, his lip curling to reveal the telltale lines of a heavy smoker around it.

"No *fucking* way." Hercules doesn't seem tired anymore. He doesn't feel tired. I wrap my hand above his elbow, because I'm almost certain he's going to kill this man. "You piece of shit."

"Shut the fuck up," spits the man. "I have nothing to discuss with you."

Hercules laughs. "Wasn't enough for you last time? Kick him over here, Gio, and I'll give him what this asshole is so desperate for."

I tug at Hercules's arm. "What are you talking about?"

He pulls away from me too fast to stop him. Hercules is at Gio in a few long steps, and he digs his hand into the man's dark hair and pulls his head up so I can see his face in the lamplight.

"You've met before," Hercules says. "Remember?"

One blink, and I see their faces as they were the night of the charity gala. Hercules's hair was much shorter, but his eyes are still the same. The bloodlust there sends a shiver down my spine.

The man, whose name is Kenneth Coleman, hasn't aged well.

Dark smudges underneath his eyes make them look wilder. There's a pallor about him, a strange color to his cheeks. The man looks *haunted*.

Not by me. He's the one who pushed me into that alcove and put his mouth on mine when I didn't want him to touch me. He's the one who called me a bitch after I bit him, trying to get him to stop.

I take a few steps closer.

"Kenneth." He pulls against whatever Gio used to tie his wrists. "You…don't look great."

"That's what you wanted, isn't it? You should be thrilled."

"What?"

"You killed my parents. You killed my *sister*."

A general murmur rises from my family. Artemis's voice is loudest. "Okay, *now* I'm putting an arrow through his eye."

"*Artemis*," warns Apollo.

"Daisy's never murdered anyone," she says, even louder, each word sparkling and clear. "What the hell are you talking about?"

"I'd *love* to know," Demmy says from off to my left.

"My sister *saw you kill me*." Kenneth grits his teeth. "You sent a curse to her in a dream."

"No, I didn't."

"Yes you *did*, witch."

I run my hands over my face. "Are we really doing this?"

"You're a fucking demon. You're a witch. She knew what you were and so you sent visions into her brain that drove her out of her mind."

"How would I have *done* that?" One slip, just one, years and years ago and suddenly I'm the cause of every bad dream and intrusive thought she ever had. I'm exhausted again. This is exhausting. "And, like, what is the criteria for being a witch? Is it anyone your sister dreams about?"

"She dreamed about you killing my parents, and then me, and laughing with your creepy, black witch eyes, and she spent *years* begging me to do something about it before it was too late. And I *didn't* destroy you first. So now my entire family is dead. Because of *you*."

"Yikes," Poseidon says softly.

There's a light calm in the room, but it doesn't feel steady, as if the person making it happen actually wants to kill Kenneth, too.

"She dreamed of me killing you?" I say, as if somehow I've already forgotten about this.

"Yes."

"But…" I lift both hands in front of me. "I haven't."

"No, you just made sure I had to live when everyone I loved was dead, but—"

"I said I *haven't*. As in, I haven't *yet*."

Kenneth's eyes widen slowly as the adrenaline of confronting me fades into awareness that I *am* the threat. How is the man so far behind the curve? He's in my father's house. Gio tied his hands. He's badly outnumbered.

I could kill him, if I wanted, and everyone in this room would help me dispose of the body.

Hercules lets go of Kenneth's hair and steps away. He stands next to Demeter and crosses his arms over his chest.

I take that as my cue to move forward, into the library. Kenneth scrambles, pushing himself harder into Gio's legs.

Demmy's husband frowns down at him. "Where do you think you're going?"

"Away from *her*," Kenneth yells. "Don't touch me."

I get closer and closer until he pulls his knees up to his chest, breath shallow. Then I crouch down until our faces are level and look him in the eyes.

He's afraid.

He thinks my eyes are creepy, too. I get it. A lot of people do, and those people aren't tied up in my parents' library. He's in too deep, at the end of the line. And he's alone.

"I've always felt bad that I accidentally scared your sister," I tell him. "Whatever curse she talked about was something that already lived in her. Nothing I put there. If a scary part of me woke it up, I certainly didn't mean to. I've spent a lot of time and effort trying *not* to scare people, believe it or not."

"I don't."

"It's not a requirement." I keep studying him. The easily breakable bones. All the soft parts of him, inside and out, that form a map I didn't know I could read until now. Sorrow. Pain. Fear, above all, a yawning chasm of it inside him. "I'm sorry to hear she died. You must feel awful."

"Just like you wanted, demon bitch," he says through gritted teeth. I'd almost admire his bravery if he wasn't trying to murder us. "I know you. You made sure I'd be the last one, so I'd suffer longer."

"So it might be…" I reach toward him, my hand a good five inches away, and he flinches. "A relief if I killed you?"

He shakes his head.

I make a sympathetic noise. "You're scared to die. I get it. But that's not your worst nightmare, is it?"

Kenneth pinches his lips together. The confirmation traces little zings of electricity through my veins.

"If I know anything about *you*, your worst nightmare is being rejected. Being worthless. Being forgotten." I lean a little closer. "That could happen tonight. You could disappear, forever, and nobody would look, because there's nobody left to—*oh*. It changed, didn't it?"

He's the color of chalk.

"You don't know what's worse. Dying here at my hands or walking free and spending the rest of your life looking over your shoulder."

"Fuck you. Get it over with."

"I have better things to do."

His voice drops again. "Bitch. I should have finished what I started at the gala."

I get to my feet and turn away. He's had plenty of chances to get back at me, and he's terrible at it.

Let him keep trying.

He can live in his nightmare, if he wants.

Every time he opens his vile mouth, he creates it for himself.

My mom brushes by me on my way to Hercules, her palm warm on my arm for a moment. Then I'm in his arms. He's here. He's *here*.

"Oh, shit," says Poseidon.

"Kenneth." My mom gets down on the floor next to him, her curse everywhere. He doesn't know what to think about her. Everyone always underestimates her, because she's beautiful, and she looks so sweet. He stays perfectly still while she reaches up and takes his chin in her hand. Then she leans in and whispers into his ear.

Hercules tenses right before she laughs.

Jesus. I feel that all the way down to my cells. It's the darkest laugh I've ever heard. It's like a nightmare.

Kenneth screams.

He keeps screaming while Gio hauls him to his feet and unties his wrists. He's begging by the time Poseidon shoves him out the door, and still babbling when Zeus drags him to the end of the driveway and tosses him out of the gates. My uncle waves down the security agents in a clear *let him go.*

Zeus watches him leave, then slips his hands into his pockets and starts back down the drive.

Castor and Pollux dart forward and open the door. "Uncle Zeus!" Castor shouts.

Zeus picks up his head and waves.

"You okay?" Castor's still shouting.

"Yes," Zeus calls back.

"If you're done crying, can you make breakfast?"

Zeus rolls his eyes. "We have a cook, Castor. He lives in my house."

"He lives in a separate house," Pollux says. "It's technically a detached—"

"We didn't want to wake him up," Castor yells over his brother. "Would've been a dick move."

Zeus stops and takes his phone out of his pocket. "He just texted me. He says to tell my nephews to shut up, or he's making a noise complaint."

"You own half this neighborhood," Castor shouts. "What is he going to—"

At that moment Ares arrives to put his hand over Castor's mouth and drag him away from the door.

"Baby." Hercules's voice, low in my ear.

"Yeah?"

"Come upstairs with me."

# CHAPTER TWENTY

*Hercules*

I ASKED DAISY TO COME UPSTAIRS BECAUSE SHE'S tired.

All the way upstairs, her hand in mine, I'm not sure how it'll play to tell her she looks exhausted. I'm actually worried she'll fall asleep into her breakfast if she insists on sitting at the table. Or in the living room. Wherever they're going to eat once Cook comes over.

We reach the landing, and Daisy's shoulders sag. She lets go of my hand and pads into her bedroom. At the end of the hall, the door to the main bedroom is open. Hades sits in a chair in his sleep pants and black T-shirt, one hand over his face. Conor rests his head on his knee, and Eleanor crouches on the floor in front of him, his other hand in both of hers.

Daisy wanders around her room, changing out of the pajamas she was wearing and into a tank top and different pants. She comes to get me like I'm the last piece of her outfit. Like I belong directly against her skin.

We get into the bed.

She curls close, pressed so tight to my side that she's basically on top of me, and gets heavy, like she's fallen asleep.

Then she pops up, one hand on my chest. "I love you."

Her hair is a blonde cloud, and her eyes are so dark, and her cheeks are so pink. "I know. Go to sleep."

Daisy pouts.

"I love you, too."

She drops her head so fast I put my hand underneath to catch it, then maneuver her into a position that won't hurt her neck.

Then there's nothing else to do.

It's like lying on that soft, soft grass.

Not *totally* like it. My shoulder hurts a little bit. It usually does when I'm alive.

Everything else feels fucking great.

I didn't know how heavy it was to carry around all that guilt about my mom and Ollie. I'm not a weak-ass prick to begin with, so it would've had to be very fucking heavy to be noticeable, but now that it's gone, I can't believe how much it weighed.

That *asshole*. Making jokes about fucking my mom.

I'm smiling at nothing for several minutes before it hits me that I haven't thought of Ollie and *smiled* since he died.

He must've known that.

*Don't come back.*

It was a real choice to say that to me, his best fucking friend. Seriously.

*Thank God it wasn't you, Herc, you'd never have been able to appreciate it.*

Thank God, he said, but I don't get the sense that he thought it was random, or lucky, that he died instead of me.

He couldn't have chosen that.

Could he?

I have a faint, vague memory of the rest of that flight. Getting to the hangar. Gearing up. Ollie's hand around a harness that he gave to me. Buckling it while he buckled his.

Did he know, even then?

He's not here to ask, but he made a point of getting to me. He wanted me to know that he's fine. That he's apparently fucking his way through heaven. Or... the underworld. Or an eternal dream. That's how he's spending his time.

And my mom is living in the cottage she always wanted, and now—if everything that happened is real and not some hallucination I had—she has a *pet*.

They're okay.

*I'm* okay.

Daisy's okay. Demeter seems convinced of that, and if the poisoner doesn't want to give her a new prescription, then I'm the last person on earth who's going to argue with her. As though I could. She reminds me of Daisy in a lot of ways, which makes sense, given that Demeter's her grandmother.

What an incredible fucking play. Everybody thinks the women of this family are pretty and delicate and breakable, and they do nothing to dispel the illusion.

I guess Persephone scared the shit out of Kenneth this morning. Her laugh scared the shit out of me. If I had to guess, I'd have said that laugh came from Hades.

Good thing I never had to guess.

Quiet voices move down the hallway. "—to eat, Hades. It's been a long night."

"I'm not—" A hitch, like he's still crying. "Hungry."

"You will be when the food is ready."

"Then I shouldn't have to go down until the food is ready."

"You don't have to go down, but I think it would be good for you."

"Good for me to cry in front of other people? You're not serious."

"I'll tell them all not to look at you."

Hades snorts. "You just want me to sit next to you."

"I always want you to sit next to me."

Their voices fade, and I'm...

Happy for him. Eleanor was Zeus and his siblings'

nanny growing up, and I've never heard any of them call her anything but *Eleanor*. Out of everything, hearing Hades call someone *mom* has probably been the biggest shock of the day.

I wait to be angry, to be jealous, but I'm not.

I lie there with Daisy, picturing the grass and the flowers and the sky, drifting.

I couldn't fall asleep for real if I tried. I want to feel her chest move. I want to keep my hand over her shoulder blades and keep track.

It's not standing guard. Not anymore. I have a deep certainty about that.

Maybe I shouldn't. Other things could always come up. No life is as peaceful as that field.

But today, nothing's coming for her.

Even if it did, I'd die instead.

Ha, ha. No. Fuck that. I'm not dying any time soon. Not if she's here with me.

I wish I could've seen the inside of my mom's cottage, but I bet I can guess what it looks like. She always wanted white sheets and gingham curtains and a braided rug. A low bookshelf. A lamp with a lampshade.

She wanted to be able to afford nice shampoo.

I'm not jealous of her, either.

I've been jealous of her before. Angry at her, too. There were lots of nights on the street when I raged at her. Dying would've been easier, I thought. It wouldn't have been so cold, or so tense. It wouldn't have hurt so much.

I didn't have anything to leave behind back then.

I was the only one.

That gives me a hint of pity for Kenneth. The foolish prick looked like complete shit. I can't help but understand that. I know what it's like to be the only one, too.

I *don't* know what it's like to be so devoid of humanity that I'd push a teenage girl into a dark alcove and kiss her until she fought me off.

Forget pity. He'll run around screaming his head off about whatever Persephone said until he gets arrested. Whatever the cops do is up to them.

The bedroom door opens and Zeus comes in, closing it quietly behind him. He carries a plate in his hand and a bottle of orange juice. His eyes are *all* red. Guy's a wreck.

"Hey."

He waves the bottle as if I could've missed the bright orange and puts it on the side table closest to me. "Cook sent bacon."

Zeus sits down on the edge of the bed and balances the plate between us.

"Is it a revenge thing? Is he pissed that your kids woke him up?"

He picks a slice and bites into it, the bacon crunching between his teeth. "I don't know. You'd have to ask Poseidon."

"...why?"

"Because Cook came with him, from his ship. He only lives at my house because it's central."

"Jesus. You didn't tell me anything, did you?"

Zeus eats another piece of bacon without looking at me. "I've always said I'll tell you whatever you want to know."

"Even if I was a prick about not wanting to know it before?"

"Yes."

I eat some bacon. It's hard to live in a guy's house without picking up some things, but there's a lot I don't know about Zeus. Even more that I don't know about his brothers. And I guess, if I'm going to be alive, it's going to be in this family. The way they move around each other was formed a long time ago. It'd probably be easier to be a part of it if I wasn't a willfully ignorant bastard.

Even this room is something new to learn, now that our darkest hour has blossomed into dawn and I can let my guard down long enough to check out the perimeter. Another one of Daisy's old, family-safe paintings hangs on the wall across from the bed. An abstract, I think.

Zeus follows my gaze and tilts his head. "Is it poppies?"

I squint at the canvas, ignoring the way he takes advantage of my focus to secure extra pieces of bacon. "I don't see it." We're quiet for a moment, until I'm ready to know. "What shook you up so bad this morning? You're a mess."

He glares at me. "Crying does not make a person a mess."

It takes me too long to realize it's a joke, but once I do, it's fucking hilarious. I nearly suffocate myself trying not to wake Daisy up by shaking with laughter.

Zeus shakes his head, smile fading, and leans back on the headboard. "I was pretty fucked when Hades screamed."

"It seemed bad, but…not out of the ordinary, right? Nightmares had to be common."

He lets out another breath and blinks, then blinks again. "It was extremely out of the ordinary."

"Guys scream, you know. It happens."

"Not Hades."

"No."

We sit in silence for a minute.

"Are you going to tell me why?"

He thinks about it. "You know he can't be in the light, and the painkillers, all that. Daisy's the same way."

"Yeah."

This bacon is really good.

"We didn't grow up in a good situation."

"Ares said something about a farmhouse. And you had a nanny." I'm not arguing with him. The bits and pieces I've overheard or ignored don't come to mind, so this is all I'm working with right now.

""I've mentioned Cronos to you before."

"Your foster father."

"He hated us."

"But you're so charming."

Zeus laughs, the sound hollow. "He was the one

who originally owned the whorehouse. I learned to run it from him. He liked for me to keep things calm so the clients would spend more money. Poseidon mainly fought with him. Cronos had some ideas about getting into shipping, but…" Zeus waves a hand. "It never happened. Poseidon was too stubborn."

I don't like where this is leading.

"Hades was supposed to take my spot."

"What does that mean?"

"He was the one Cronos wanted at the whorehouse, for whatever reason. It didn't work out that way."

"Because?"

"Because he figured out that if he took Hades into the sun, he'd have a seizure. And all that—" Zeus puts a hand to his chest, like he can feel the unforgiving pressure. "Would go into the ground and become diamonds."

"You're fucking with me."

"Not even a little."

"Is that why…" I think of everything I've heard about the mountain where Hades used to live. How luxurious a prison it was. "Is that why he went to the mountain?"

"It didn't come with diamond mines when he bought it, if that's what you're asking."

"Christ."

"Yeah. I thought he'd die before Demeter grew those poppies. I asked every doctor I thought I could trust at the whorehouse for ways to slow it down, or stop it, but the damage was done by the time I had any real sway there."

"How long…" I don't know which question to ask, or which answer I'm looking for. "His whole life?"

"I'm not sure how early Cronos knew. And when Hades was small, so were the diamonds."

"Meaning…"

"They were worth less money. Cronos needed more of them to make it worth it."

I could throw up. Being on the street and getting beat to shit wasn't pleasant, but I wasn't small. Not that thirteen is anything close to an adult.

Still. *Still.* I've always been strong.

"Anyway." Zeus sounds like he'd rather move on to another topic. "He was used to it when we were very young. The last time he screamed was the year we turned seven. Never again after that. So when I heard it, I thought…"

He doesn't say, in the end.

I take the opportunity. "How long ago was that?"

Zeus looks me in the eye.

I look back at him, keeping my face as innocent as possible.

"Fifty years," he says slowly. "Give or take."

"You *cannot* be more than forty. I don't even think you look *that* old."

He shrugs, and hope creeps in so slowly I don't recognize it at first.

"So you…" I don't dare say it out loud. "And Daisy?"

"My theory is that Cronos kept time," Zeus says, like he's discussing an HBO limited series. "And we killed him. So."

They—fuck. Eliminating the enemy is second nature to a soldier, but they weren't soldiers. They were a bunch of messed-up kids who grew up trying to survive the bad hand they were dealt in a man who kept time and loved cruelty.

"So if you keep Hades alive—"

"If you keep *her* alive, I would guess she'd live for…" He lets out a short laugh. "A very long time."

Okay.

*Okay.*

"I should have said more to you when you came here."

Takes me a second to stop thinking about how I've never been able to die and catch up. "Why?"

"You thought I was trying to make up for what I'd done at the whorehouse, and you were right, but I was also trying to make up for something else."

"What?"

"Cronos liked to kill the women." His tone goes flat, like it's too hard to talk about when he's at a party. "He didn't want me to walk around with bruises, so he used them against me. If he caught me helping Hades or Poseidon or Demeter, he'd torture the women in front of me. Ares was pissed when I told him about that. He thought I should've died instead, and I agreed with him. I should have."

Hearing it from Zeus is another shock. He's so *wrong*. "You couldn't do that."

"I know. I knew, on some level, that killing me wouldn't stop him from killing any more women, but it would mean my siblings had no chance. Poseidon would disappear. Hades would die."

"And your sister?"

"I can't—" A shivery shake of his head. "That'll have to wait for another day."

"Okay."

"What I mean is that I understand the impulse to lay down your life for the people you love. And I understand how hard it is *not* to do it, too. So…thank you. For doing both for Daisy."

Dying for her was as easy as breathing. "It was nothing."

"Hercules, it was everything. I don't think Hades is going to stop crying any time soon."

"It's weird," I whisper. "I didn't think he could cry."

"I thought the same for a long time, and guess what? He can."

"Damn right."

"I'm more surprised by what I can't do."

"Yeah?" I feel okay enough to eat bacon again, which is a relief. "What's that?"

"I always thought the hardest thing was staying alive for them, but it's not. I could stand that. Even if it was fucking terrible. I couldn't stand losing them. That would kill me. I never would have survived losing my brother and my niece." Zeus looks me in the eye. "I owe you."

"Well…maybe not."

"Hercules, you're worth—"

"I saw my mom when I was there."

"You—you mentioned that."

"She's super fucking happy. She has a cottage and now, I guess, Hades's dead dog. I saw Ollie, too, but mostly I got to talk to my mom."

"How did that go?" Zeus is cautious about this. I've shut him out for a long time, and I can feel how much he wants to know the answer, and how willing he is to live without knowing.

"It was great. I asked her about you."

"Oh, God."

"She didn't say anything bad."

"What *did* she say? If you don't mind my asking."

"I asked her why she didn't tell you about me, since that was—" I wave a piece of bacon in a circle in his direction. "—your whole thing. And she said she might've stolen from you."

His eyes go wide. He's got golden eyes. "What could she possibly have stolen?"

"It wasn't sperm. Calm down."

Zeus rolls his eyes and lets his head *thunk* on the headboard.

"She said the night I was conceived—which I'd rather not think about, so move the fuck on from that— she felt you freak out."

He opens one eye. "Freak out?"

"Lightning in her room, or something like that. It went into her body somehow—not like sperm, Zeus, Jesus Christ."

He wipes the expression of horror off his face. "That's not what I was going to say."

"She *said*." I eat the rest of the piece of bacon. "That it stayed with her, and she didn't want you to think she'd stolen any of your…energy. Then, later, I was born."

"And she realized she was wrong?"

"And I had your weird-ass golden eyes, so then she *really* didn't want to tell you about me."

"Oh." Zeus nods. I don't know what he's doing with his head like that, or with his face. Is he *happy* about this? "Understandable."

"Obviously…" Obviously *I'm* the one who's going to have to bring this home. "She *did* take something from you. So we could probably call it even."

"No, that's—no. I *owe* you." Worry flickers across his eyes. "It was no simple thing you did."

"Okay." My heart jumps, beating faster with sudden, inexplicable nerves. I'm not nervous about this. Why would I be? Everything turned out fine. "Then I know what I want."

"Name it." Jesus, his face is so open. He thinks I'm going to ask for money. A house. A car.

"Would you mind if I called you Dad?"

Zeus is completely still for one, two, three heartbeats, and then his face crumples. "Oh, shit."

"Look—you can keep crying all day if you want, but can you tell me if—"

"Of course you can. You didn't have to ask, Hercules, but yes. You can. Fuck." Zeus leans over, crushing a piece of bacon in the process, and gives me a hug. It doesn't feel awkward at all. "I have to go. Come downstairs if you want. Breakfast is in twenty." He's already off the bed and across the room. Zeus opens the door and pauses with his hand on the frame. "I love you, Son. Bye."

"Bye, you fucking weirdo."

"Mom!" Poseidon yells downstairs, and Daisy startles against me. "Eleanor didn't say you were coming. Rude as hell of her!"

"*Poseidon*," Hades snaps.

"I'm just kidding, Hades, calm down. My mom's here, everybody. Is it time to eat?"

# CHAPTER
# TWENTY-ONE

*Daisy*

**M**Y DAD CRIES FOR AN ENTIRE DAY.

I always thought that *if* he ever did that, then it would be the end times. The Four Horsemen of the Apocalypse couldn't be a clearer sign than tears on his face.

But, of course, he's my dad, so he does it in his weird, non-crying way. He forgets to drag his sleeve over his eyes until Poseidon starts following him around with a dish towel, and then he just cries and glares at the same time, which is objectively hilarious.

Everybody spends the first few days after what Pollux calls *the Ordeal*—in air quotes, naturally—resting. At least, that's what Hercules and I do. We take lots of naps, and in between, he covers my mouth with his hand and we fuck like we almost ran out of time.

Artemis and Apollo are *not* fucking, but they do spend a lot of time draped over each other, her head on his shoulder, like they need each other to feel whole.

I've been back in the land of the living for a week when he rolls his naked, tattooed, perfect body off me and reclines on the pillows like someone tore him out of an ancient Greek fresco. He even has one of his legs folded, a hand propped behind his head, so the resemblance is uncanny.

I don't know how long I spend staring. Hercules doesn't open his eyes, and he looks so hot and at peace that I want to make a painting of him.

Except I haven't had any nightmares since *the Ordeal*—for God's sake, Pollux—and I'm not sure I can paint without them. Also, I have no idea how to paint a human man instead of the spectral form of death.

I'm still staring when his lips part. Okay, well, even if I can't paint nightmares anymore, I can learn to paint him. He's barely moved, and I'm stricken by his perfection.

"Baby." Hercules peeks at me from the corner of his eye and startles. "Jesus. How long have you been watching me?"

"Since you bit my neck while you came inside me and rolled away like a fainting Victorian woman."

He lifts his chin, leaning harder into the pose. "Did you paint me yet?"

"No, but I was thinking about it."

Hercules shakes his head, *fast*. "No. Nope."

"Oh my God. You don't like my paintings?"

His body glistens in the pre-dawn sun filtering in through my window, movement and muscle until his hand is in my hair, and his lips are on my cheek. "Baby."

"*Yes?*"

"Those paintings were the creepiest fucking things I've ever seen in my life. I'm begging you." A kiss at the corner of my mouth. "Don't paint me like that."

"Why? Would you be scared?"

Hercules pulls back, his eyes solemn. "It would be a nightmare."

It's hard to pout and kiss him at the same time, but I lean in and try it anyway. "I wasn't going to do it like that. I was going to learn a new style. Maybe take a class or two."

He pulls back *again*, his neck at an awkward angle. "You *have* taken art classes before, haven't you?"

"What kind of question is that? Of course I've taken art classes."

Hercules's eyes narrow. "Were they painting classes, Daisy?"

"They were…related to painting."

His hand is so serious and soft on my face. "Baby."

"Yes?"

"Don't lie."

353

"I'm not lying."

"Where did you take classes?"

"At Berkeley."

"*At* Berkeley? In the buildings?"

I let my head fall back into his hand with a dramatic sigh. "I don't know what the buildings would have to do with—"

"Did you get an art degree online so nobody would see your creepy paintings?"

"Excuse *me*. I submitted some of my creepy paintings to get into the advanced classes."

"I'm sorry," he murmurs against my temple. "Baby. Don't be angry with me."

"Why? Because I'm—"

"Because you're *scary*," he says, in a voice so innocent that I lose it completely and laugh until I cry and eventually I'm forced to climb on top of him and fuck him slowly.

We have all the time in the world.

"I wanted to talk to you about something else," Hercules says the next week in the shower. He runs the washcloth over my shoulders, my hair wrapped around his fist. It's like when he came to California, only better, because I can look at him all I like now. I want to jump him *constantly*.

I'm so busy acting casual about how gently he's

pulling my hair and how much I want him to pull it harder that I forget I'm supposed to answer.

Hercules tugs, and I can *feel* him smiling. Or is he smirking? Probably smirking. "Baby."

"Yes? Yes. What? Ask me."

"Should we fuck first?"

I turn around and jump him like I wanted to, and it's quite some time before my feet are back on the floor.

"Okay." I let the water stream through my hair, Hercules's hands on my waist. "What was your question?"

"Do you want to go back to California?"

Back to California. Not back home.

I open my eyes and blink away the water. Hercules's cheeks are flushed from the heat of the shower and from the way he fucked me up against the wall, and he looks…surprisingly vulnerable. Like he's trying his hardest to keep his face neutral, in case I want to get on a plane within the next hour.

"Do *you* want to go back to California?"

"That doesn't—"

I put my hand over his ridiculously perfect lips. "Don't you dare tell me that what you want doesn't matter. Do you want to go back to California, or would you rather live here?"

Hercules looks away and opens his mouth.

"Don't tell me yet. Really think about it."

His eyes crinkle, the gold turning wicked and dark, and he licks my palm with his entire tongue.

"*Ew.*"

Hercules grabs my hand before I can pull it away and sucks on one of my fingertips. "How's this?"

"Also gross."

"Baby."

I laugh at him, because he is *not* doing this right now. "Stop."

"Don't lie. You like it."

"Now you have to answer me. What do you want? It seems like you want to live here."

He shrugs, and even his *shrug* is beautiful and a little shy. I don't know if I've ever seen him shy before, but it's hot. God, why is he *so* hot?

"I think it would be good to stay. My dad is here."

I cannot help what happens to my face. I'm literally helpless. Hercules watches it happen, his eyebrows raised, and when I'm about to perish in the shower from the sheer cuteness of the moment, he sticks out his index finger and pokes at my bottom lip.

"Wow. I didn't know you could get your lip that far forward."

He pokes it again, and I open my teeth and bite his finger. Hercules laughs. "You look like an emoji."

"I feel like an emoji! Did you just call Zeus your dad? You want to stay here for *him*?" I put both hands over my heart. "I'm going to cry."

"Don't."

"There's no way I can stop it. There are tears." I point

at my eyes, which are generally wet from the shower, but I can feel the emotions gathering.

"Baby." He takes my face gently in his hands. "At least cry for a good reason. Here. Get on your knees, and you can choke on my—"

I let out a scandalized gasp, which Hercules completely ignores in favor of pushing me to my knees. Somehow, he's already hard again. His penis is practically godlike.

"You can choke on my cock," he finishes in that same soft voice.

I look up at him through the water droplets and the warm haze of joy. His eyes look lighter than usual. Happier. They're glowing with affection, and he's just told me I can choke on his cock.

I love him.

"I want to stay, too."

His grin is the nicest thing I've ever seen.

I only have a few seconds to memorize it, and then my tears are being put to good use.

"We're staying here," Hercules announces the next day at dinner. It's chaos in Zeus's giant living room, everybody walking around with plates and bickering over the best places to sit.

On the opposite side of the room, Zeus's mouth drops open and his eyes go wide and he looks so genuinely, childishly delighted that I laugh out loud. My uncle turns his back, pretending to be interested in the drinks fridge.

Nobody else answers.

"We're staying here," Hercules shouts.

"We get it," Castor shouts back. "What did you want, a round of applause?"

"Kind of," Hercules answers, equally as loud.

Pollux jumps to his feet and starts clapping. Artemis cackles, grinning at Calliope, and joins in. Apollo looks at Artemis like he's never been fonder of another person in his life, catches himself doing it, and beams at Hercules instead.

Poseidon starts a pirate chant that seems mostly directed at Zeus until my dad slaps him on the back of the head.

"No chants," he orders, but he looks happier than I've ever seen him.

Ares claps the longest with my mom and Brigit and Ashley.

Demeter wanders in from the dining room, Gio trailing behind her, looking flushed and satisfied. I look away on instinct and pretend I didn't notice.

"What's all this?" Demmy looks over the room with a skeptical arch to one eyebrow. "A collective hallucination? It's dinner, isn't it?"

"Hercules and Daisy are staying," my dad tells Demeter as my mom comes to his side and wraps her arms around his waist.

Demeter stares at him, shaking her head slowly, as if

she can't believe she's still putting up with him after all these years. "Obviously? They've been here two weeks. Did you think they left?"

"Oh, for fuck's sake, Demeter."

"No," my mom says. "I think he means they're staying in the city. They're staying close to us."

"Isn't that lovely." Demeter shoots Gio a look. "People make the most interesting choices, don't they?"

"Demmy, do you want some food?" Zeus asks, grinning at the plates in his hands. "Shells and cheese, if you want."

"Ooh. *Yes.*" Demeter goes toward the plate, and my dad breathes a sigh that sounds relieved.

"Were Demeter and Gio fucking in the garden?" Hercules murmurs in my ear.

"Probably."

"Good for them."

"Oh my God. Stop."

"No," he says. "I won't."

After we've spent a week house-hunting and twenty minutes deciding to move across the street from my dad and fifteen seconds signing paperwork on my phone, Dad announces that we're having the annual end-of-school pool party at Zeus's house, the way we always did after we moved to the city.

"Dad, it's July. And we're not in school."

"I know. I don't care."

He spends several days calling and texting his friends from the city. My dad doesn't invite them to the pool party. He demands that they come, and every one of them says yes.

I would, too.

I spend that time having stuff packed up in California, including Shane. He doesn't go in a moving box, but he and the rest of my team are coming to New York to guard our new house.

The day of the pool party is a perfect July day. It's too hot to wear anything but bathing suits and cover-ups, and all my dad's friends come out of Zeus's house ready for the pool, and the whole patio is filled with people shouting and laughing and teasing one another.

I lie underneath the giant sunshade on the opposite side in my bikini, wearing the largest pair of sunglasses I have ever owned, in the most comfortable lounge chair available on the market, listening to the party.

I could watch, if I wanted. The painkillers are working again, and the sunshade was designed for me and my dad, but I've spent enough time in the dark to know that the visual isn't everything.

They sound so happy.

I wouldn't go so far as to take credit for it. My parents are thrilled that I'm moving back, of course, and Zeus is beside himself, but that's also about Hercules.

He's the happiest I've ever seen him.

It's bittersweet. Sometimes, he seems tentative

about it, like he's not quite sure that it's real, or that it'll last. There's no such thing as a guarantee in life, but he feels like one to me.

I hope I feel like one to him, too.

And not just me. All of us. The whole family. I didn't understand why he was so hesitant to be part of it before. Last week, when we were talking in the middle of the night, he told me that he worried about betraying his mom. Forgetting her.

He's not worried anymore.

See? Nightmares have silver linings, too.

Just kidding. Those things are the worst. I would be fine if I never had another one for the rest of my life. Or if I had a *normal* one, the way other people do. I'd rather dream about being late for math class or being lost in a maze or having my phone quit working.

The pool party gets a little quiet, the chatter ebbing the way it does sometimes. I don't open my eyes. I'm enjoying the entire range of sound. Shrieks and belly laughs and my old friends chatting and *can I hold her? She's darling* and Castor and Pollux in the pool, and, and, and...

"Hey."

Hercules's voice is close to my ear. I still don't open my eyes. I know what he looks like in his bathing suit, and I can't have sex with him right now. Not unless we go upstairs, and everybody at this pool party will know what we're doing.

"Hi."

"Daisy."

"Yes?"

The lull in conversation is a real lull now, and I want to know what's going to break it up. Is it someone's birthday? I didn't think so, but now would be the ideal time to bring out a cake.

"Baby."

"*Hercules*. What?"

"Open your eyes."

He's on one knee at the side of the lounge chair, hope in his eyes and that shy, knock-me-out-in-a-good-way smile on his face, and he's holding a ring.

A *ring*.

It's a tiny black diamond in a lovely, delicate setting. It's how I've always wanted to feel, made into a ring.

"Oh my God." I scramble up on the chair and shove my glasses gracelessly up onto the top of my head. "What are you doing?"

"Proposing," he whispers. Then he clears his throat. "Daisy, I love you. I would literally die for you."

I cover my face with my hands, but then I can't see him, and I'm *going* to see this. My face burns. I can feel everybody watching. That's not what makes my heart race. It's him. It's always been him.

"You could at least give me a courtesy laugh."

The giggle that exits my mouth sounds frankly deranged, and Hercules pauses to bite his lip and look down at the tiles until he can continue.

Finally, he takes a deep breath and meets my eyes. I

could look at that honey-gold color forever. It wouldn't be long enough.

"I love you so much, baby." This part's only for me, but Artemis squeals somewhere nearby and I *know* they all heard. "Will you marry me?"

"*Yes.*"

I jump into his arms, which is awkward on account of the lounge chair, and Hercules catches me on his lap.

The entire pool party cheers. It's so loud. So joyful. He puts the ring on my finger while he kisses me, and I know there are going to be a million pictures of this moment—me, making out with my new fiancé, straddling him at the pool party in front of everyone.

This is it.

This is the dream.

And it's all mine.

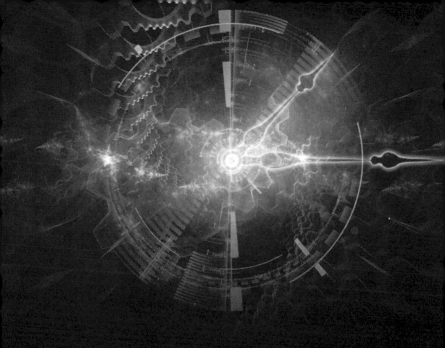

# EPILOGUE

*Artemis*

NOTHING IS MORE ROMANTIC THAN A proposal.

Did my best friend and closest cousin Daisy plan on getting engaged in a bikini in front of sixty people? No! I don't think she did. Actually, I think she never planned on getting engaged at all, because she's always thought she was too scary to be lovable.

I've never been able to convince her that's complete nonsense. She is living proof that scary things can be lovable. I mean, has she *met* her dad?

Beyond that, has she met her *grandmother?* The only reason Uncle Hades is the original scary thing is that he was born first, and most of the time, Demmy looks pretty harmless.

I said *looks*. Okay? I know she can be dangerous if she wants to be.

Right now, she's out by the pool, her curly hair shining in the sun, ready to make out with her own husband while she claps for Hercules and Daisy and keeps a sharp eye out for *weeping*.

I clapped until my hands hurt, but then I got sunstroke.

Or—that's what it feels like. My stomach twisting. I'm a little dizzy. The heat got to me.

I head through the kitchen in my parents' house, away from the pool. I need a shadier room. Somewhere I can collect myself.

From the sunstroke. I don't have a jealousy problem.

There's no *reason* for me to be jealous of Daisy. It would be callous to ignore all the stuff she's gone through in her life because of her brain, and I am not a callous person.

I wanted to shoot *one* person in the eye with an arrow. That's it. And he deserved it.

The farther I go down the hall, the cooler and quieter it gets. After an hour on the pool tiles the carpeting feels like heaven's grass, and the air conditioning feels like heaven's breeze. When I go back out, I'm getting *immediately* into the pool with a big sunhat on.

I can do that, because it's not my event to run. When the family's not in crisis, I use my looks, borrowed from my mom, and my charm, borrowed from my dad, to host social events.

Never you mind if those events are usually for another purpose. Nobody needs to know.

When I go back out, I'll feel fine. I just need a few minutes. I haven't consciously chosen a room, but I have a feeling, way below my thoughts. If I was into meditation, I'd probably be able to figure out where that feeling was leading me, but I'm not into meditation. I like archery.

I turn into a den off one of the longer hallways in the house, already relishing the shadows. The subtle, whisper-quiet pull at my spine exhales.

"Artemis."

A terrified, girly shriek flies out of me like I notched it on my bow. It's so *weird*, because I *am* startled, but underneath that, I'm not surprised. My back knocks against the wall from my panicked jump.

"Holy crap, Apollo, you scared me."

"Did I?" He sets his drink on the side table and unfolds himself from the couch. "I thought you came to find me."

It's a simple thing to say, and it doesn't mean anything. Not anything romantic, anyway, and why would it? Apollo is in my family. Aside from Daisy, he's my best friend in the world, and he has been since the day I met him.

"I came to avoid death from sunstroke."

"What?" He's across the room in a few steps, his

hand on my cheek, my forehead. "You don't feel like you have heat stroke."

"I got overheated after the proposal."

When he's this close, it's impossible to ignore how beautiful he is. Apollo is a strikingly beautiful man. An unfairly beautiful man. He looks like royalty, with dark hair and blue eyes and a fine bone structure, but he also looks like he could be deadly. I know for a fact that he's as good with a bow as I am, which is why it's only fun to play dangerous archery games with him.

Apollo's equally skilled with conversation and brokering agreements and negotiating, which is why he spends too many hours every week at his think tank, influencing policy. And, like my social event business, his outward work deflects attention from his real talent as a backchannel negotiator for the government and other groups who like some discretion dressed up as a gorgeous man.

"But…" I let out a breath. "You left the whole proposal scene before I did."

His hand lingers on my cheek. It always takes him a few extra seconds to let go. That's not because I'm in love with him.

I mean—that's not because he's in love with me. We are not in love with each other. We love each other, obviously, because we're family, but we're not in love. I don't have a massive crush on him. I don't feel sick if I spend too long away from him. I wouldn't know anything about that.

"I was jealous," he admits.

It's not what I expected him to say. Apollo hasn't ever talked to me about getting engaged or getting married, and why would he? It must be the sunstroke making my face so hot.

"I was, too."

This is when he straightens up, puts his hands in his pockets, and says *one day, you'll get your own proposal, Artemis. Whoever proposes to you will be so lucky.*

He doesn't do that.

Apollo moves his hand from my cheek to the wall behind me and leans in.

And I just…freeze.

I don't want to move, because I don't want him to remember that we're friends, we're family members, and if we've looked too long at each other, if we've stood close enough to touch on purpose, if I came looking for him—

His eyes move over my face. My lips.

I can't breathe. My only choice is to say something, or else become a statue forever.

"Do you wish it was you?"

"Do I wish *what* was me?" I've spent hours upon hours of my life talking to Apollo, and I've never heard his voice like this. Low and warm, soft like a secret arrow through my heart.

"Do you wish you were the one proposing?"

"Not to Daisy."

"Did you have somebody on your mind?"

"No," he breathes, and it's a lie, it's a *lie*. I know he's lying. I've known him for so long, and he's lying.

I don't know which of us moves first, him or me, but the next second I'm crowded against the wall, his hand in my hair, his mouth on mine.

It's a feral, stolen kiss, and forget about breathing—I can't even think. He tastes so good, like citrus and sparkling water, and I want my nails in his shirt. Then my nails *are* in his shirt, and I'm—

Climbing him?

Climbing him.

One of my legs wraps around his waist, then the other, and he puts an arm under my ass to support me and pushes me against the wall so he can kiss me even harder.

I never want this to end.

Apollo tips his face to mine, tasting, searching, and I lock my arms around his neck like this is possible, like this is the start of something. He makes a wordless, sexy sound into my mouth. It's everything I've ever wanted from a man, and nothing I've ever taken, because I've never wanted anyone but—

"Apollo!" His brother's voice echoes down the hall.

For a split second, Apollo kisses deeper—*please don't stop*—and then he puts me on my feet and steps back, the distance between us cold. His hands work over my bikini. He tugs my cover-up into place.

He touches my cheek one more time. "Fuck," he says, under his breath.

"It was the heatstroke," I blurt out. "I got heatstroke. It was an accident. It didn't happen."

There's a flash of pain in his blue eyes, and I want to take it back.

"Apollo? Where did you go? We're going to play cards."

"It won't happen again," Apollo corrects. "It was just this once."

"Never again," I promise.

"Never," he whispers. His chest heaves with a deep, ragged breath, and then he tears himself away from me. "I'm right here, Ares. Who's playing?"

I stand perfectly still in the den, my heart pounding and pounding and pounding.

*Never again.*

Apollo and I have another thing in common now. We're both liars.

Thank you so much for reading HERO WORSHIP! If you liked Daisy and Hercules, you'll love Artemis and Apollo. Read their angsty, sexy, forbidden friends-to-lovers romance in TWIN FLAME.

They can't be apart, and they can't be together. Artemis and Apollo have been inseparable since childhood, and they're the perfect pair. Both of them are smart. Talented. Gorgeous. That's what Artemis believes, but it's not true. Apollo has hidden the truth for years. He's damaged goods, in more ways than one. Artemis can never know. And he can never have her.

Read TWIN FLAME now!

# ABOUT
# THE AUTHOR

**Amelia Wilde** is a *USA TODAY* bestselling author of steamy contemporary romance and loves it a little *too* much. She lives in Michigan with her husband and daughters. She spends most of her time typing furiously on an iPad and appreciating the natural splendor of her home state from where she likes it best: inside.

For more books by Amelia Wilde,
visit her online at

www.awilderomance.com

Made in the USA
Monee, IL
08 November 2023

46015234R00219